The Chain

By

Jeffrey M. Preston

BEARHEAD PUBLISHING LLC

- BhP -

Louisville, Kentucky
www.bearheadpublishing.com/jeff.html

The Chain

By Jeffrey M. Preston

Copyright © 2009 Jeffrey M. Preston
ALL RIGHTS RESERVED

Cover Concept & Design:
David Mullett

Cover Layout:
Bearhead Publishing LLC

First Printing - October 2009
ISBN: 978-0-9824373-3-9
1 2 3 4 5 6 7 8 9 10

NO PART OF THIS BOOK MAY BE REPRODUCED IN ANY FORM, BY PHOTOCOPYING OR BY ANY ELECTRONIC OR MECHANICAL MEANS, INCLUDING INFORMATION STORAGE OR RETRIEVAL SYSTEMS, WITHOUT PERMISSION IN WRITING FROM THE COPYRIGHT OWNER

Disclaimer
This book is a work of fiction. The characters, names, places, and incidents are used fictitiously and are a product of the author's imagination. Any resemblance of actual persons, living or dead is entirely coincidental.

Proudly printed in the United States of America

The Chain

By

Jeffrey M. Preston

12-12-14

Jim & Kim —

may every word on every page make you want to read more. With great love

Jeff Preston

Dedication

This book is dedicated to God,
because without Him there is nothing.

Acknowledgements

Special thanks to David Mullett, who designed the cover artwork, and supported me from the beginning. Additional thanks to Julia Tussey, Mark Preston, Gary D. Drechsel, Mary Drechsel, and my friends and family that supported me throughout this endeavor.

Chapter One

The DJ spoke, "Here's a classic for everyone to enjoy!"
Stevie Nicks and Lindsey Buckingham sing, "*Listen to the wind blow. Watch the sun rise…*"
The chill was still in the air, but Stan Weaver knew it was time to get his rig moving. Being an over the road trucker paid the bills, and Stan had plenty of those. He had a hardened face and eyes that assured you he was smarter than he portrayed. His demeanor was quiet, but it was clear he had his reasons.
He knew this rest area well, and made his way to the restroom. He washed his face, and bee lined to the coffee vending machine. The advertisement stated "Every cup was fresh," but Stan knew better.
Making his way back to the truck he displayed a hint of a cowboy's natural swagger. Unfortunately, a bad hip helped contribute to that facade. Pulling out a crowbar from inside the cab he made his rounds tapping each of the eighteen tires with a resounding thump ensuring there would be no problems on his trip home.
Carefully, he inspects the back doors of the trailer. The white doors were surely fastened by the metal latch. Finalizing his inspection he gives the truck a nod as if they share some secret language between man and machine. Moving toward the cab the sun shows his outline, and for a moment he resembles the Marlboro man. In a maneuver clearly performed daily, he climbs into the cab, puts on his seat belt, and pulls down his Ray Ban's from the visor. With a turn of the key, Stan starts the truck and stares at the visor for a moment. Kissing his pointer and middle fingers he touches a worn-out Polaroid clipped to the visor. With his morning routine complete, he completes his ritual by making the sign of the cross.

The Chain

He slides on his sunglasses as he takes I-90 directly into the rising sun. Several gears later he makes his way east through the badlands.

Stan sips his coffee scanning the sparse morning traffic as the radio begins playing Kashmir by Led Zeppelin. He turns up the volume and plays the steering wheel like a rock and roll drummer following every beat.

He flashes back to the memory of a birthday party. All of the little girls dressed in party dresses racing around the yard tumbling in the grass, and the boys chasing after them. They were a collage of shiny patent leather shoes reflecting in the sun. It was one of those late summer days where you would need a windbreaker by dinner time. But the children didn't know and didn't care. Those were things that adults worried about. It was like a picture from a fairy tale.

"Oh let the sun beat down upon my face..."

Halfway through the song the radio cuts out with static. Frustrated Stan yells "No! No! No! This is Satellite Radio damn it! This isn't supposed to happen!" He starts fiddling with the radio turning it off and on again. As he rounds a slow bend near a pass the radio kicks back in. "All will be revealed…"

He sings along with the music *"Talk and song from tongues of lilting grace, whose sounds caress my ear…"* as he shifts the rig into a better cruising gear all the while keeping the beat on his steering wheel. Stan was in a trance swaying his whole body with the song.

"Sing it Plant!" Stan said.

"Oh, I been flying...." the song continued with the Moroccan percussion weaving in layers behind the crashing orchestral events.

The truck picked up speed as Stan allowed himself to absorb the hypnotic melody. The morning sun continued to rise in the distance oblivious to Stan's display of percussive genius.

There was a crackle again on the radio, then silence.

"Damn it all to hell!' Stan hissed as he hit the dash.

"What's up with this friggin station? Why does this happen with the good songs!" Stan complained to an empty passenger seat.

The radio crackled again

Robert Plant continued the ballad *"Oh, pilot of the storm who leaves no trace, like thoughts inside a dream"*.

"Hell yeah! Stan said with appreciation, regaining his composure and grasping the steering wheel with confidence.

"Heed the path that led me to that place."

Suddenly Stan's world goes into slow motion. As the rig rounds a curve he spots something out of the corner of his eye. Standing on the side of the road in a perfect party dress with flowing blonde hair was a little girl, motionless, her face without expression. Her hands were interlocked by her two looped pointer fingers across her waist.

"Yellow Desert Stream…" The hypnotic song continued.

Stan stomped on the breaks and gasped, "Oh my God, Kylee!"

The behemoth screeched and moaned under the intense weight of the trailer in a horrific demonstration of inertia and mass.

The music continued in a haunting progression, *"My Shangri-La beneath the summer moon will return again…"*

The back end of the truck slid into the passing lane before finally screeching to a stop.

"Sure as the dust that floats high in June. When movin' through Kashmir"

The music crescendos with a sweeping orchestral arrangement that makes the listener wish it would never end.

Stan jumps out of the truck and runs back in the direction where he saw… her.

"Kylee!" he yells. The music could barely be heard as he continued towards the back of the truck.

As he rounds the back of the trailer he sees an older couple getting out of a yellow Honda Accord.

"Are you okay?" They ask Stan with sincere looks of concern.

"Where is she?" Stan asked out of breath.

"Where is who?" The man asked.

"Kylee, the girl in the dress! Didn't you see her? In the dress with the blue flowers. She was there on the side of the road!" he pointed as he surveyed the land.

"Kylee!" he called out again. But there was no sign of her.

The woman approached him.

"Are you okay sir? We saw no one on the side of the road. Can I get you some water?" she asked.

"But… I saw her. I know I saw her." Stan mumbled as he walked to the place where he believed his daughter had stood.

"Yes, Deloris, get him some water. He is probably just a little dehydrated. You know that happens out here some times." the husband said sternly as he walked over to Stan.

The Chain

Deloris followed behind with a bottle of water, the entire time, babbling about how dangerous it was to travel without water in these parts.

Stan accepted the bottled water and apologized, "I'm so sorry. I could have sworn I saw someone on the side of the road."

He took a swig and at the same time realized his truck was strewn across two lanes of highway.

"I need to move my truck," Stan sighed.

He realized he probably appeared a little crazy to these people. He never saw their car behind him. That wasn't like Stan.

"Thanks again for the water and everything. I need to get going. I'm glad you all are okay. I don't know what got into me."

Stan's mind reeled as he ran to the truck.

"You drive carefully now, Stan," yelled Deloris as Stan raised his hand in a wave and climbed back into the rig.

The radio cried out "Satellite radio. Where you need to be!" Stan smacked the on/off switch and dropped the rig into gear.

"What the hell just happened here?" he thought shaking his head.

He started back down the highway watching in his rear view mirror for the older couple to follow. As he pulled away they were still talking outside of their car. He imagined the wife still babbling on about dehydration, etc. He rounded a curve and headed down a long hill, continually checking his rear view mirror. He expected them to come over the hill behind him, but they never came. It was then that he realized that the woman had called him "Stan", but how could she know his name? He now looked for a place to turn around. He was desperate. He found an old weigh station and managed a fumbled u-turn. As he made his way back up the hill and around the curve he started to wonder if this were some strange dream. He returned to the place where he saw Kylee and pulled the rig over to where the older couple had parked. He half expected to see them still arguing, but their car was gone. It was quiet. There was no sign of them at all. Climbing out of the truck he mumbled to himself trying to make sense of it all. Strange that they and Kylee were both there and now gone, and how did that woman know his name?

Then it hit him. He spoke aloud "They must have her! They have Kylee!"

"Son of a bitch!" he growled as he jumped back into the truck, He slammed it into gear and raced down the highway oblivious to the diesel engine roaring with complaints. Car or not, he would catch them.

He picked up his CB mike and asked for anyone on Highway 90 that may have seen a yellow Honda Accord heading west. An east bound trucker indicated he hadn't seen anyone in 25 miles and had just passed Stan's rig.

"Where could they have gone?" he sighed hitting the steering wheel with his hand.

Stan reached for the water bottle Deloris had given him, but it was gone! His hand recoiled as if he had reached for a rattlesnake.

"Was there ever really a water bottle?" he wondered, or did he imagine all of this?

He pulled over and decompressed.

"Man, what the hell is wrong with me?"

Gathering his thoughts he climbed out of the truck. He removed the crowbar once again and made his way around the rig performing his standard wheel inspection. Not that they needed it, but it helped him to think and to calm down.

He talked to his truck, "Now we both know I can act a little crazy, but that's acting. I don't drink, and I haven't smoked grass since I was twenty. Now I do miss Kylee, but we both know I had to let her go. I had to..."

He paused to take everything in and spoke again. "So obviously, something is up. I just need to figure out what's wrong."

"What seems to be the problem?" a voice spoke from behind causing Stan to startle.

Stan turned to see a highway officer. The sun shining bright behind him made it hard to see his face. But he was tall and broad, and not someone that Stan wanted to upset.

"Oh, I thought one of my tires might be acting up," Stan said.

"Where are you headed?" the officer asked.

"Back east to pick up a load. I'm just returning from Wyoming."

The officer cocked his head a little and said, "If that's the case, then why are you headed west?"

Stan didn't mind the law, but knew how patrolmen could be at times. He looked towards the front of his truck and saw a sign that read "Sonny's service station" off in the distance.

Pointing at the sign Stan said, "Well, I passed this service station earlier and was going ask them to take a look as well." In his mind he thanked God that the station was in sight.

The Chain

The officer moved closer and said, "You sure you didn't fall asleep at the wheel or something? I saw skid marks on the highway a few miles east of here, and I can see where a large vehicle made a quick u-turn in the middle of the highway."

It was clear he didn't trust or believe Stan. Stan drew closer and said, "Honestly, I was wide awake. My tires are just acting up. That's all."

The officer looked him over and said, "Well Sonny's station doesn't open for another thirty minutes. Why don't you go have a cup of coffee over at the Truck Stop till he opens up shop?" He said pointing; then quickly added "And if you don't want to wait for him to open up, how about you have the coffee anyway?"

The officer placed his hand on Stan's left shoulder and gave a reassuring smile. Stan breathed a sigh and said, "I think I will. Thanks for your help."

The policeman nodded.

As he walked back to the cab of his truck he considered the idea that maybe he had actually fallen asleep at the wheel. He put the rig into gear and headed for the truck stop.

As he pulled up to the coffee shop he thought, "It's never a bad time for coffee."

Chapter Two

"Morning, sunshine," the waitress said with a big smile. "What can I getcha?"

"Western Omelet and a cup of coffee please?" Stan said as he placed his sunglasses on the counter and took a seat.

"White, wheat, or rye toast?"

"White," Stan said.

She yelled to the back under the heat lamped opening separating the cooking area from the counter, "Joe, I need a 'white western' please".

Stan watched as she made her way along the length of the counter, refilling coffee, and delivering plates of various breakfast concoctions to patrons. She was older than Stan, but younger than his mother. It always amazed him how waitresses in these places had never really changed over the years. She had on white sneakers and a pink waitress outfit with a small apron in the front. She had a name tag that read "RITA". He was sure in her younger years she was a much smaller size and probably got much larger tips.

She placed a thick plain white coffee mug in front of him. Stan often wondered if coffee was actually better in these places, or was it those cups that seemed to be able to hold the heat for just the right amount of time.

"That's fresh. Here's some cream and sugar if you need it. Your food should be up in just a minute," she said as she dashed away to attend to the other patrons.

Stan nodded as he looked around the room. There were two couples at booths. One couple sat quietly while sharing the morning paper. Their plates were empty, and they looked to be in no rush to get back on the road. The other couple was a bit younger. They were laughing as they

The Chain

were clearly excited about the mini jukebox mounted to the wall of their booth.

Breakfast was normally a weekend thing for Stan, as most mornings it was two cups of coffee followed by an afternoon of soft drinks. Stan sipped the hot coffee. There was no question that this was the real stuff compared to the mud he purchased earlier from the vending machine.

He was off in deep thought reviewing the morning's events looking for logic or a hint of explanation. As he was stepping through the events in his mind, Rita appeared with his food.

"Here's your omelet, Hon," The plate landed hard on the counter top.

"And here are some butter packets for your toast. Is there anything else I can getcha?" she asked as she moved a small basket containing various jellies just above his plate.

"No thanks," he responded with his hungry eyes focused on the omelet.

"Well, here's some salt and pepper," she said pulling out two small shakers from behind the counter. "Joe doesn't salt things like he used to, ever since his doctor put him on high blood pressure medicine. He thinks he's responsible for everyone's salt intake now," she winked.

Stan gave a light smile and started to eat his omelet.

His mind was on the morning's event. He entertained the idea that teenagers possibly tampered with the coffee machine at the rest area this morning. Maybe they put drugs in the machine or something? The idea that kids would tamper with the vending machine in such a way was horrific. It would seem a little isolated to be any type of terrorist attack. It made no sense as he always stayed at that rest stop. Purchasing coffee from that coffee machine was just part of his weekly routine. The kids must have gotten in there and put something in it like PCP or one of these new drugs on the market like ecstasy. It all seemed so real.

"Where could she be?" he whispered to himself.

"Where could who be, Honey?" Rita asked.

Stan was dumbfounded and stared at Rita. Was this a continuation of his insane morning?

You said, "Where could she be?" Rita looked at him with her bright blue eyes and gleaming smile.

"Were you needing me?" she asked.

"Oh" he laughed lightly. "I was thinking of someone and, well… Did you ever accidentally speak what you are thinking and ahh… well..." he said looking down at his plate feeling exposed and stupid.

"All the time, Hon, it's called old age. I'd like to officially welcome you to the club, but just remember that membership has its privileges", she winked at him.

They both chuckled.

The counter was slowly clearing of patrons. Rita approached Stan to refill his coffee. She leaned closer to him and said, "You looked like you'd seen a ghost when you came in earlier. I was worried about you. You okay?"

"A ghost is right!" Stan thought. Heck, more than one.

Stan looked into his coffee cup, swirling the remnants.

"I lost someone, and well… You know," he said, hoping she wouldn't probe deeper.

"Well, of course. I understand," she smiled as she started gathering dirty plates from the counter where the exiting patrons had been seated.

"Pancakes are up!" Joe called from the back.

Stan watched as Rita picked up the warmed syrup and made her way to a table occupied by an older man and his wife. He watched Rita as she walked back behind the counter a few moments later. As Stan sipped his coffee he saw something out of the corner of his eye towards the restrooms. He turned to see the ladies' room door closing and the edge of Kylee's dress. He stood up and stared with his mouth agape.

Rita walked over to Stan and placed her warm hand on his arm. "You ready for your bill?"

Stan spoke very quickly never taking his eyes off of the bathroom door, "Rita, can I ask a big favor of you?"

Stan was shaking and Rita could see he was clearly upset.

"Sure, Hon, what is it?" she asked.

"Could you go into the ladies' room and see if my daughter is in there. She has blonde hair and a dress with blue flowers on it" he asked.

"Your daughter?" she asked, searching the room with a puzzled expression. "I didn't see anyone with you. Was she asleep in your car or something?" She looked at his troubled face glued to the door.

Stan just stood there as if in a trance.

"Well, of course. I will be right back. What is her name?" Rita asked.

The Chain

"Kylee", he said in a broken voice, lost in the moment.

Stan's eyes were riveted to the door as Rita entered the bathroom. Immediately Stan's world shifted into slow motion as he saw Deloris follow Rita into the ladies' room with her bag in tow. It happened so fast. Stan dashed for the ladies' room. As his hands reached for the door, a bright explosion of light accompanied by a loud "Boom!" erupted from inside. He was thrown to the ground.

Joe, a portly man with a soiled apron, came running from the back and darted into the ladies room. Stan groaned and got to his feet. He followed Joe. They both almost tripped over Rita who was moaning and struggling to get up from the wet floor. Water splashed and gushed as it overflowed from the sinks onto the floor.

Rita was holding her hand over a gash in her head as Joe helped her to her feet. Stan made his way to the sinks and one by one shut them off. He turned to the stalls and looked underneath. There was no one to be seen. Each stall was open, except one.

Joe said, "What the hell are you doing!" He was clearly upset from all of the commotion and had grabbed a clean towel to hold against Rita's head.

"Someone is hiding in there!" Stan said as he kicked in the locked stall door. The door flew back with a loud "Clank!" as it slammed against the inside wall of the stall.

Standing on the toilet with her back to Stan was a little girl crying and withdrawn. Rita made her way to the stall with Joe.

Joe shook his head and said, "Patty Ann Compton! You are in big trouble! How many times do I have to tell you that the bathroom isn't a playroom?"

"Now, now, Joe," Rita said as she reached for the little girl.

"Come with Nana Rita, Patty. It's okay. Now, now... Come on." She said in a soothing voice. "We will just get a mop and clean it up and find some coloring books for you to play with," Rita said as she made her way back out to the patron area, leading the little girl by the hand. It appeared Rita's bleeding had stopped.

Stan just stood there in rigid shock.

"Who were you looking for?" Joe asked.

Dumbfounded, searching for an explanation he finally said, "I was waiting on my bill and saw Rita go into the ladies room. I heard this loud thud. I ran to check on her and the next thing I knew I was falling to the ground."

"Yeah, I saw the door whack you right in the head. Rita must have fallen into it as you were approaching. You okay? My insurance is already through the roof." Joe said with a very concerned face.

"Yeah, yeah, no worries," he assured him, waving his hand, "Just tell me how much I owe you."

"It's on the house. Sorry you took that spill," Joe said as he grabbed a mop and started cleaning up the water.

"That is kind of you." Stan said as he made his way to the counter and left a five dollar tip.

Rita was at the counter with the little girl getting her started on her coloring books. She saw Stan leave the tip and leaned over to Stan and said "Thanks, Hon, and good luck," she smiled.

Stan smiled at her and out of routine said "thank you."

He noted the bump on her head. It was bleeding earlier, but now it was just a bump. She wasn't hurt as bad as he first thought.

Stan turned and left the diner. Climbing into the sanctuary of his cab, he started the truck and pulled out of the parking lot heading east.

Behind in the diner, Joe has come out from the bathroom and walked up to the counter asking, "Rita, how did you know about that mess in the bathroom?"

"Oh I didn't. I was helping that man find his daughter."

"His daughter?" He asked with creased brows. "I didn't see anyone in there besides Patty."

"Her name is Kylee. She was adorable. She had pretty blonde hair and that little dress with blue flowers. How could you miss her? She must have run out scared when I slipped and fell. One minute we were talking and the next minute all I recall was a flash of light. The next thing I knew I was waking up in a puddle of water with you looking over me," she explained.

"Let me take a look at your head," he said.

"Oh, it is fine, Joe. Really," she protested, waving him away.

"Rita!" Joe exclaimed.

Stepping closer and pointing to her head he said, "It is gone. There isn't even a sign of a cut. I could have sworn you were bleeding."

"Well, I was, I think?" she said as she pulled out the hand towel she had held against her head. They both looked at the blood on the towel, puzzled.

Joe's eyes looked haunted as if he had seen something supernatural.

The Chain

Putting on his best masculine front, he cleared his throat and said, "Well, you are fine now, and that is all that matters!"

He kissed her, smacked her on the butt and said "Now go make some tips. We're eating out tonight!"

They both chuckled.

Chapter Three

Steve Miller's voice sang through the radio.

*"Well I ain't superstitious, and I don't get suspicious,
But my woman is a friend of mine.
And I know that it's true that all the things that I do
will come back to me in my sweet time
So keep on rocking me baby..."*

Stan knew this highway well. He always stopped and slept in his cab at the same place each time. Well, he did as of today, but after today's events that was going to change. He made this trip twice a week hauling mining supplies to a warehouse in Casper, Wyoming. He usually had a load to return, but this trip his trailer was empty. It didn't matter to Stan. He got paid the same either way.

Stan flashed back to happier days with Maggie and Kylee, snowed in at the Mall of America. He recalls Kylee on the kiddy rides and Stan trying to fit in the seat next to her. He remembers Maggie taking video of them laughing the whole while. In his memory he is carrying his exhausted daughter, fast asleep in his arms. He breathes in her smell. Every parent knows the smell of their child. It is a fresh clean smell that is unique to each child. It was at that moment Stan snapped out of it.

"I smelled her!" he said aloud. "First on the side of the road, and then in that bathroom!" He said in an exciting tone to the empty passenger seat. He realized that in all of the commotion he had smelled Kylee. He sniffed his shirt and realized that in addition to the "day old truck driver" smell that he smelled Kylee. *But how? And where was she?*

"Where are you, Kylee?"

The Chain

The radio sings,

*"People are strange when you're a stranger
Faces look ugly when you're alone."*

Stan was heading east on I-94 toward Eau Claire. Thirty minutes out of St. Paul he picked up his cell phone. He stared at it for a moment and put it back down. He smacked his fist on his steering wheel. He needed someone to talk to. Someone to confide in, but since the loss of Kylee and the split with Maggie, there was no one left. He had no family. He needed someone to tell him he was either crazy or sane. There was only one person he trusted, and that was Maggie.

Stan touched his finger to the photograph clipped to the dash. It almost seemed to him the image was clearer. He picked up the phone again, and dialed the number. It rang three times. He was about to hang up, when the answering machine replied," Hello, I'm not home right now, but if you will leave a message I will get back to you. *beep*"

"Maggie, I... I..."

Stan was at a loss of words, he didn't know what to say. Then he heard a click on the line.

"Stan?" Maggie asked in a suspicious tone of surprise.

A tear rolled down Stan's face. He was frozen as memories flooded his mind.

"Stan, are you okay?" she asked. "I can hear you breathing!" she spoke tersely into the phone.

Finally, overcoming his fear, he replied. "Maggie, it is me."

"Where are you?" she said in a sarcastic tone as if he had been out drinking again and needed her to get him out of some jail.

The phone was silent.

"What's wrong?" she asked impatient.

"Maggie... Maggie... can I come and see you please?" Stan asked. He didn't know what to say and he didn't want her to know he was crying.

Maggie was blindsided by this idea. After all they had been through, out of the blue, he calls, and he sounded horrible. Though she wanted to see him, and know that he was okay, she also didn't want to invite the thing he had become, back into her life. That was a past life she was desperately trying to overcome.

"Come and see me? Stan? Come and see me? Now? After all this time?" she yelled into the phone her face reddening and the veins on her neck filling.

"I just need to see you, please Maggie. It's important," he asked. He knew he was failing, and he was sure she probably heard the tears in his voice. She would reject his request, and again he would be... alone.

"Damn it, Stan. You're scaring me," she said. She had never heard him talk like this. He could be drinking, but he wasn't that kind of a drunk.

He said nothing.

Maggie decided to put on her professional persona and address him as a business associate.

"Well alright. When do you want to come over?" she asked, relieved that she didn't give him any sense of control.

"Now please?" he asked.

Stan waited for the rejection.

She could tell he was upset. He had never cried till the day of the funeral. Not that she or Stan ever really buried Kylee. It was her family's idea to have the funeral to have them both get past it and move on. On that day, he went to Kylee's room and sobbed for hours. Kylee had been gone for ten months by then, and the detectives told them that she was either dead or brainwashed and living as someone's sex slave somewhere. Not long after that, their relationship dwindled. Until then, they had spent every free moment looking for Kylee. They followed every lead. They were so frustrated. Stan started drinking. He blamed himself for what happened, as did she. The relationship ended when Stan got drunk and took out his anger and frustration on Maggie's cousin, Michael.

Michael was the black sheep of their family. He was "openly gay". Michael was effeminate in a soft spoken timid kind of way, but never overly flamboyant. He was a quiet sensitive boy that always preferred to be with the girls. It was no shock when he "came out" to his parents later in life, but they were quite unhappy with it. He would spend lots of time at Maggie's house to avoid the daily conflict at home. His family finally realized that nothing they were going to say or do would ever change things.

Michael eventually moved out to his own place and opened his own landscaping company. It proved to be quite successful.

Michael was like a moth to the flame when he learned about Maggie's pregnancy with Kylee. He was elated and would check on her every

The Chain

couple of days. They would sneak out and get a milk shake at the local Baskin Robbins. Michael would always order them root beer floats, and Maggie would always request an extra scoop of vanilla for hers.

He was at the hospital when Kylee was born, and he had five outfits picked out for her. They were hand wrapped in his typical "over the top" fashion. Maggie loved it and giggled with him about it.

Kylee loved Michael, and he loved her as well. When Stan and Maggie would go out for a rare date night, Michael was the only one they trusted to watch Kylee. He would come for dinner, and Stan would have to drag them both from Kylee's room. They would play dolls, and dress up, and he would teach her how to act like a lady. For weeks, Kylee demanded that the family have afternoon tea at the house. Maggie purchased sugar cubes, and Kylee would say "One lump or two Madam?" It was all in fun. She would call Michael to come over for "Afternoon tea" periodically. He would never miss it. Stan was never jealous of Michael, because in Stan's mind Michael was more like a big sister, or as Michael would say "I'm Kylee's Auntie." Though Michael was really her cousin, it was easier to just go with the flow, though Stan would have preferred Kylee called Michael Uncle.

Stan and Michael were close, but when Kylee disappeared Stan became leery of everyone. The detectives kept trying to point a finger at Michael. They told Stan that it was most likely a sexual deviant and would then follow up with questions about Michael. They reminded Stan often that most abductors knew their victim.

Eventually, Stan confronted Michael at his landscaping shop. Stan had been drinking too much. His mind was reeling from the detectives continually drilling him about Michael's "obvious" involvement. They reminded him that, though Michael was at the party, he was mysteriously missing for fifteen minutes after her disappearance. And that a lot could happen in fifteen minutes.

It was after hours, but Michael was still there watering the flower beds. Michael saw Stan approaching and asked with concerned dark brown eyes, "Have you heard anything?"

Michael stood 6' 2" and outweighed Stan by at least seventy pounds. Stan couldn't be wavered and grabbed Michael throwing him to the ground.

"Yeah, I have heard things." He growled through his gritted teeth.

"Stan. You've been drinking," Michael pointed out, unable to miss the strong smell of alcohol on the Stan's breath. Backing away he asked, "What the hell is wrong with you?"

As Michael brushed off his clothes he was stunned when Stan threw a punch hitting him squarely in the face. They both heard the bone in Michael's nose shatter. Michael screamed in a deep voice as blood rushed from of his nose down his face.

"Stan! No, no! Why are you doing this?" Michael screamed in a gurgling voice as he lost his balance and fell to the ground.

"I loved her, Stan! I loved her! Why would you hurt me?" Michael whimpered and cried.

Stan suddenly realized his mistake. He turned and trudged off to his vehicle, carrying the weight of the world on his shoulders. He drove around for a long while realizing that he probably made the worst mistake of his life.

When Stan arrived home, the sheriff was waiting for him. They took him to the police station and let him sleep off his drunkenness.

Though he had every right to press charges, Michael never did. Stan called him several times, but Michael wouldn't take his calls. Stan showed up to apologize, and Michael told him to leave or he would call the police. Shortly after that, Michael sold the business and moved away.

Maggie and Stan's relationship was strained after that. Stan and Michael never spoke again. Stan would ask about Michael, and Maggie's aunt would only say that he moved out to California. Losing Kylee and Michael was hard on both of them.

Chapter Four

Maggie was stirring the stew when the doorbell rang. She replaced the lid, and took a big breath. She looked at her reflection in the Microwave. Her face was clean, and her highlighted hair was in place, but not overly styled. She looked at the reflection of her teeth in the glass. There was no food in her teeth. If there was anything that she was obsessively compulsive about, it was clean teeth.

Happy with what she saw, she made her way down the hall to the front door.

The doorbell rang again.

Opening the door, as expected, standing before her was Kylee's father. His face looked tired, and he looked as if he needed a shower.

He reached his hand out very formally and with a smile said, "Hello, I am Stan Weaver."

She reached her hand out, shook his and said, "Well, I am Maggie. Maggie Franklin." His hands were calloused but warm. She always loved his ruggedness.

They looked at each other and smiled then finally Maggie said, "Mr. Weaver, you need a shower." They both laughed and shared a friendly hug.

"That I do. Would you mind if..." he started to ask.

Turning to walk away she said, "Of course not. Everything is where it used to be." She realized he was quiet and turned back to look at him.

"Maggie, do you smell anything?" he asked hoping she would note the smell of Kylee on him.

"Are you making fun of my stew?" she asked with a pointed finger.

"Oh like something is burning?" she looked at him alarmed.

"No, no, Maggie. Please do something for me," he asked with a serious face.

"Um… Okay," she said in an uncomfortable tone.

He took her hand and drew her close and said, "Close your eyes and tell me. Do you smell anything familiar?"

She closed her eyes and inhaled. Then she did it again. There was something familiar about him.

Finally she asked, "Diesel truck with a hint of spilled coffee?"

He rolled his eyes at her as she grinned and made her way back to the stew.

"You can shower in the master bedroom. It has fresh towels et cetera."

In the bedroom, everything looked just like it did when he left. She kept a nice home. It was comfortable and welcoming. He undressed and laid his clothes on her bed. He made his way into the bathroom and started the shower.

She came into the bedroom and yelled from behind the door, "What was that whole 'smell' thing about Stan? What did you think I should recognize?" She seemed annoyed, but was doing her best to hide it.

He poked open the bathroom door and said, "Kylee."

She froze with an expression on her face that looked like she had just eaten something rotten.

He closed the door and said, "I will explain when I get out."

He entered the shower and washed away two days of exhaustion

Thoughts raced through Maggie's head. Everything came flooding back to her from the day of the party, the explosion of light, and the many interviews with the detectives.

She turned to look at Stan's clothes laid neatly on her bed. She reached down and picked up his shirt. She held it to her face and inhaled deeply. An alarm went off in her soul. There was no denying Kylee's smell. She loved that fragrant clean smell of life. It is that same smell that is so strong in an infant and carries through the rest of their life. No mother can forget the smell of her child. She gathered the rest of his clothes and ran up the stairs for Kylee's room. She ran to the dresser and frantically reached to the back of the top drawer. Folded nicely were Kylee's pajamas. Though not really pajamas, it was actually an old white

The Chain

tank top of Stan's. Michael and Kylee decided she needed something 'En Vogue' so they gathered up rubber bands and dye, and created a tie-died T-shirt. Kylee treasured it and used to tell Stan that when she was a teenager it would fit her like a top and she was going to wear it everywhere. Stan would just role his eyes. Kylee slept in it every night, and it was the last thing she wore before the birthday party that day. Maggie could never bring herself to wash it. She always felt that if she washed it, it would somehow wash away her memories of Kylee too. Maggie would often go to Kylee's room and breathe in the T-shirt because she was afraid she would forget Kylee's smell.

Maggie held Stan's flannel shirt and breathed it in, then she held Kylee's Pajama T-shirt and breathed it in. Stan's flannel shirt definitely smelled like Kylee, and was a stronger smell.

Had he abducted their daughter? Had he been hiding her away? She folded Kylee's Pajama T-shirt and put it away. She then took Stan's clothes and made her way down stairs. The shower water was still running as she ran to the kitchen opening drawers till she found a large butcher knife. She heard the shower turn off. Stan entered her bedroom with a towel wrapped around his waste.

"Maggie, did you take my clothes or something?" he called out.

She entered the bedroom with his flannel shirt in one hand and a butcher knife held high in the other. She glared at him, her eyes resembling a woman gone mad.

"Stanley Weaver, I don't know what kind of games you are playing, but I will cut you apart, piece by piece, until you tell me what is going on here! Where the hell is my daughter?"

She hoped he believed her, because she knew there was no way she could go through with such a thing.

Stan was stunned. He had never seen Maggie act this way. He took a step backwards and looked directly at her.

"I don't know where she is"

"Stan, don't mess with me! I know what I smelled on your clothes. That was Kylee! Now where is she?" Maggie demanded as she moved closer slightly waving the knife in the air.

"Maggie, something happened today. I saw her twice, but it was strange… she… she disappeared," he exhaled and sat on the bed with his head down.

"What do you mean disappeared? Are you telling me she is a ghost? Is that it? You are seeing ghosts now?" she yelled with tears in her eyes losing hope in the idea that Kylee might still be alive.

"No! Yes! Hell I don't know!" he yelled at her, cradling his head in his hands.

"Maggie, I think she is alive and is trying to make contact with me," he said.

Maggie paused to gather her thoughts. She needed to present a feeling of calm.

"Let's make this easier. Where did you see her?" she asked in the tone of the many detectives that interviewed her and Stan.

"I-90 in South Dakota"

"Okay, that is a start. Where in South Dakota?" She asked in that same steady tone.

"Southwest, near the Badlands."

"And what was she doing?" she asked as she started to sound like herself.

"Standing by the highway."

"And did you talk to her?" she asked hanging on every word he spoke.

"No, when I stopped the truck and went back she was gone."

He knew she probably thought he was crazy at this point.

"Oh, Christ, Stan!" she wailed, lowering the knife and turning and making her way back to the kitchen. Her mind reeled from the things Stan had said. None of it made sense. Hell, none of anything since that day made sense. Maybe he is suffering from some type of mental illness. Maybe something triggered this reaction in his subconscious. Either way, he seemed harmless. She set the table and sensed something behind her. She turned to see Stan still garbed in a bathroom towel.

"My clothes?" he asked, looking pitiful.

She said, "Oh, wait here." Clearly still very upset with her head down.

She came back with a T-shirt and pair of sweats.

"Use these. I will wash your other stuff after dinner."

"Thank you, Maggie" his eyes showing the true gratitude he felt as he turned for the bathroom to change.

He came back to the kitchen, and Maggie had traded the butcher knife for a large spoon. She was very quiet, and was clearly using this time to gather her thoughts.

The Chain

Stan asked, "Is there anything I can do to help?"

She turned to face him. Her sweats were a bit short on him. The ankle bands announced a flood was eminent.

"Preparing for the flood I see," she smiled looking at his legs.

He pondered her comment then looked down at his legs. "Well, I have Yoga later," he joked.

They looked at each other without saying a word, and then both laughed.

"Would you mind cutting the bread?" she asked.

The bread was on a wooden cutting board and Stan cut thick slices. She set the whole pot of stew in the center of the table with a large ladle. Maggie took a bowl and filled it. She placed it in front of Stan, and then filled a bowl for herself.

She said, "Let's say grace."

He took her hand and said, "Lord, we thank you for this food and the gifts we are about to receive." He wanted to say so much more in his prayer relative to Kylee and Maggie, but knew it was best to go slow with Maggie.

Maggie responded, "Amen."

And Stan completed the prayer with "Amen"

He had forgotten what a good cook she was. It was such a hearty meal, and he hadn't eaten since the truck stop breakfast.

"The food is delicious."

"Thanks," she tried to smile.

Stan broke the ice asking about her family. They talked about old friends and the house. They were careful not to touch on anything too complex or emotional. He helped her clear the dishes and started cleaning the pots and pans in the sink.

The phone rang.

"Hello."

"Maggie, this is Beverly Clayton."

"Oh, hello, Mrs. Clayton," Maggie rolled her eyes at Stan.

"Honey, Just tell me if you can't talk. If you need me to call the police or something just say 'thanks for calling' and hang-up the phone. That way I will know you are in trouble." Mrs. Clayton said in a hushed voice.

"Oh, thanks for checking on me. Stan came over for dinner. Everything is fine." Maggie grinned at Stan.

Stan yelled out "Hi, Mrs. Clayton!"

Maggie waved for him to hush.

"Well I must say, it is mighty fine to see you two talking again. I will leave you alone. Just call if there is any trouble."

"You are very sweet, Mrs. Clayton. Thanks again." Maggie said trying to get her off the phone.

"Okay, goodbye honey." Mrs. Clayton hung up.

"Bye" Maggie sad.

"I see your watchdog is still around," Stan joked.

"You better be careful, Mr. Weaver. She is tougher than any Sheriff around here," Maggie grinned.

Maggie yawned, "If you don't mind, I'm going to go take a shower." She left the kitchen and looked forward to the time alone to gather her thoughts for more questioning.

Stan wasn't sure where her head was at, and he had so much to tell her. He finished drying off all of the pots and pans, and hung them back on their rack.

Stan found his way up to Kylee's old room. The door was ajar, and he pushed it open. It was like time stood still in there. It was as it was the day she vanished. Her tea set neatly displayed on her dresser. Her Barbie dolls sitting around the tea set. Her dresser neatly decorated with her brush and mirror. It was then that he saw her diary. When she learned how to write, Michael bought her one. He told her that she could now keep a journal of her life. Stan sat on her bed and turned the pages to read her last entry.

We had a tea party today. Auntie Michael came, and Mommy did too. Daddy had to work, so I invited Barbie to take his seat. Michael decided it was a two lump day, and Mommy and I agreed.

Tomorrow is Anthony's Birthday party and I get to wear my new dress. Michael says the blue flowers are beautiful, and I will look like a forest princess.

I think I will surprise Daddy with a tea party this weekend so he can have some too.

Tears rolled down Stan's face as he slowly fell apart in shuddering gasps. That is how Maggie found him. She reached down, and put her hand on his shoulder. She reached for the box of tissues on Kylee's dresser and handed one to Stan. Numb, they sat there and cried.

Maggie took the diary and put it back in its place and then took Stan by the hand and led him to the den. She sat him on the chair, and left for the kitchen. She came back with a bottle of wine and two wine glasses.

"I thought we could use this," she said.

He opened the wine, and she made her way to the fireplace and started it.

"Whoa! Upgrade!" he said.

"Yeah, I don't like hauling around wood, so I had a gas line installed." She said.

He poured her a glass of wine, and they sat next to each other staring at the fire.

After a long silence, Stan said, "I know you have a lot of questions, and I have a lot to tell you. I just ask you to be patient with me and let me tell it all. Many things have happened that I don't understand, and there are a lot of things I can't explain because I just don't know the answer."

"Of course," she said sipping her wine. She knew she must be patient as Stan was never the great orator.

"Before I begin, when is the last time you saw Kylee?" he asked.

She looked at him with a shocked expression. "Well, at the party, that day, just after they cut the cake," she said.

"So you haven't seen her since?" he asked. He knew he must sound ridiculous to her, but he also knew she would absorb everything before drawing a conclusion.

"No, only in my dreams," she said as she pulled her feet into an Indian sitting position.

He proceeded to tell her about the events of the day. How he went through his normal routine that has been the same for almost two years, and how today had been drastically different.

Finally Maggie stopped him and asked, "Stan, do you think you saw her ghost?"

"It's strange, but no. I'm telling you it was her," wishing he could give her a solid reason.

"Then where is she?" Maggie asked as if asking the wind.

"I just don't know," he said.

"You do realize she would be fourteen now, Stan. She would never be able to fit into that dress at that age," Maggie said in a matter of fact way.

"Yeah, that is exactly what I was thinking, but..." he said not sure how to explain it.

"But what Stan?" she asked hoping for something more, something that would lead her back to Kylee.

"The smell" he sighed.

"My god you are right! Let me think here," she said as she got up and paced around the room searching for logic or a hint of reason.

She stopped and stared at the fireplace and said, "Do you think she is trying to reach out to us from the dead or something like that?"

"I really don't know," he said.

She turned to Stan and stared at him, deflated.

"Why now Stan? What's changed? Why would she appear now? Why not last year, or two years ago? What has changed?" she asked looking for a clue.

Stan just shook his head and sighed, "I don't know."

She turned to face the fireplace and search for answers in the flames. Stan stood up and went to her side.

Their hands touched and he asked, "Do you believe Kylee is still alive?"

Maggie took his hand and turned to face him with tears rolling down her cheeks she said, "I know she is."

He held her as she sobbed into his chest. Offering comfort he drew her close. Her body pressed against his. He had forgotten how much he loved her. How he had missed her sweet smell and soft skin. Their lips met and they entangled in a beautiful embrace melting away the painful past that had driven them apart. They made their way to Maggie's bedroom and made love through the night. A love that once seemed extinguished was denied its death.

Chapter Five

Conrad Jenkins had a typical government office tucked away at Schriever Air Force Base. His metal desk was long past its expiration date. The room was lit by exhausted fluorescents. Though his window served neither as a light source nor as a corporate picture frame to the beautiful world outside, it was still his. The walls were decorated with old pilot photos from his early military years. The room was typical in so many ways, but it was the contents of the locked cabinets behind his desk that separated him from the rest of the staff in that building.

He was a well dressed man and carried himself in such a way that people naturally respected him. While at Shriever he wore his office "blues". The patch on his shoulder announced his rank as Colonel. Being a full bird demanded respect, but he didn't require it. Being well acquainted with protocol he often wondered how many other offices around the world were populated with agents just like him. He never thought it would be this easy portraying this façade, but it was, and that made his job that much easier.

The phone rang.

"Jenkins," he responded.

"Is this line secure, Sir?" the woman's voice asked

"Yes, it is."

"Sir, we have a situation that requires your attention relative to the Unity Project."

"I'm listening." He reached into his briefcase and pulled out a folder labeled "Unity" on the tab. He paged through photos, and coordinate information. He tapped on a photo.

"Sir, it appears that the secondary nodes have re-acquainted."

"Are they together now?" He frowned as he looked through the pages of the folder.

"Yes. They are at their original residence," she said.

Jenkins was silent for a moment as he played with the tab on the folder. He finally spoke into the phone. "I will be putting the teams on standby, please keep me appraised of the situation."

He placed his hand on the receiver to end the call and dialed the phone. A voice answered on the other phone "Yes?"

Jenkins spoke clearly into the phone, "Do we have a secure line sir?"

"Yes," the voice said

"Sir, we have some activity relative to the Unity Project. I would like to activate two teams."

"Of course. What kind of activity?" the voice asked.

"The secondary nodes seem to be re-acquainting, Sir."

"Interesting. Keep me posted please, Mr. Jenkins."

"I will, sir."

Conrad heard the receiver on the other end hang up. He immediately dialed an on base number.

"Yes, sir," the voice answered.

Conrad spoke into the phone, "I need two teams. We need to blend in on this one, Tony, so bring the ladies."

"Yes, sir."

"Tony, I need our eye on the sky to be watching the following coordinates." Jenkins read off the coordinates to the man on the phone.

"May I confirm, Sir? Those coordinates appear to be Eau Claire, Wisconsin? Shall I use the same coordinate for the teams?" the voice asked.

"That is correct on both questions. Contact me when the teams are assembled and twenty minutes out from the destination. This is NOT a hot zone. I repeat NOT a hot zone." Conrad was perspiring and wiped his brow.

"Understood, Sir."

They both hung up the phone. Conrad knew things would be getting busy soon.

Chapter Six

Stan salivating to the smell of fresh bacon, made his way down the hall after a brief pit stop to the bathroom.

"He lives!" Maggie smiled at him as he entered the kitchen.

"Just barely," Stan grinned, stretching as he yawned.

"How would you like your eggs? Over easy, scrambled, sunny side up?"

"Scrambled, please," he replied, pulling out a chair taking his place at the table.

"I have to go put on make-up et cetera, and I will be right back down." She whipped past him to the bedroom with a bounce in her step.

"You are up early. Where are you headed?" he asked amazed at what a happy bird she was this morning.

"I have a load to haul out west," she said in a serious tone.

"What? Did you take up truck driving?" he asked sounding cynical.

She poked her head around the corner and said, "No, you did! And as long as you keep seeing Kylee, I won't be satisfied until I see her too! So, either you are crazy, or you are on to something." She dashed back into the master bathroom to finish up.

Stan examined the eggs and smiled as he saw the steaming cup of coffee sitting in front of his plate.

"Well, here's to me not being crazy," he said as lifted his coffee in a toast.

After they ate breakfast, Stan took a quick hot shower and found his clothes cleaned and laying out for him. Maggie had packed a large overnight bag, and filled a container with various food items.

"Let's get this straight, Mr. Weaver. I don't shower in truck stops!"

"Well, Mrs. Weaver, for your information, I don't either," he grinned.

She interrupted him and said, "Mr. Weaver that was quite evident when you came in last night." Maggie bonked him on the head and chuckled as she made her way down the hall.

Stan grabbed his things and followed Maggie to the front door. They moved to the side of the house where Stan's truck was parked. He helped her into the truck cab, and walked around the truck finally reaching the driver door. He climbed into the truck and looked at her. She could tell by the look on his face that he was entering his trucker mode. He would adorn this organized tactical look on his face like he was preparing for an important military mission.

"I filled up before I got here last night," he said pointing to the gas gauge pointing to the large letter 'F'. Staring out through the windshield he mumbled, "So I just need to get the trailer loaded, and then we're out of here."

"Ten Four, Good Buddy," she responded, saluting him. Then she asked in her best trucker voice, "and what exactly are we hauling?"

"Bowling balls," he said, starting the rumbling truck and throwing it into gear.

They both laughed as he drove away from the house.

"Bowling balls? That's the best you could come up with?"

"Well, actually I'm hauling fasteners used for mining," he said in a matter of fact way.

"Stick with the bowling balls. It makes for a better story," she grinned.

* * * *

"You're all set, Stan," the dock worker said.

Stan signed the papers and stuffed the rest in his clip board. As he got back into the truck he saw Maggie with something in her hand.

"Whatcha got there? He asked.

"I always loved this picture of us. I had no idea that you had it"

"Yeah, it is my good luck charm." He smiled.

She handed it back to him and he slid it back into the visor.

"You need to go to the bathroom or anything. We have a long haul ahead of us."

"No, I'm good."

The Chain

He buckled his seatbelt, and pulled out his Ray Bans. Kissing his pointer and middle fingers, he touched the Polaroid, and made the sign of the cross.

Maggie took his hand and kissed his fingers and said "Me too" with a smile.

Stan put on his sunglasses and headed west. He hit the power switch on the radio.

> *"Saturday, in the park I think it was the Fourth of July*
> *Saturday, in the park I think it was the Fourth of July*
> *People dancing, People laughing, a man selling ice cream*
> *Singing Italian songs"*

Maggie watched the endless highway roll past her. The grass wasn't as green as she recalled in the past. An unusual summer drought had hit the area, and it looked more like autumn, than mid summer. It was hard for her to imagine that Kylee would be anywhere on this stretch of highway. After leaving St. Paul, her belief that she would actually see Kylee dwindled.

"Are you getting hungry?" she asked.

'Well, I could eat. I don't usually stop till Sioux Falls, but if you want something I can pull off," he offered.

"No, I brought some snack stuff for us. It's nothing too exciting, but something to tide us over for now," she said, as she turned to get things out of one of her bags. "I'm more concerned with my bladder holding out till Sioux Falls," she laughed, as she kept rumbling through the bags.

"Oh, just let me know when you need to stop."

"Oh, I will," she insisted.

Stan turned to see what she was up to. He was greeted by the Wrangler's jeans tag on her back side.

"Nice Wranglers," he laughed.

"Trust me, it could be worse," she reminded him.

"I don't think it could get much better."

She turned back around with a couple of oranges and some yogurt cups. Her smile was as bright as the sun.

"Well, time for the breakfast, or, in this case, make that the 'snack of champions'," she smiled.

"Oranges and yogurt," he said in a fake smile. "Now I remember why I usually skip snacks," he laughed

"Stan Weaver, we're not getting any younger and we need all the help we can get. Yogurt really helps the digestive system, and you always loved oranges," she quipped.

He was holding the orange in his hand with this "what do I do with this?" expression on his face.

"Oh, give me that. I peel. You drive," she sighed.

"Sounds like a deal," he agreed.

The radio said "Satellite Radio. Where you need to be!"

> *"Are you reeling in the years?*
> *stowing away the time*
> *are you gathering up the tears?*
> *Have you had enough of mine?"*

Stan couldn't remember an orange tasting so good, and the yogurt wasn't so bad. Maybe, she is right. He wasn't getting any younger, and he should take better care of himself.

"Thanks, that wasn't half bad," he said, flashing a smile.

She got them both a bottle of water, all the while her bladder reminding her that it would need relief soon.

She reached her hand in front of his face and said, "Open up and swallow". He opened his mouth, and felt a large pill hit the back of his throat. He started to cough, and took the bottle and swigged it down.

Still coughing, he said, "What the heck was that?" trying to gain his composure.

"Multivitamin. See?" she said, as she held one out in front of him. She popped it in her mouth and swallowed it down with some water.

"For all I know, you could have drugged me," he said with a wink.

"You wish, Mister!" she teased.

"So, you are a health nut now?" he asked with eyes showing friendly surprise.

"No, I'm taking care of the engine," she said, patting her heart. "It is getting older, and I want it to run for a long time. You should too." She gathered up the debris from their snacks and put it in a plastic bag.

"Well, I hate to be the bearer of bad news, but my bladder has just sent me a message with a timer."

"No problem, my bladder is talking too," he said.

The Chain

Stan pulled off of the highway and turned into the closest truck stop. Stan asked Maggie to wait as he got out and made his way around to her side of the cab. He opened the door and helped her out. Stan always was a gentleman, and Maggie enjoyed being the recipient of his attentions once again.

Maggie made her way into the truck stop and bee-lined for the ladies' room. She was thankful that she had the restroom to herself. As she sat there, she heard someone enter the bathroom. "So much for privacy," she thought.

"Honey, try and go to the bathroom before we get back on the road," the older woman said.

Maggie finished as fast as she could. Her heart was racing. She had this fantasy that Kylee would be standing there. She flushed and headed out to the sink to wash her hands. The woman was in her fifties and had white hair. She was slightly overweight and wore a dress reminiscent of Edith Bunker. Maggie moved, hoping to catch a glimpse of the girl. She slowly dried her hands and smiled at the woman.

The woman spoke to the girl behind the door, "You really need to get moving, honey. Uncle Rudy is waiting for us in the car."

"Kids, can be such a challenge" Maggie said to the woman.

"They sure can. I never remembered being as much trouble as they are today."

Just then, a little girl came out of the bathroom. She was obviously a Downs kid. She had pretty dark hair, and was older than she appeared.

"Come on, honey, let's get those hands washed," the woman said.

Maggie smiled at the girl and headed back to the truck. Stan was checking the tires with his crowbar.

"Don't you need to go?" she asked.

"Already been," he said with a shrug.

"Pffft," she responded as she climbed back in the truck.

Back in the restroom, the elderly woman was saying, "Make sure you dry them off and be sure to shut that water off this time. You know what an awful mess you made last time at the diner," the elderly woman said.

"Yes, Aunt Deloris," the girl said.

Chapter Seven

"So you drive this every day?" Maggie asked looking over the farm fields.

"Yes, Ma'am," Stan nodded.

Stan wondered if this were some strange dream. Here he was with is ex-wife driving to Wyoming in his rig in hopes of discovering his daughter, who has been missing for six years. Maggie had made a good point the night before. *What had changed? Why had Kylee surfaced now? Was she trying to give him a message? A warning?* It seemed she was trying to reach him, but couldn't make it to him. And why hadn't she tried to reach Maggie? Could it be he was hallucinating all of this? No one else actually saw Kylee except him, but then he recalled the smell, and he knew he wasn't going crazy.

Stan reached for the radio power button to turn the radio back on and was greeted by Jackson Brown singing.

> *Doctor, my eyes*
> *Tell me what is wrong*
> *Was I unwise to leave them open for so long...*

"Where is your head, Stan?" Maggie asked.

He never even heard her as he continued staring through the windshield at the highway.

"Stan? Hello?" Maggie persisted, a hint of aggravation in her tone.

"Oh, sorry," he said with true repentance in his glance, "I was off in another place."

"I could see that, can the rest of us go there too, or is this a 'solo thing'?" she stared at him, annoyed.

The Chain

Looking back at Maggie, he moved his hands around the steering wheel and said, "This whole thing is really odd. I have been going over it all in my head. None of it makes sense to me. I have looked for anything that might make sense. I'm sure I saw her, Maggie," he said with confidence, meeting her eyes. He returned his focus to the road, and in a haunting voice added, "I just know it was her, but the fact that she hadn't aged a day? How could that be? And who were the two people that looked like they could be Archie Bunker's neighbors?" Stan stared off into the highway like a person mesmerized by it's never ending qualities.

Maggie re-positioned herself in her seat so she could face Stan. She then started to speak.

"I have been thinking a lot about your story. Is there anything about both experiences that were the same?"

Stan was quiet for a moment retracing the events.

"Well, both times I saw her. I smelled like her afterwards. And both times I saw her, I saw that couple, well, at least Deloris."

Maggie interrupted him, "Stan, I just realized something. Remember the day Kylee vanished? Remember that flash of light? It knocked people to the ground. Did you experience that flash of light when you saw her these two other times?"

"Well..." he stammered, carefully thinking it through. "Yes and no, the first time was such a blur... I almost jackknifed the truck, and... Well, hell maybe there was a flash. I do know there definitely was one at the restaurant. I think that is what knocked me off my feet. Christ, what could that mean?" He shook his head.

After a few moments, Maggie gathered her thoughts and spoke, "I have a theory. You may not like it, but with everything you have told me and all that you have experienced I believe we have to consider the idea of something extraterrestrial here".

Stan was quiet, contemplating her comments. Under interrogation by detectives, both she and Stan individually told them they thought a UFO had taken Kylee. The flash of light, people falling to the ground, the whole experience was very strange. Everyone was in shock after that moment. People walked around in a daze. It wasn't until Stan found Maggie that they both panicked and started calling out to Kylee. The whole area smelled of ozone. Everyone was frightened. It was as if it happened yesterday. Stan had lived that day over in his nightmares many nights.

"Let's assume what you are saying is true," he said his eyes expressing his sincere concern. "What can we do about it? Obviously they are of a higher intelligence, and more evolved. What chance does Kylee have of escaping them? Or us retrieving her for that matter?"

Maggie displayed a confident demeanor. She repositioned herself to face forward and pulled one leg up underneath the other.

"Well, I have been thinking about that too, especially this couple that keeps showing up. Could it be that aliens are trying to return her to us, and this couple is trying to intercept her? Or them? Heck, maybe those two are aliens themselves, or government agents. You hear about people being abducted all the time, and the conspiracy theories. Aren't aliens supposed to be able to travel through time and space? It seems to me it's the only way Kylee could still have the appearance of an eight year old." Her troubled blue eyes were darting to and fro frantically scanning the roadways and fields for any sign of Kylee.

"Either way, they seem to be showing up every time you have an encounter with Kylee." She searched for a meaning to it all.

Maggie realized at that moment that Kylee hadn't ever tried to reach her. None of it made sense. Wouldn't she want to be with her Mommy? Maggie wondered if she would have believed Stan from the beginning, but smelling Kylee on his clothes changed everything. She knew she had to find the truth.

Miles of highway passed below them. There was a steady stream of truckers making their way in both directions accompanied by cars full of families travelling to vacations unknown. They had stopped for a lunch and grabbed some drinks earlier in the day, and the sun was sinking slowly in the western sky. The blue sky had slowly dimmed with no cloud in site. Stan pulled off the highway and went north on Highway 63.

"What's up here?" She asked.

"Good food and restful sleep," he smiled

"Stan, she is out there somewhere," she said, looking out all of the windows again. Maggie wore a forlorn expression. "We'll miss her, we should keep going."

"Maggie, it's getting dark. Do you really want to take the chance of driving by and missing her?" Stan reasoned, his brown eyes projecting his seriousness.

"No, no. You're right," she said nodding her head. "I'm sorry," she conceded.

They pulled into the small town of Philip, South Dakota.

Chapter Eight

The next morning, Stan slid out of the bed and made his way to the shower trying hard not to wake Maggie. They had gotten a room just after a hearty meal, and literally fell asleep as soon as they climbed under the covers. He had forgotten how nice it was to sleep next to her soft warm body. He had forgotten how much he still loved her.

When he came out of the shower, wearing a towel, Maggie had already brushed her teeth and made the bed. She was funny about that. Stan remembered how she always did that when they traveled, all the while knowing that a maid was going to strip it and make it again.

"Oh, I see the maid has been here already," he joked looking from her handiwork back to the smile on Maggie's face.

"Yes, and she wants in the shower now mister," she teased as she moved past him. Just before the door closed she pulled off his towel and closed the door, applying the lock. She laughed loud and giggled the whole time she was in the shower.

Stan yelled out, "I'll get you and that little dog Toto too!"

"And Toto too?" she teased.

Stan threw on his boxers, and slid on his wrangler jeans. He proceeded to brush his teeth.

"Is it safe to come out?" she asked.

"Is it ever!" He chided.

"Look, I just want my damn ruby slippers, then I'm out of this town, Mister!" she teased.

She came out of the bathroom looking like a swami. The towel wrapped around her head and the other covering her breast down to the very edge of her bottom.

"So what do you think? Is this the wrong color for me?" She posed.

He drew her close and said, "Every color looks good on you!" They kissed in a long embrace until she finally spun out of his arms and quickly slid on a pair of panties, followed by a pair of jeans.

Stan was amazed how she seemed so ageless. He was so thankful he had called her.

Stan threw on an aging cotton T-shirt, and a pair of work boots, and Maggie put on a pastel blouse and a pair of walking sneakers. They packed the rest of their things and headed to the truck. Stan drove them to the McDonald's parking lot and pulled off to the side. He gave Maggie cash to go and purchase some breakfast. He took out the crowbar and checked his tires while he waited for her return.

Maggie came around the front of the truck as he finished checking the backdoors of the trailer.

"Sir, would you kindly open the door for a lady in need?" she asked in a very noble accent, juggling her bags.

"Well, yes, madam." As he lifted her to the cab, he goosed her.

"Well, I never!" She exclaimed with a teasing smile.

"Oh, yes you have, lady!" he teased back

The sun was still rising, and shone brightly in Stan's eyes. He was thankful for the company. He performed his ritual and kissed his fingers and the photos, and Maggie added her two fingers.

"Ok, good buddy, have I got the breakfast of champions for you!" she spoke in her best trucker voice.

"Oh, boy," he glanced at her with a fake smile.

"When will you have faith in me, mister?" She teased as she pulled out a large coffee.

"Mmmm," he responded with great appreciation.

"Oh, yeah, I know what a trucker needs." She teased as she sipped her coffee.

"I went southwest on you this morning and brought you back 'Breakfast Burritos'. They are the new rave below the border."

"Hmm, smells good, I will give you my critique." He grinned as he devoured the food.

Stan turned on the radio. Lynyrd Skynyrd was playing.

Ooooh that smell
Can't you smell that smell

The Chain

Ooooh that smell
The smell of death surrounds you"

They found themselves singing along with the song when all of a sudden Maggie stopped with a look of great fear. She hit the power button on the radio, bringing an abrupt silence to the cab.

"Stan, that smell! Oh my God… That smell!" She said as she stared right through him.

"Maggie? Are you talking about Kylee's smell? What's wrong?" He asked with concern in his eyes, lightly touching her arm.

"No, okay, wait," she said opening and closing her hands. "Let me gather my thoughts. Remember the first time you saw her since her disappearance? You said you ran to the side of the road where she was standing? Did you smell ozone?" she asked, her eyes searching his for an answer.

"Well, hmm… I… maybe," he said.

"How about at the restaurant?" she asked frantically.

"Well, come to think of it yes. Oh, wow, just like the day she disappeared. I forgot about that ozone smell," he said.

Maggie gasped and spoke very forcefully to him, "Tell me about Deloris."

"Tell you about Deloris? Umm, it isn't like I really know her or anything, but..." he started to say as she interrupted him.

"Just tell me, Stan, what did she look like? What was she wearing? What color hair? Just tell me everything you remember please!" she emphatically requested.

"Well, she had on one of those old lady dresses. It was sort of an off white or ugly yellow. She had white hair. I guess she was like 60-65-ish. You know I'm not good at this stuff," he said.

"Did the dress have a little string belt around the waist? And did she have black shoes, and did she carry one of those big beach purses?" she asked.

Stan looked at her amazed.

"Well, yeah, she did. Do you know her? Did you see her?" he asked as he looked in the rear view mirror.

"Oh, my God! I did see her I think! She was in the bathroom with a little Downs Syndrome girl. She was telling her not to play with the water and make a mess again and Uncle Rudy was in the car, and oh, my God, Stan!" she said as she stared off.

"Maggie, how can you know it was her?" Stan asked with a frown.

"The smell, the ozone, I noticed it in the bathroom. Dear God, should we go back?" she asked, looking at Stan for the answer.

"That was yesterday and several hundred miles back. Do you think they are following us or something?"

"Well have you seen them on the highway?"

"No, I haven't. I don't think they have her. Let me drop off this load in Casper and we will keep watching for Kylee." He was worried that any decision was the right decision.

There was no denying Stan was right. These people seemed to arrive when Kylee appeared, so either they were following now or would arrive when Kylee appeared again. Stan planned on making sure that the next time Kylee appeared that she left with him and Maggie.

The highway was mostly empty minus the vultures along the way picking apart road kill. The road was mostly occupied by the truckers and the occasional family vehicle. They had both agreed to grab lunch after Stan was done unloading the trailer. Stan could see that Maggie was starting to lose the vigor she initially had when they started the journey. He wondered how much more she could endure.

He turned on the radio and noticed Maggie had dozed off. She woke up once, and Stan told her to go back to sleep. He would keep an eye out for Kylee.

Stan backed the rig up to the loading zone. Maggie was fast asleep. He got out of the cab and took the manifest to Roy Duncan. Roy quickly unloaded the truck with a propane powered forklift.

"Do you have anything going back?" Stan asked.

"Nothing with a manifest, but Mrs. Bauer wanted to know if you would mind dropping off some paperwork for her when you got back to town? Roy asked.

"Sure, no problem."

Stan entered the building and was greeted by Mary Bauer. Mary was a well dressed lady with a bright smile. She kept her hair short, and colored dark brown, though the grey hairs fought their way to the surface. She wore bifocals, and though functioned in a professional capacity, maintained her matronly image.

"Hi there. Would you be so kind to deliver this to the other office for me? I missed today's mail, and I would really appreciate it." She asked as she handed him some large envelopes.

The Chain

Mrs. Bauer was a polite woman he guessed would have been the same age as his mother if she were still alive today. Mrs. Bauer favored Stan and would periodically make him cakes and pies.

"No problem at all, Mrs. Bauer." Stan smiled.

"Oh, and this is for you and your friend" she winked as she handed him a loaf of banana bread and looked over his shoulder.

"My friend?" He turned to see Maggie behind him.

"Oh, her? That's just my ex-wife. Part of our divorce agreement states that she retains the right to ride with me one day a year and nag me the entire time."

Stan braced himself for Maggie's smack on his arm.

"Stan, you dog!" Maggie said as she pushed him out of the way.

"Hello, I'm Maggie. I apologize for my ex-husband's lack of manners." She shook Mrs. Bauer's hand.

"It is nice to meet you," Mrs. Bauer said with a warm smile.

"My, you are a beautiful lady," she complimented. Then giving Stan a chastising stare she said, "Stan, how could you let this precious gal get away?"

Sweeping her gaze back to Maggie, Mrs. Bauer professed, "Ahh, men, I tell yah. Sometimes, they just got no sense."

Maggie nodded at her then winked at Stan.

"It was nice to meet you, Maggie." She winked as they exited down the hall making their way to the truck.

"Do you need to use the restroom before we leave?" Stan asked.

"Roy showed me where it was. I'm set to go."

"Okay, let's get some grub." He said as he helped her into the truck.

****

Maggie looked clearly disappointed as the waitress brought the bill. Stan had to finally tell her to eat her sandwich. He realized she was constantly watching for Kylee. When they arrived at the restaurant, Maggie purposely waited for the booth at the front door and took a seat where she could see everyone that came and went. Her three visits to the bathroom were a clear sign to Stan that she was about to pop.

She was fiddling with her nails and fidgeting. Stan took her hands, and she started to shake. Tears streamed down her cheeks. He moved to her side of the booth to hold her. She tried to push him away, but she gave in and sobbed quietly into his chest.

"Ma'am, are you okay?" a voice boomed from the end of the table.

Stan and Maggie both looked up to see a local police officer. He was a pear shaped man that obviously spent a lot of time eating the truck stop's donuts and coffee. He eyed Stan, and finally rested his hands on his holster.

Maggie waved her hand and shook her head at him. "No, no, I just found out a family member passed away. This is my husband," she confirmed squeezing Stan's arm.

"Well, could I see some identification please?" the officer asked.

Stan stood up to retrieve his wallet from his back pocket. The officer was poised ready to respond had Stan made one questioning move. Maggie dug through her purse for her wallet. They both handed over their driver's licenses. The officer looked them over.

"Okay, Mr. and Mrs. Weaver, I see you live at different addresses?" he asked.

"Yes, we're divorced, but we're trying to work things out," Maggie responded as she pulled a tissue from her purse and blew her nose and trying to regain her composure.

"Ma'am, could you step outside with me for a moment?" the officer asked.

"Really, I'm okay." She said

"Ma'am, please?" he insisted.

Stan started to get up with her, and the officer indicated with his turned down hand for Stan to stay seated.

Stan watched as Maggie walked outside with the officer. They talked for a few minutes and she walked over to Stan's truck. The officer came back inside and moved towards Stan.

"Mr. Weaver, your wife is pretty upset. Can you tell me whose death she is mourning?" he asked.

Stan's mind raced. He had no idea what she told the police officer. Did she make up a story? She wasn't one to lie, but then how much did she actually tell him? Stan didn't want trouble, but this could go bad really fast if they weren't careful.

Stan placed his hands on his face searching and finally said, "Yes, her name was Kylee." He sighed and covered his face hoping to appear like a father who had endured a great loss.

The Chain

The officer placed his hand on Stan's shoulder, and said, "I'm very sorry for your loss. I hope you understand that you all looked suspicious. Mrs. Weaver is outside waiting for you. Again I'm sorry about your loss."

Stan rose slowly slumped over. He left a tip on the table, stepped to the counter to settle their check, and made his way out of the restaurant.

Maggie was in the cab fixing her makeup that had run. Her eyes were still bloodshot, but her nose appeared to have stopped running.

He put the truck into gear and said, "That was quick thinking to come up with a story about mourning Kylee's death."

"Is that what this is to you, Stan? A story!" she blasted him with angry, hurt eyes. "It's a friggin' nightmare, damn it. I'm mourning. It was the only way I could get past the pain. These last six years I had to pretend that she really is dead. Hell, for all we know she is!" she snapped at him.

"Now hold on just a God Damn minute. Kylee is not dead!" he snapped back.

"How do you know? How do you know, Stan? You don't! You know no more than you did six years ago!" she yelled.

"Our baby is alive! I know it! You know it, and we are going to see her again!" he yelled back at her.

Maggie turned facing the passenger door with her knees drawn up to her chest.

Stan started the rig and pulled back out on to the highway. He would look over at Maggie, but she was in a far away place staring out the window.

Maggie watched as the mile markers ticked away, the never ending grasslands blurring into each other, all the while hoping Kylee might be standing next to one.

The silence was deafening. Stan knew it was best to let her cool down. Maggie had a way of drawing in to herself when she was upset. He reached to the turn the radio on, but her hand caught his and held it. The feeling was like an old favorite fragrance that he had long forgotten. Her soft hands seemed to melt through his callous skin. They were kind and loving, and they reminded him how much he loved and missed her. He kissed her hand and placed it back on her seat as he contemplated what would happen when they returned to Eau Claire without Kylee.

Chapter Nine

Maggie went to the back of the cab and started shuffling through her bags. She seemed on a mission and finally appeared with two bottles of water and an orange.

"Snack time." She said as she handed Stan a bottle of water.

"That is for you and this is mine. She placed her water bottle in the cup holder and began to peel an orange. Breaking apart the orange sections, she placed them on a paper towel in her lap.

"Okay, one for you, two for me" she giggled.

"Hey, wait a minute," Stan smirked.

"First things first, open wide." He reacted without thinking as she popped a vitamin in his mouth and told him to swallow.

"I feel healthier already," he joked as she pushed an orange section in his mouth.

They both loved fruit. Maggie fed him his share of the pieces in a teasing manner. He never got tired of her. He wondered what ever happened that caused them to go their separate ways.

"Okay, I get to pick the radio station now."

"Be my guest."

"How does this thing work?" she asked staring at the radio as if it were a foreign object.

"Here use this." He pulled down her visor and handed her the radio guide.

"Oh, wow, this is great. I had no idea. Oh... oh my!" she said as she giggled while looking over the various radio stations genre.

"Oh, no." Stan sighed knowing that she was sure to be selecting something that wasn't his style.

thump thump thump thump

The Chain

Oh yes it's ladies night
And the feeling's right
Oh yes it's ladies night
Oh what a night (oh what a night)
Oh yes it's ladies night
And the feeling's right
Oh yes it's ladies night
Oh what a night…

"Oh, God, Maggie, you have aged us for sure," he laughed, but even Stan couldn't stop from tapping his foot. It brought back memories of good times with Maggie dancing the night away.

The miles and memories intertwined for a long time. Stan was glad she was over her downward spiral. Though he would never have picked the station, he knew it helped them both lift their spirits. He planned on pulling off soon as it was getting dark, and Sioux Falls wasn't too far away.

"It's your song, Stan!" Maggie laughed as she sang, "I'm just a loving machine…"

The radio popped and cracked.

"Hey!" What's up?" she asked, frowning.

"I don't know. Sometimes it just goes nuts. Try changing the station".

"Well, crap, I liked that song," she said.

All of a sudden, they both heard a very loud "THUD!" Stan hit the breaks and slowed the truck, making his way off to the shoulder.

"What was that?" She asked with eyes full of concern.

"Not sure, maybe a tire." Stan shrugged, as he put the truck in park and turned on his hazard lights.

"Want my help?" she asked as he got out with no sign of traffic

"No, just stay in the truck," he said as he closed the door.

"Stupid radio," she said as the radio kicked back on.

"You can ring my bell. You can ring my bell. You can ring my bell. Ding dong ding ahhh ring it."

Out of the corner of her eye, Maggie saw her. She was standing just over a hill with her blonde hair blowing in the wind. It was Kylee. Maggie gasped as her world went into slow motion. She opened the truck door, almost fell out of the truck, and started to run. Her heart raced as tears poured down her face.

She screamed, "Kylee!" falling into some brush, but she wouldn't take her eyes off of her daughter. She rose to her feet and continued her run.

As he came around the back of the truck, Stan heard Maggie's scream. He saw Maggie running and watched her fall to her knees. It was then he saw Kylee. He could only see her head. She was looking toward them as if in a daze. He ran across the hills chasing after Maggie, and caught up to her as she crossed over the last hill where Kylee stood. It was just as before. Her clothes were in perfect condition and her hair was flawless. Her thumb and pointer fingers made little circles and were locked together. As they drew close, Stan realized he could smell the ozone and finally Kylee.

Maggie dropped to her knees ten feet in front of Kylee with her hands outstretched. Tears were rolling down her face and all she could do was cry. She finally said, "Kylee".

Kylee just stared off in the distance as if she couldn't see Maggie and Stan.

"Kylee, honey, can you hear Mommy? Come here, baby," Maggie called to her with open arms.

Kylee looked down into her mother's eyes with a calm emptiness.

"Kylee!" Maggie called to her sternly.

Kylee's demeanor changed and she looked at Maggie and said, "Hi, Mommy."

A smile filled Kylee's face that felt like the morning sun as she ran to Maggie.

Maggie embraced her breathing in Kylee's scent.

Stan wrapped his arms around the both of them and sobbed.

"Don't cry, Mommy. Daddy, don't cry."

Stan's mind was racing. This is happening. This is really happening!

Maggie started examining Kylee and said sternly, "Are you hurt? Did they hurt you, honey?"

Kylee responded "I'm thirsty, Mommy."

"Of course you are, Kylee. Come on, let's go back to the truck," Maggie said, but Kylee just stood there and looked at Stan.

"Honey, come on," Maggie said

"Kylee looked at Stan and said questioning, "Daddy, my new shoes and dress?"

The Chain

Maggie looked at Stan, puzzled. Stan looked at Maggie and winked. Obviously, he knew something she didn't.

Stan gave Kylee a big smile and said, "Of course. What kind of gentleman would let a fair lady take the chance of getting her fine dress and shoes dirty?"

Stan stooped over and hoisted her up.

Kylee reached down with a hand cupped over her mouth and whispered into Stan's ear, "Thank you, Daddy."

The sun was going down as they loaded into the truck. Maggie fastened Kylee in the front seat and moved to the back.

Maggie was full of adrenaline as she searched through the bags in the back of the cab.

"Damn it! Where is it?" Maggie scowled as she continued to search.

"Mommy! Potty mouth!" Kylee giggled.

"Yeah… Mommy!" Stan chided her.

"Oh, gracious, I did potty mouth," she said, placing her hand over her lips. "I'm sorry. I lost something, but tada! I found it!" Maggie said as she loosened the cap on the water bottle.

She handed it to Kylee and said, "Here, honey, drink this."

Kylee drank the water bottle as if she were famished. It was disturbing, and Maggie looked at Stan with raised eyebrows. She finished it in a very short time and asked for another. Maggie gave Kylee the last water bottle and watched as her daughter devoured it.

"I'm tired, Mommy," Kylee said.

Maggie looked at Stan in a questioning manner as she spoke, "How about we stop at a hotel and rest for the night, Daddy?"

"Yes! One with a pool, Daddy! Please!" Kylee asked.

"Oh. I see, two against one. Well, looks like I have been outvoted!" He winked at Kylee.

Kylee and Maggie cheered together!

Stan knew his way around Sioux Falls and knew the perfect place. He pulled the truck into the Ramada and went inside to check on rooms. He came back to find Kylee sleeping in the front seat, and Maggie laying next to her with tears rolling down her face.

"Come, Maggie, I got us a room!" he said in an excited whisper. He unbuckled Kylee and carried her. Maggie grabbed a few things. The front desk clerk ooh'd and ahh'd when she saw Stan carrying Kylee in her party dress to the room.

Stan laid Kylee on the bed and Maggie began digging through a bag she laid next to Kylee.

"You stay with her while I get the rest of the stuff, okay?' Stan asked.

"Of course," Maggie said as she never let Kylee leave her eyes.

Maggie looked fondly at Kylee's patent leather shoes. She remembered the day Michael, Maggie and Kylee went shopping for the outfit. Michael kept going on and on about the shoes.

"Kylee, honey, remember it is all about the shoes. Basic black goes with everything. A little heel goes a long way," Michael smiled at her all the while getting looks from Maggie as she rolled her eyes.

"Mommy, what kind of shoes do you have on?" Kylee asked.

Everyone in the store looked down at Maggie's feet, and Michael rolled his eyes.

"What? What's wrong with my shoes?" Maggie asked.

"Well, nothing at all Ethel. Are you and Lucy making dinner for Fred and Ricky later?" Michael teased.

"Yeah, Ethel!" Kylee giggled. Kylee then asked Michael, "Who is Ethel?"

"Who is Ethel?!" he declared. "Why she is the best friend of Lucy, a fine lady and a true Diva," Michael stated as he made his way through the various shoes.

"Are you and Mommy best friends?" Kylee asked as she looked back and forth at both of them.

"Well, yes, honey, and Michael is also my cousin," Maggie explained.

"So, does that mean you are a Diva too, Auntie Michael?" she asked him.

"Absolutely, darling, and one day you will grow up to be one too!" he gave a pearl clutching wave and fake smile to an invisible audience. Kylee tried to mimic him; then they all burst out laughing.

Maggie shook off those treasured memories and looked down at her precious daughter lying on the bed. She slid off Kylee's shoes, amazed to see hardly any wear on them.

Kylee started to wake and asked for a glass of water. Maggie brought her two cups of water, and finally asked Kylee to get out of her dress and put on her pajamas. Kylee slid into her tie-died pajamas and went to get another glass of water.

The Chain

"Not too much, honey", Maggie told her. Maggie was amazed at how much her daughter was drinking. She was concerned.

Stan came in with a handful of luggage from the truck. He saw Maggie and Kylee talking on the bed. "I have a surprise," he said

"Hmmm, what could it be?" Maggie asked looking at Kylee like she knew.

"Oh my, Daddy! What is it?" Kylee asked.

"Close your eyes, everyone," Stan said as he unloaded several little boxes of rice and Chinese food and placed them on the table in the room.

"I smell something, Kylee. Do you?" Maggie asked.

"I do, Mommy. What is it?"

"Okay, open your eyes," Stan said.

"CHINESE! Yeah!" Kylee screamed.

She started jumping on the bed, and they all laughed.

Stan handed bottled water to both of them, and everyone sat down to eat. Kylee drank her whole bottle before she even started to eat. She ate the sweet and sour chicken and skipped the rice.

Kylee hummed as she ate her food, finally breaking into song, "This is so good. I want to be Chinese!"

Everyone laughed.

Kylee refilled her bottle from the sink two more times during the meal. Maggie nudged Stan under the table during her second trip to the sink.

He nodded at Maggie making a gesture to not worry.

After the meal, Kylee said, "I'm going to fill my water bottle in case I get thirsty in the night. Okay, Mommy?"

"Sure, honey". Maggie looked at Stan for a reaction.

Stan and Maggie tucked Kylee into bed and kissed her on her forehead. They said their prayers together and followed the same routine they had up to six years prior. It was as if time hadn't passed, but it had, and Stan and Maggie knew better.

Kylee fell asleep quickly. Maggie cleaned up the boxes of rice and Chinese food and put them back in the paper sack. She didn't realize how hungry she was till she ate the food. Her mind was racing with a million thoughts, but most of them were centered on her concerns for Kylee. Her excessive dehydration was worrying Maggie.

She whispered to Stan, "The extreme water drinking has me concerned, Stan. She isn't exhibiting other signs of dehydration, but she is a child and very resilient."

"Don't diabetics drink a lot of water?' Stan asked.

"Well, that is a sign, I believe. When we get back, I'm going to arrange a doctor's appointment for her," Maggie said.

"Maggie, are you sure you want to do that? Think about it. She has been missing for six years, and she hasn't aged a day. What will people say? How will you explain that to the doctor?" Stan asked.

"True, but she needs to be evaluated. Something isn't right. We can not hide her forever, Stan," she said.

"And what will you tell the newspaper, and television reporters? Oh, I saw her on the side of the road and everything is better now. Please leave us alone?" Stan hissed at her.

Stan was right, and she knew it. She hadn't considered what they would do if they found Kylee. Though she followed Stan on this journey, maybe she really never anticipated success, but hope drove her to where she was now, and she was thankful for it. The police would surely frown at their story and suspect something whether it was the truth or not, but they never believed what they heard six years ago either.

Stan and Maggie got ready for bed. He held her close, and knew she would hardly sleep this night.

She turned over in the bed to face Stan and said, "Forgive me. I should have believed you from the minute you walked into the house. How could I have not smelled my own daughter? It was all over you that day. I'm an awful mother."

She wept as Stan held her close.

"Now, now, Maggie, that isn't true. First of all, you say you didn't believe me, yet you packed all of Kylee's clothes, and it took me two encounters to realize what I smelled. And relative to you being a good mother, you are the best anyone could ever hope for." He said as he kissed away her tears.

They embraced and started to kiss as she climbed on top of him. They were lost in a deep passionate kiss when Kylee said, "Mommy, I need more water."

Maggie giggled and whispered into Stan's ear, "I will make this up to you. I promise."

Maggie got out of bed, and took Kylee into the bathroom to fill her water bottle.

The Chain

"You sure have been thirsty, Kylee. Do you need to pee, honey?" Maggie asked.

"Yes, Mommy, can I have my privacy," Kylee asked.

Kylee came out and Maggie saw Kylee had her bathing suit on under her pajama top.

"Kylee, are you planning on going swimming?" Maggie asked with a smile

"Yes, Mommy. Tomorrow Daddy said he is going to take me to a magical pirate ship like the one Peter Pan and his friends were on."

Maggie giggled and said, "Oh that sounds like a lot of fun. Now, let's get you back to bed."

Maggie heard Stan snoring as she tucked Kylee in. She kissed her on her forehead.

"Mommy, could you sleep with me tonight?" Kylee asked.

"Aww, sure, honey," Maggie said as she climbed into the bed.

"Plus, Daddy snores so loud," Kylee whispered. They both giggled and drifted off to sleep. Maggie couldn't remember a happier moment.

Chapter Ten

Maggie woke from a very peaceful sleep to the scream of a child. She reached for Kylee and realized she was no longer in the bed. With the window shades and drapes all pulled, the room was completely dark. She called out to Stan in loud whisper, "Stan!"

There was no response as she made her way around the dark hotel room searching for a light switch.

She stumbled across the room feeling for a light switch on the wall by the door. She was greeted by an empty room. She called for Kylee and Stan, and still no response. Then she heard Kylee scream. She opened the hotel door and stepped out into early morning sunshine. Maggie was greeted by yet another scream by Kylee. She cried out, "Kylee!"

Kylee cried back, "Mommy, save me! Captain Hook is trying to make me walk the plank" as Kylee slid down the sliding board from the large Pirate ship centered in the Hotel Pool.

"I'll get you, Peter Pan!" Stan yelled as he saw Maggie standing outside the hotel room in her underwear and a long t-shirt.

"And your friends too!" he winked at Maggie.

Just then, Maggie heard the sound of her worst fear as the hotel room door closed behind her, and she had no key. She quickly pulled her T-shirt down around her panties as she realized the pool was full of children and their parents. It was then she realized everyone was looking at her.

"Stan! I need your help here," she grinned with brightly colored cheeks.

"Oh, so you need Captain Hook's help, do you?" He laughed at her.

"Stanley, now please," she pleaded, looking down at her feet.

The Chain

Just then, Maggie heard the wheels of a cart and looked up to see a maid making her way down the hall. The woman smiled knowing all too well what had happened. She took out her pass keycard and let Maggie back into the room.

Seeing Maggie make into the room, Stan went back to playing with Kylee in the pool. He was chasing after her, as she pretended to use her sword to defeat the foe, when all of the sudden, Maggie grabbed his foot from underwater and pulled Stan through the water. He pleaded aloud that a great crocodile had him by the leg and was unable to break free of its grasp. He turned to see Maggie and held her close. She was in a pair of shorts and her t-shirt.

"Nice bathing suit." He teased.

"I was just about to say the same to you," she said as she looked at his frayed jeans shorts.

They realized that they had lost track of Kylee. They called out to her and she waved back to them from the seats next to the pool. She was talking to a little boy. He had dark skin and black hair. He was sitting in a wheelchair next to his mother who was fully clothed in Islamic attire. Her hair was covered, but you could see her face. She had lovely skin, but her face seemed so downcast.

Maggie climbed out of the pool and went over to Kylee and the people she was visiting with. "Hello, Kylee, who is your new friend," Maggie asked.

"His name is Ahmed, Mommy," Kylee said. "His family is from Michigan. He is one of Peter Pan's friends. We are working together to deal with Captain Hook.

"Oh, good thing you two are working together," Maggie said as she turned to greet Ahmed's mother.

"Hello, I'm Maggie. Kylee's mom," she said feeling completely naked in front of this woman draped in stunning mysterious clothing.

"So sorry. My English not so good," the woman said.

"This girl," she said, pointing. "She is yours?"

"Yes, she is my daughter," Maggie said with pride.

"And this Captain Hook is your husband?" the woman asked.

Maggie laughed, "Yes that is him."

"He very nice man," the woman said with a smile.

"Thank you?" Maggie asked waiting to hear her name.

"My name is Sameera. Ahmed is my son. He has sick legs," as she looked at him with great love.

Maggie watched Sameera as her face changed from love to curiosity. Maggie turned to see what had Sameera's attention. Kylee was standing next to Ahmed talking, and there was a small sparrow on her hand chirping away. Ahmed's face lit up as she placed the bird on his hand. The bird seemed very content and chirped a song as he looked at Kylee. He then flew back to Kylee's hand. It appeared she was talking to the bird, and finally, the bird lifted from Kylee's hand. It flew around the pool area finally disappearing into the rafters.

"Oh, wow," Maggie said as she approached Kylee.

"That was exciting," Maggie said.

"Hi, Mommy, Ahmed's legs are asleep, but they're gonna wake up," she said with a happy nod.

"Oh, they are? Are they?" Maggie said as she smiled at Kylee.

"Honey, I think we should probably go dry off and get some food. What do you think?" Maggie asked Kylee.

"Okay, Mommy."

"Ma il Salamma," Kylee said to Ahmed with a giant smile on her face.

Ahmed said, "Shookrun. Ma il Salamma."

Maggie waved goodbye to Sameera as she gathered Stan out of the water. They made their way back to the room.

The room was cool from the air conditioning, and Kylee said, "Mommy, it is freezing in here." Her teeth chattered.

They quickly dried off and got into clean clothes. Maggie brushed Kylee's hair and said, "Honey, what did you say to that little boy when you left?"

"Oh, I said 'Ma il Salamma'," Kylee said in a matter of fact way.

"It means 'Peace be with you' in Arabic. He taught me how to say it. Isn't that cool, Mommy?" Kylee asked.

"Wow that is very cool," Maggie said.

"And what did he say to you when we left?"

"Oh, he said 'thank you and peace be with you'," Kylee said.

"Wow, he taught you a lot of words," Maggie said.

Maggie continued to brush Kylee's hair and asked as if to continue the conversation, "And what was your new friend thanking you for?" Maggie asked.

"Oh, for waking up his legs. They have been asleep since he was born, but they are waking up now, Mommy," Kylee said

The Chain

Maggie stopped brushing and looked at Kylee in the mirror. She thought for a moment then said, "Kylee, do you know how Captain Hook is pretend?"

"Yes, Mommy."

Maggie started brushing again as she spoke, "Well, you realize that you were just pretending to wake up his legs, honey? He has some type of disease or birth defect that is stopping him from walking."

"Yeah, he has Muscles Disandfree, but I woke them up now, Mommy," Kylee said.

"Muscles Disandfree? You mean Muscular Dystrophy?" Maggie smiled at Kylee in the mirror.

Maggie continued the conversation while brushing her hair.

"Now, Miss Kylee, why do you think you can wake up your friend's legs?" Maggie asked.

"Because the Big Man said I could."

Stan came in and said, "Okay, we are all packed. You two ladies ready to go?" he asked.

"We're hungry!" Kylee yelled.

"Yeah, Daddy!" Maggie sounded concerned.

They were startled by a woman's scream from the pool area. Stan ran out the hotel room door and headed towards the commotion. Several people were gathered around the pool. It was empty with the exception of one child.

Maggie and Kylee caught up with Stan, and everyone watched as Ahmed made his way out of the pool water and up the steps. His mother was on her knees with her hands in the air, and Ahmed stood before her with a great smile on his face.

Maggie grabbed Stan and pulled him away saying with panicked eyes, "We must leave now!"

They made their way to the lobby. Stan went to the counter to pay the bill while Maggie led Kylee out of the lobby. They moved at a heightened pace towards the truck.

"Mommy, what is wrong? Why are we running? Did you see, Mommy? Ahmed's legs woke up! Yippee!" Kylee said as she was being pulled along by her mother.

Stan paid cash for the room. He turned to leave the lobby and found himself face to face with Sameera. She was crying with a great smile on her face and said,

"Thank you, Captain Hook! Thank you!"

She kissed both his cheeks. Stan smiled and waved goodbye as he made his way out of the lobby and to the truck.

As he got into the truck, he noticed Maggie sitting in the back looking out the back window of the cab as if she were afraid. Kylee smiled at Stan.

"You're the best Captain Hook in the world, Daddy"

"Apparently, your friend's mother thought so too, "he said as he looked to Maggie for an answer.

"What happened back there, Kylee?" he asked.

"Ahmed's legs woke up! They were sleeping a long time." She spoke like she was telling a story to her Barbie doll at Tea time.

"Wow, how did that happen?" he asked as if were having a child conversation.

"I woke them up, Daddy," she said.

"The Big Man told her she could do it," Maggie said looking at Stan concerned.

"The Big man…Well, that is great. How about some food?" he asked. He gave Maggie a questioning look.

"Stan, can we just get something to go? I want to get back."

Maggie's mind was far away. She was frightened. Her maternal instincts warned her that they were in danger, and she wasn't going to lose her daughter again. She struggled with what to do and where to go. It seemed they needed to make a plan. Everything had happened so fast, she wasn't sure which way to turn. Her fears doubled when she considered Stan's comments about a flood of reporters and TV news crews at her door. That is the last thing she wanted for Kylee. Either way, she needed to get home and get things figured out. More importantly, she needed to start getting answers from Kylee about this "Big Man."

A short ways up the road, Stan pulled into a truck stop and went into the store to get some food and drink for everyone. Stan returned and climbed back into the truck and handed Maggie a bag full of items he bought at the store. Maggie pulled out water bottles for everyone, and distributed fries and cheeseburgers. Stan got the truck going again, as Maggie picked through the bag sorting out the other munchies Stan had purchased.

Kylee sat in the back and ate her cheeseburger as she hummed a song.

"Kylee," Maggie said.

"Yes, Mommy."

The Chain

"So tell me about the 'Big Man'.

"He is nice, Mommy."

"I bet. Where did you first meet him?" Maggie asked.

"He was at Kevin's party," Kylee said as she sipped her water.

Maggie turned pale as she and Stan exchanged glances.

"Is that the first time you met him?" Maggie asked.

"Yes, Mommy"

"Where did he take you when you left the party?" Maggie asked.

"Up into the sky, Mommy."

Stan looked at Maggie in the mirror very concerned. So it was true. She really was abducted.

"Did he hurt you, Kylee?" Stan asked very irritated.

"No, Daddy," Kylee laughed.

Maggie gave Stan a look that said, "Shut up and let me handle this!"

Maggie asked, "Did you have fun up there, Kylee?"

"Yes, Mommy."

"What did the Big Man look like?" Maggie asked.

"He was very tall, and bright. He had a white uniform on."

"Was he dressed like a doctor?" Maggie asked.

"Yeah sort of. I don't want to talk about this anymore, Mommy."

Maggie struggled with letting the conversation go. This was the first time Kylee ever discussed that day and what happened. Maggie just had to know what was going on.

"Well, I guess you don't want the surprise that Daddy bought us," she said as she rummaged through the bag peering inside oohing and ahhing.

"A surprise! What is it?" Kylee was excited.

"Kylee, I know you are tired of talking, but do you remember what the 'Big Man's" name is?" Maggie asked.

"Mommy! I must never say it! Never!" Kylee said in a very matter-of-fact way.

"Why not?" Maggie asked.

Kylee's demeanor changed. She looked catatonic as if she were lost in her thoughts. She finally spoke in a very monotone voice, "It is a name which is not to be spoken."

"Did he tell you not to say his name, Kylee?" Maggie asked.

Kylee just ignored her and looked out the windshield at the highway in front of them. Maggie finally gave Kylee a candy bar. It was a

Kit Kat bar. They were Kylee's favorite. She would often serve them at her Tea parties with Michael.

Kylee broke the two strips of the candy bar into halves and shared them with Maggie and Stan. She ate half of her piece, and wrapped the last piece up in a napkin, and put it away.

"Do you not want the last piece?" Stan asked.

"I'm saving it for Michael, Daddy."

"I see," Stan said as he looked back to the highway, still not sure how he would explain what happened with Michael.

After driving for some time, Maggie realized that Kylee had drifted off to sleep. She stuffed one of Stan's undershirts with clothes to make a pillow for Kylee and propped her head.

Maggie leaned forward to whisper into Stan's ear.

"What are we going to tell her about Michael?" she asked.

"The truth. That he has gone away."

"This whole 'Big Man' thing is crazy, Stan, "Maggie said.

Stan nodded and said to her, "I think we need to come up with a plan. We are being entirely too reactive."

"You are right," she said.

"Let's just get home. We can rest for a few days. That will give me time for us to pack. We can go away for a while and try and get our heads together."

"I don't have a lot of money, but I can get the time off," Stan said.

Maggie smiled at Stan. He had been the pillar she always relied on. Even after six years of separation, she still found herself needing him… wanting him.

Not long after, Stan looked over and saw that Maggie had drifted off to sleep. He tried hard to figure out his next move. Getting off from work for a week shouldn't be too difficult. He would drop off the paperwork at the office in the morning, and tell them he had to take a medical leave. He had never taken off before and was sure they would be suspicious, but they had other drivers and things were slow. He had money in savings, but it wouldn't last them long. The real question in his mind was where to go and who could they trust? He was sure they would reach Eau Claire by nine o'clock. For now, he would have to figure out a place to go.

Maggie and Kylee both woke around dinner time. Stan found a nice little restaurant that offered trucker parking. They filled up on meatloaf and macaroni and cheese. Even Maggie splurged when the waitress

The Chain

brought fresh apple pie with a large scoop of vanilla ice cream to the table.

Kylee said, "A la mode. I want to be French, Mommy!"

Everyone chuckled.

Chapter Eleven

"Mommy, can we go to the bathroom?" Kylee asked.

"Sure we can, honey. Mommy needs to powder her nose." Maggie said with a wink to Stan.

Stan paid the bill and waited outside the restroom door. He was watchful for any signs of Rudy and Deloris. But it was uneventful. Maggie came out with Kylee, and they all walked out of the restaurant and over to the truck. Stan escorted them both and helped them into the cab. As he got into the truck, he could see the frightened look on Maggie's face.

"What's wrong?" he asked.

She looked at Stan worried, "Smell it?"

She was right. There was a strong smell of ozone in the air. Just then a large bolt of lighting came down out of the sky and hit the telephone pole across the street. Maggie and Kylee screamed as fire streaked the sky, the ground shook. The loud rumbling echoed in their ears. Stan threw the truck into gear, and pointed it back in the direction of Eau Claire.

"Go, Stan! Faster!" Maggie urged him.

More flashes of lightning decorated and illuminated the sky, and then they all heard a large whoosh sound. They were immediately enveloped in a downpour. Stan slowed the truck and continued his way down the road, his wipers struggling to keep the windshield clear.

Finally, Stan looked at Maggie and said, "It was just a storm. That's all."

Maggie looked at him, then at Kylee, who was clutching her hands to her face, and then she and Kylee burst into laughter.

"Why were you screaming, Mommy?" Kylee asked.

"I don't know; why were you screaming?" Maggie asked her.

The Chain

"I screamed because you screamed."

"I scream, you scream, we all scream for ice cream," Maggie sang.

"A la Mode," Kylee giggled.

Ten miles down the road, the rain had become a light drizzle. The radio had just finished playing Disco Duck.

In the quiet of the moment, Kylee asked, "Daddy, where are we going?"

"We are going home. To our house, so we can sleep in our beds," he said.

"We shouldn't go there, Daddy." Kylee said with a distressed look as she dressed her Barbie doll in a different outfit.

"Oh and why is that, pumpkin?" he asked.

"Because they will find us, Daddy" she said.

"Who will find us?" he asked.

"The Seevers will find us."

"Are you talking about the 'Big Man', Kylee?" Maggie asked.

"No, Mommy, they hate the Big Man."

"Daddy will protect us from the Seevers. Right, Daddy," Maggie prodded Stan.

"Of course I will, honey." Stan glanced at Maggie and realized that neither of them really could protect her.

The rest of the ride was very quiet. They ended up getting home later than Stan anticipated. The storm clouds seemed to follow them right into Menomonee. Stan pulled up to the side of the farmhouse getting the cab as close as he could to the front porch. The downpour was like buckets of water being dumped from overhead.

"What all needs to go in the house?" Stan asked Maggie.

"There is nothing we need right now. I can get it out tomorrow," she said.

"Well, then it is time to make a run for it. Soldiers are you prepared?" he asked in his best Drill Sergeant's voice.

"Sir! Yes, Sir!" they responded.

"We move out at the count of three. One. Two. Three! Move out!" Stan ordered.

The girls laughed and ran with their hands over their heads. The rain was deafening. The front door was locked, and Maggie fished her keys out of her bag. They entered the small entrance hall taking deep breaths. They were soaked.

"No one move!" Maggie shouted as she ran into the bathroom to get towels.

"I don't want water all over the house."

"Okay, soldiers. Here are some nice clean towels. Please get out of those clothes and, I'll get you some warm dry ones," Maggie said as she started to undress as well.

Maggie handed Kylee a pair of pajamas.

"Mommy, I want my good pajamas. Not these," Kylee complained as she stood there wrapped in an oversized towel.

"Oh, they are in the truck. Can you wear these just for one night?" Maggie asked.

"Those are dorky pajamas. I don't want to look like a dork, Mommy."

"A dork? Who said these pajamas look dorky?" Maggie quizzed her.

"Michael did, "Kylee said in a very matter-of-fact way and handed them back to Maggie.

"I'll run and get them," Stan interrupted as he opened the door to the pouring rain.

"It's in the small red suitcase," Maggie called out.

Stan made his way back to the truck and saw movement in the window at Mrs. Clayton's house. He climbed into the cab, and opted not to turn on the interior lights. He rummaged through the back till he found the small suitcase. He was about to open the passenger door to exit the truck when he noticed a black sedan at Mrs. Clayton's house. It wasn't her car, or at least not the car Stan recalled her driving. He watched from the cab as he saw a man on the phone talking in the kitchen window. Immediately, all the lights went out in Mrs. Clayton's home. Lightning traversed the sky like a mangled piece of barbed wire. Stan made his way back to the house.

Maggie saw the lights go out and immediately reached into a drawer in the little entrance hall table. She had a small flashlight and used it to track down matches and candles. Kylee followed her around the house as she lit candles. Stan came through the front door, and was soaked from head to toe.

Maggie offered him a towel, and a change of clothes.

"What a storm," Maggie said as she dug Kylee's tie-died pajamas out of the small red suitcase.

"Put these on, and we will light a fire in just a minute."

The Chain

Stan had a strange look on his face.

"What's wrong, Stan?" Maggie asked.

"Did Mrs. Clayton purchase a new car? A black sedan?"

"Not that I know of. She was still driving that old Crown Victoria as of last week.

"Well, she has company, and it is a man."

"Hmm, that's strange. Maybe she got lucky," Maggie teased.

"Maybe she won't be the only one," Stan shot back.

"Where's Kylee?"

"She's... she's... well hmm..." Maggie said as she made her way towards the kitchen. She saw a candle go out and heard movement in the dark.

Maggie whispered, "Kylee?"

Kylee whispered, "Shhhh."

Maggie and Stan followed her voice.

Kylee was standing with her back to the wall next to a window. Maggie approached her and whispered, "What's wrong, honey?"

"There was a man in the window. I saw him when the lightning lit the sky. We should leave here, Mommy."

Stan whispered, "I'm going to check. Draw the blinds and lock the doors."

He made his way out the front door and went around the opposite side of the house. He was careful not to move too quickly in hopes of catching the man off guard. He hoped it wasn't the 'Big Man'.

He peaked around the corner towards the window. There were bushes there and the rain made it hard to see. Stan realized he had no weapons, and no plan. He moved out from the house and towards the window. The white noise of the rain made it hard to hear anything out of the ordinary. He looked for signs, in the mud and grass, for footprints, but saw nothing. He turned around and made his way back around the house, still waiting for someone to jump out of the shadows. He finally reached the front door and knocked.

Maggie handed Kylee a rolling pin, and Maggie grabbed a butcher knife. They made their way to the front door. She unlocked it, and waited in the candlelight.

Stan opened the door and said, "It's me Stan."

Maggie let out a sigh.

Stan looked at them both and chuckled. "What are you supposed to be? The butcher and the baker? What am I? The candlestick maker?"

Maggie said, "Real funny. Did you see anything?"

"No. Can I get dry now?" he asked.

"Oh, sorry. Here" She handed him a towel.

The lights came on and Kylee and Maggie both screamed at the same time.

Stan took away their kitchen weapons and said, "Here, let me take those before someone gets hurt."

Kylee and Maggie laughed as Maggie locked the front door. They made their way upstairs careful to blow out the rest of the candles. Kylee asked if she could sleep in their bed tonight.

Maggie said, "Sure, honey" as she smiled at Stan.

They cuddled in Maggie's bed in the soft country quilts made by Maggie's grandmother. The rain continued on the tin roof. Stan was the first to doze off. Maggie and Kylee continued to whisper to each other.

"Oh no, Mommy. He will be cutting wood soon"

Maggie kissed Kylee on the head and said, "You are right. Let's try and fall asleep fast"

Chapter Twelve

The rain poured down, saturating his dark clothing, as Keith Ross climbed down from the tree. The dark night and curtain of rain allowed him to function flawlessly in his element. His teammates called him "Panther" due to his natural agility and nerves of steel. His ability to remain unseen was what made him special. So many others had to learn this ability, but it was natural to him. He learned the importance of leaving no tracks or trails. They said he seemed invisible, but for all of his natural abilities, he couldn't escape the night vision goggles in Keeper's hands.

Conrad spoke into a headpiece, "Panther, come home."

There was no response, nor was one required. Panther stayed low to the ground as he saw the lights of the house come on. He heard a scream and froze. Had he been discovered? Then he heard laughter, but could it be there were more than two people in the house? He only had a short time in the home, and his exit through the basement window was challenging. He escaped into the wooded area behind the house and paused to listen for movement. The white noise of the rain would allow for many things to move freely in the night. Thus, he shared his advantage with other creatures of the night.

Jenkins hissed at the rain. He preferred the drier climate of the high desert, but he knew that his teams were trained to work in all weather conditions.

Mrs. Clayton made coffee and tea for her guests. Jenkins gave her a nod of appreciation as she made her way back to the den.

"Are our ears in place?" Jenkins asked.

"Affirmative, but only two," Ross replied.

"That should be plenty," Jenkins nodded.

"We are in 'watch and wait' mode from here out. We don't anticipate any activity, but I want both teams in place just in case." Jenkins spoke clearly to the two team leaders.

"Team one is assembled; Team two is on standby at the airport," said an attractive young woman.

She appeared to be right out of college, but that was what made her so valuable. She could appear to be many things at the drop of a hat, and that is what Jenkins liked about her.

Beth Foster was hand picked by Jenkins. Many thought it was the perfect figure and stunning smile that made Jenkins choose her over so many others, but the truth was she was deadly with a firearm, and could shift into any role at any time. Her team name was Chameleon.

"Beth, we still want to maintain a very low profile here. We have no reason to expect activity, but just in case I need your team to be ready to move quickly. Our eye in the sky will give us limited advantage. Please remind your team that we don't anticipate this situation turning hot."

She nodded.

"Ross's team has established light surveillance of the area, and we have two sets of ears inside. We're not sure why the secondary nodes have re-acquainted, but we will be keeping a close watch. This could be temporary and mean nothing, but I want us to be prepared to intercept the primary node. Understood?"

Panther and Chameleon nodded.

Chapter Thirteen

Stan woke to the feeling of someone in the room. He could see the silhouette of Kylee standing next to the bed.

"What's wrong, honey?" he whispered.

She placed her hand over Stan's mouth and motioned for him to follow.

Stan slipped out of bed and walked with Kylee to the hallway. A glow from a low energy blue night light lit the hallway. Kylee sat in front of it. Stan started to speak, but she placed her hand back over his mouth and pointed at a tablet on the floor.

Stan picked up the tablet and read.

"They are listening. Don't talk Daddy. They can hear us. The Big Man told me in a dream. We shouldn't have come here. We should leave now, Daddy."

Stan started to speak again, and Kylee quickly put her hand over his mouth and handed him a pen.

Stan wrote on the tablet.

"Who is listening? Is it the Seevers?" he asked.

"No, it is the Watchers," she wrote back.

Both of them were startled when they looked up and saw Maggie.

She looked at Kylee and Stan and whispered, "What is going on?"

Stan put his finger over his lips and motioned Maggie to read the tablet.

Maggie took the tablet and read it all. She then motioned for the pen and wrote, "How can they be listening to us?"

Kylee wrote, "They put ears in the house."

Maggie wrote, "Do you know where the ears are in the house?"

Kylee led them downstairs into the den. She pointed at a lamp on a table.

The morning sun was just starting to rise, but it was still too dark in the house to see. Stan grabbed the pen and told them to go upstairs and not to talk.

As they left, Stan checked the cord from the wall to the lamp looking for anything out of the ordinary. The lamp was nothing special. It had a ceramic base. He looked at the lamp shade following every piece of metal from one end to the other. He could see nothing out of the ordinary. He was about to take off the shade when he saw a small metallic wire just barely sticking out under the lip of the shade. Had he not looked on the inside, it would have escaped him. He moved slowly away from the lamp, and made his way upstairs.

He moved to Maggie and took the pen and paper from her.

"We need to get out of here. She was right; we shouldn't have come back. I found something in the lamp. It could very well be some kind of listening device. I'm not sure who, but obviously someone is interested in us. We need a plan," he wrote.

Maggie wrote, "If we are going to get out of here, we will need some kind of diversion. How could they know we have Kylee?"

Stan Wrote, "Maybe they don't know? Let's create a diversion. How about we pretend to wake up in what appears to be a typical morning scene. You turn the radio on loud and we start the shower and plan behind all the noise. Kylee <u>must not</u> say a word."

Kylee nodded that she understood.

Maggie spoke out loud. "Stan, wake up sleepy head or you're going to be late for work. "

She went downstairs and started the coffee like she usually did. Then she headed to the den and turned on the stereo. She turned up the volume very loud.

Stan yelled from the bedroom, "Damn lady, you like your music loud!"

Kylee grinned as they entered the bathroom. They shut the door and turned on the shower.

When Stan and Kylee came back out of the bathroom, Maggie returned to the bedroom. Stan walked over to her and placed his mouth against Maggie's ear and started to speak, "We need a diversion. I propose an ugly fight between us. I will make my way to the truck and make a loud and ugly departure. Kylee can sneak and hide in the backseat of

The Chain

your car. No matter what, don't use your cell phone. I'm sure they are listening there as well. Go to Wal-Mart and purchase two throw-away cell phones. Use cash so they can't track your purchase. Kylee must not be seen."

Maggie whispered into his ear, "Where are we going to meet?"

"I'll meet you in the Wal-Mart parking lot. Can you get cash?" he asked in a whisper.

She nodded.

Everyone showered and packed. Kylee followed Maggie and went to her bedroom. Kylee watched as Maggie opened her closet door and started digging through the twenty purses hanging on the back of the door. She finally pulled out a large gaudy purse that resembled something Christy Love wore in the 70's.

Kylee opened her mouth and stuck her pointer finger into it indicating her dislike, but Maggie showed Kylee the inside. It was full of cash, and lots of it. Kylee had a huge smile and gave her the thumbs up.

Stan brought the tablet to Maggie and wrote, "Kylee, Mommy and Daddy are going to have a pretend fight with lots of potty mouth words. We don't talk that way, but we have to in order to fool the watchers. Okay?"

Kylee nodded.

They assembled in the kitchen.

"Did you make coffee?" Stan asked in a moody voice.

"Yes, Stan. It's on the counter. Could you just get going? I have to get to work." Maggie shot back.

Stan drank some of the coffee and spit it out. "Christ, woman, are you trying to poison me?"

"Look, asshole, just get your shit and get out. This was all a mistake!" She yelled at him.

"Well, you married this asshole, so I guess that makes you bride of asshole," he said as he slammed down the coffee mug.

"Get the hell out of my house," she screamed at him.

"Listen, bitch. You are nothing but a cheap ride. I'm thankful that our daughter never grew up to see what you became," he yelled back as he went out the door, slamming it behind him.

Maggie made her way to the door and screamed, "FUCK YOU! And don't ever come back Stanley Weaver! Ever!"

She slammed the door and fell to her knees sobbing.

Kylee came over to comfort her, and when Maggie looked up, Kylee could see she was actually giggling. Maggie pointed for her to go out the back door.

Stan started the rig. A loud, 'Rum, rum, rum' filled the air as he revved the engine. Dark smoke from the diesel shot into the sky and smelled up the air. He punched the pedal and headed for the road.

Kylee slipped out the back door with her little red suitcase.

Stan slammed the truck brakes on and made an ugly scene at the road. He revved the truck beeping his horn and gave the finger in the general direction of Maggie's house. By now, all eyes were on him. Kylee hunched over and snuck to the car. She tried to open the back door, but it was locked. She tried it several times. Maggie watched from the window over the kitchen sink in panic as she realized that Kylee couldn't get in. She dug through her purse for her car keys, and hit the electronic lock button. The locks all clicked open and Kylee was finally able to open the door. She slid in, softly closed the door behind her, and hid on the floor behind the back seat.

Stan continued his show with the eighteen-wheeler and finally made his engine roar once more as he drove off down the road.

Maggie's phone rang.

"Maggie, this is Beverly Clayton. Is everything all right?"

"Hi, Mrs. Clayton. Yes, everything is alright. I thought Stan and I could…work things out, but well… As you probably heard. That isn't going to happen." Maggie sobbed.

"Oh, honey, I'm so sorry. Should I come over?" Mrs. Clayton asked.

"No, no. I'm going to work. It'll make the day go faster."

"Okay, honey, you just call me if you should need anything."

"Thanks, Mrs. Clayton. Goodbye now." Maggie hung up the phone, happy with her performance. She made one last trip through the house and shut off the radio. Everything was where it should be. She grabbed the tablet and her oversized purse and made her way to the car.

Chapter Fourteen

Maggie walked to the car. The small red suitcase sat in the backseat. It took everything she had to not look behind the seat and confirm Kylee was there. She started the car and turned on the radio. Maggie looked in the mirror as if she were checking her makeup. She was trying to think of what her normal routine was each day. It was strange how she went through the same steps everyday, but when forced to think about it, she drew a blank.

The car rolled down the dirt and gravel driveway ending at U.S. Highway 12. Maggie liked living here, but today she was looking forward to getting as far away as possible. She turned east onto the highway, thankful that Wal-Mart was in the same direction as her office. She tried to look normal, but found herself looking in the rearview mirror repeatedly searching for a pursuer. There were none, at least none that she saw.

* * * *

Stan travelled through town taking the most direct route to work. He backed the empty trailer up to the loading dock wanting to keep the appearance of his typical routine. He got out of the truck and approached the dock where Sam Gentry stood.

Sam opened the trailer doors and said, "I see you have an air delivery."

"Well, I like to travel light." Stan handed Sam the envelope from Mrs. Bauer.

"Would you mind not loading me up today? I'm going to go inside and see about taking a few days off."

Sam scratched his head and said, "Well, that's not like you. Where are you off to?"

"I have a date with a fish," Stan smiled.

"Well, I hope she is a pretty one." Sam winked.

Stan went inside to talk with Jed Fisher. Jed was a short man standing 5' 6". He was in good shape for someone in their late fifties. He walked three miles each day, and focused on a healthy diet, but everyone knew he had an affinity for ice cream.

"Hi, Stan. How goes it?" Jed asked with a warm handshake.

"Hello, Mr. Fisher. I know this is last minute, but is there any chance I could take some time off?"

"Well, I would think you have surely earned it," Mr. Fisher smiled.

"When did you want to take off?" Jed Fisher asked.

"Well, actually, I know this is very short notice, and I'm really sorry, but I wanted to take a week off starting today?"

Jed Fisher looked at Stan with an odd glance.

"I don't mind at all as long as we have coverage. Tony's due in this morning. Could you work it out with him? I'm sure he would appreciate the travel pay."

"Thanks, Mr. Fisher. I really appreciate it."

"Not so fast Stan. Where are you headed that you need to take off today?" Jed Fisher asked with an inquisitive smile.

"Fishing trip with some buddies. One person backed out, and I was asked to fill his slot," Stan said hoping he wouldn't push further.

"Well, that makes sense, because the only other acceptable answer was woman troubles." He looked at Stan seriously then broke into a laugh.

Jed Fisher patted Stan's back and told him to have a good time.

Stan returned to the loading dock and saw Tony talking to Sam on the dock.

Tony smiled at Stan and said, "I hear you are trying to get off because you have a date with a fish."

Stan laughed and said, "Well, hopefully more than one fish."

"Where you headed?"

"Canada," Stan answered.

"Watch the flies. They are awful this time of the year."

"So I hear. Does that mean you can cover for me?"

The Chain

"Yeah, I could use the travel time. I hate desk work. Sam says I can fit it all, and Casper isn't that far out of the way."

Tony delivered weekly to a copper mine in Butte, Montana. There was a time when they both delivered goods daily, but the competition in mining supplies had increased a bit and Jed Fisher's company was feeling the strain. Stan had seniority, so he took the full time delivery slot, and Tony filled in where needed. Jed Fisher paid his people well, but that didn't change Tony's feelings about a desk job.

"Tony thanks for doing this for me." Stan said with a handshake.

"No worries, Stan, you know I hate being in the office, "Tony said trying to hide his excitement. They said their goodbyes as Stan closed the back doors to the trailer. He dropped down from the loading platform and prepared to drop the trailer.

Stan insured that the brakes were set, and then uncoupled the air and power lines. He lowered the trailer's landing gear, and finally pulled the fifth wheel release. The movement of metal against metal was mineralized by the lubricant on the hitch. It always amazed him that this small release arm determined whether a trailer was attached or not. He made his way to the cab. The swishing sound of Stan dropping the airbags told him it was time to pull away from the trailer. Slowly the truck cab pulled away. It was a naked feeling for a driver, and they all knew the dangers of driving a truck without an attached trailer. The vehicle was designed to pull great amounts of weight over large distances. Without that extra weight the truck became a dangerous vehicle as it was dependent on the weight balance that a trailer provided.

Stan pulled forward about thirty feet and put the truck in park. Getting out, he proceeded to perform his typical inspection after disengaging from a trailer. He could see that it was about time for a lube job, but it wasn't urgent. As he made his way around the back of the truck, he made careful note that none of the lines were dangling. He looked under the chassis to make sure there were no outstanding issues.

Stan's mind was far away. He was concerned about Maggie and Kylee. He, Maggie and Kylee had to stay on the run, and continue moving, but to where, and for how long? Money was eventually going to run out, and then what? They would have to stop running and face their demons. He needed a fighting chance. He needed help.

His thoughts returned to the truck, and he reminded himself that "she needed a bath". A frown appeared on his face as he realized something looked out of place. It is a strange thing how the subconscious sees before the conscious recognizes an oddity. Stan re-scanned the area he was looking at. He thought of the sesame street song.

One of these things is not like the other…

Then his eyes caught sight of it, a small black box. It was very non-descript and unimposing, yet Stan felt violated, and his face reddened as he realized that it was some type of transmitter device. It had no markings, but the small antenna assured him that someone had been keeping tabs on him. The question was who, and why? He pulled on the device. It was held in place by a magnet. He noticed that the place where the magnet adhered to his truck was just as dirty as the rest of the surrounding area. It was obviously attached recently. Stan's mind raced as he thought of Maggie and Kylee going to Wal-Mart. He was sure their vehicle had a similar device attached.

He looked around to see if anyone was watching. Paranoia had taken over. He had to get to Maggie and Kylee and get them out of here. He was about to smash the device when Tony's truck got his attention. He knew Tony would take Stan's same basic route. He made his way over to the other rig and attached the device to the underside of the vehicle.

As he turned to return to his truck, he came face to face with Tony.

"Whatcha up to, bud?" Tony asked looking not so happy.

Stan stared at him and was at a loss of words.

"Now, look here. I know I'm not the senior driver here, and we both know I want your spot, Stan, but don't worry, bud. I'm willing to wait my turn."

Stan was overwhelmed, and just needed to get out of there. He reached his arms out and wrapped them around Tony and hugged him.

"Thanks so much. Drive safely."

Tony stood there like an unmoving tree, dumbfounded, and said, "No worries. Ahh umm."

Tony pulled away and said, "Now, you umm…have a good time…uhh fishing."

Stan nodded and had an uncomfortable look on his face as he looked down and made his way back to his truck.

Tony yelled, "Have a good time!"

Stan beeped his horn and pulled out. He saw Sam and Tony talking on the loading dock. They waved as Stan's truck left the loading area.

Sam looked at Tony, "So, what was that 'Brokeback Mountain' hug about?"

The Chain

Tony looked at Sam with a disapproving comment. "Apparently, fishing has him stressed out."

They both laughed.

Chapter Fifteen

"OK, folks, I want answers. What the hell just happened there?" Jenkins asked in to the radio headset.

"Looks like the secondary nodes have parted their ways." Ross answered into the radio.

"Ross, get over there and see if you can dig up anything." Jenkins sighed into the headset.

"10-4," Ross responded.

"What the hell, they slept in the same bed last night, and this morning they are at war!" Jenkins said to no one specifically.

"Love can be ugly," Mrs. Clayton said.

"How did she sound on the phone, Beverly?" Jenkins asked.

"Like a woman broken, and angry," she said.

"Was there anything out of the norm?"

"Not that I could tell, but he hasn't been at that house for years."

Jenkins phone rang.

"Jenkins," he said.

"Is this line secure, Sir?" the voice asked.

"Yes."

"Sir, the eye in the sky shows activity," the voice said.

"Where?"

"At the coordinates you gave us to monitor, Sir"

"How many Bogeys?" Jenkins asked.

"There are two entities; they're on the ground now."

"Dear God," Jenkins said as he stared out the window toward Maggie's house.

"Panther, we have guests. I repeat we have guests. Use extreme caution," Jenkins spoke into the headset.

"Affirmative," Ross replied.

The Chain

"Chameleon, get the bird here now," he spoke into the headset.

"Already on it, sir. ETA ten minutes."

Ross didn't work well in the daylight. He preferred the darkness, but he had no choice right now and had to make the best of it. He traversed the racks of canned vegetables in the basement all the while listening for movement above. It sounded like two people, but he couldn't tell. Slowly he climbed the stairs careful to evenly displace his weight. Reaching the top he looked under the door. There was movement. Whoever it was they were being loud and clumsy, and obviously hadn't heard him, or just didn't care.

"Here, Kitty Kitty" a woman's voice called.

Ross placed his hand on the doorknob and slowly turned it until he felt the door slightly give.

"Here, Kitty Kitty. Come on now. Momma's not going to hurt you," the woman said.

Ross felt the hair stand up on his neck. Primal fear began to overtake him. Seated at his twelfth vertebrae just above his kidneys, his adrenal glands secreted adrenalin into his blood stream.

As in an automobile accident, Ross' life went into slow motion as the door swung open.

Deloris was leaning over with her hand down to the floor from across the room. She was rubbing her pointer finger and thumb together. She stared at him with a grandmother's smile and called to Ross.

"Here, Kitty Kitty. Come here, honey. Momma won't hurt you," Deloris said as Ross found himself crawling to her.

"Good, Kitty. Come sit on Momma's lap."

Ross crawled over and rested his head on her lap.

"That's a good kitty. My, you are a sweet panther, aren't you?"

"Now what were you looking for down there in that basement, Kitty?" she asked.

Ross made a guttural sound as if he were unable to speak.

"Now now. Cat got your tongue?" she laughed.

"Bas Khalas!" Rudy yelled.

"Wen il ha-deyah?" Rudy said to Ross.

"I don't think the kitty understands you, honey," Deloris said.

"Where is the gift, Panther?" she asked as she scratched behind his ears. "Kitty, momma is talking to you. Now where is the gift?" Deloris asked as she gripped his hair in her right hand.

76

Ross's life came out of slow motion, and he felt control of himself again. He felt his return to focus.

"Who are you people?" Ross asked in a strained voice.

Like a mere rag doll, Deloris hoisted his body up and tossed him across the room. In his muddled mind, as he flew through the air, he was a leaping black panther. He crashed head and shoulder into the wall with a loud 'thud'. There was a pronounced crack as something broke, and his desire to vomit confirmed this painful fact.

Deloris appeared next to him. He wasn't sure how she crossed the room so quickly much less had the strength to toss him. He felt like he was in one of those dreams where you try to scream and nothing comes out of your mouth. He realized his head was in Deloris's lap again. She was once again petting him behind his ears. In a strange way, he liked it, but he knew he was in great danger.

"Momma is asking the questions, kitty. Momma knows best."

The sound of a helicopter got Rudy's attention. Rudy looked up at the ceiling as if he could see through it.

"We have guests, Mother," he said.

"It's not here. They must have it," Rudy said to Deloris.

She leaned over and whispered into Ross' ear, "You be a good kitty. I'll be keeping my eye on you. We want the gift. Tell Keeper to stay out of the way or momma will have to pay him a visit."

Deloris stood up and walked across the room to Rudy. She turned to face Ross and waved goodbye to him like a grandmother leaving from a visit with her grandchild. He watched as she turned away from him and disappeared.

"Panther, are you there?" Jenkins spoke into the earpiece.

Ross tried to speak, but could only muster a moan. Beth's team came in through the front and back of the house simultaneously. Their dark green flight suits were specifically designed for agility and contained many pockets for storage. Their clothing swished as they moved through the house with weapons drawn.

Beth passed through the kitchen, and heard Ross moaning. She came around a corner expecting to shoot her way through God knew what, but instead found Ross curled in the fetal position on the floor. His arm was broken and laying in a strange angle on the floor.

Beth spoke into the headphones, "Panther is down, but alive."

Jenkins sighed.

The Chain

"And our guests?"

"No sign, but the house smells like ozone." She looked around the room.

Jenkins phone rang.

"Jenkins!" he said into the phone.

"Sir, is this line secure."

"Yes, you know the Goddamned line is secure!" he yelled.

"Sir, our guests have left."

"Did you record it all?" Jenkins asked.

"Yes, Sir."

"Have it cleaned up, encrypted and uploaded to me ASAP!" Jenkins yelled as he slammed the cell phone shut.

Jenkins spoke into the headset "Chameleon, our guests are gone. Get Panther medical attention, and have the teams clean that place up. I want no signs we were there. Understood?"

"Affirmative," Beth said into the headset.

"Can you feel your legs, Ross?" Beth asked Ross.

He nodded yes.

"I need to move you, and it is going to hurt. Your arm is broken and possibly your clavicle as well."

Beth called to a member of the team "Gopher, help me with Ross."

Gopher was the quiet one on the team. He wore glasses that tamed his bright green eyes. He sported a red toned beard that he kept closely trimmed. He was her all round team member. Besides functioning as a supply office he was very organized, and she knew she could depend on him. He came to her side to assist.

Ross hissed and screamed as they turned him over onto a stretcher. As Beth saw that Ross' pants were wet in front, her sense of smell confirmed that he had urinated in his pants. She glanced at Gopher who raised his eyebrows. He threw a blanket over agent Ross. Agent Foster called over one of the agents to assist in transporting Ross to the waiting helicopter. She gave instructions to her team, and had them leave the house.

"Panther's loaded and ready for delivery. Will you be accompanying Chameleon?" a voice spoke into the headset.

"Negative," she responded.

Beth needed time to figure out what happened here. She knew Agent Ross came in through the basement. But why were they here?

And why had he been attacked. That wasn't typical procedure. Actually, there was nothing typical about any of this.

She made her way through the house looking for anything that might be out of order. She searched each room for anything that might give her a clue. This was a well kept home. There wasn't a lot of clutter or doodads all over the place. It was clear that a single person lived here. She noticed that the closet doors in Kylee's room were open. There were empty hangers in the closet. She swept the room and realized that this room had been empty for a while. Dust had settled just enough that you could see darker wood on the bedside table after wiping a finger across it. Agent Foster examined the child's dresser and saw that there were items that used to sit on top of the dresser that were now missing. There were blatant dark spots where dust had yet settled.

She whispered "God, help me find something," as she made her way to Maggie's room.

Everything had its place here. Its owner was clearly a perfectionist. Agent Foster opened Maggie's closet door and every garment faced the same direction sorted by color order. There was a definite break between casual and formal. She was about to close the door when she saw that the inside of the door was covered with a large pile of hand bags and purses. They hung from a single large hook affixed to the inside of the door. It was a peculiar image as they weren't sorted by size, style or length. She started pushing purses aside looking for anything out of order. These were just off the rack hand bags and shoulder bags from the 70's. They were nothing special in the way of vintage, and definitely not designer. Agent Foster first thought the owner was a collector, but a collector would have taken better care of their collection. She continued digging through them when something caught her eye. Balanced between two handbags was something that resembled a small book. She reached for the item, but it fell to the ground with a thud. Agent Foster pushed the door open further to reveal a stack of twenty dollar bills still in their paper wrapper on the floor.

She carefully placed the stack in a zip lock bag, happy with her find. She mouthed," Thank you," through the ceiling towards heaven.

Maggie Weaver must be on the run. But why? And where?

"Keeper, can you tug the leash and tell me where the secondary nodes are?" Agent Foster asked.

"Affirmative."

The Chain

"Nodes are still separated. Node two is at "Wally world", and node one is on a westerly route as was suspected."

"Got anything?" Jenkins asked.

"Possibly."

"You coming in?" Jenkins asked.

"Affirmative," Agent Foster said as she made her way through the kitchen.

She looked around the room, saddened what this family had endured. Walking over to the window above the sink she wondered what she would have done if she were in Maggie's situation. She looked down in the sink and saw an empty coffee mug. It didn't sit well with her. Is this the sink of a perfectionist? She opened the dishwasher and looked inside. Her mind was searching for any clue to what was going on. The dishwasher appeared empty. She pulled out the top drawer and saw two cups. A coffee mug and a juice glass sat in the back. She carefully removed them.

"Keeper, do we have an accurate guest count?" she asked into the headset.

"The eye reported two, but the media should be cleaned and uploaded shortly. You got something?" Jenkins asked.

"Possibly," she responded.

Chapter Sixteen

Maggie looked around before she got out of the car. She then opened the back door to get Kylee's attention and motioned for her to follow.

Kylee stepped out of the car and followed Maggie.

"Where are we going, Mommy?"

"We need to get some supplies, and then we are out of here."

"We really should leave soon, Mommy" Kylee said as she reached for her mother's hand.

"I know, baby. Daddy will be here soon and we will be gone. For now, we need to get you a disguise."

"Nice, like a costume? Can I be a princess?" Kylee asked excitedly.

"Well, for now, let's get you a hat and some sunglasses," Maggie said with a grin.

"Oh, like Jackie O?"

"Jackie O?" she said with a quizzical expression on her face. "How do you know who she is?"

"Michael told me about her. He said she was one of the prettiest women to ever live. He said she dressed impactably," Kylee said.

"Impeccably, Kylee," Maggie said as they both laughed.

They went straight to the sunglass section. Kylee saw a pair of sunglasses that had lenses in the shape of stars. She tried them on. They were a little large for her face, but Maggie thought they would work.

"What do you think, Mommy?" Kylee asked.

"Perfect, now let's get you a hat."

Kylee picked out a hat that read "Surfs Up!" Maggie helped Kylee pull her hair up inside the hat.

The Chain

They made their way to electronics where Maggie picked up two disposable cell phones as Stan requested. She also grabbed a six-pack of water, and some food.

Maggie continued to look over her shoulder constantly expecting someone to pounce on them, but her trip to Wal-Mart proved to be safe.

The woman at the checkout counter looked at Kylee and said, "Wow you are a star and a surfer! Where are you headed, little lady?"

Maggie began to panic as she found herself at a loss of words, but Kylee said, "We are going to California to a place called Malibu."

"Take off your hat and glasses for the cashier honey so she can ring them up."

"No need, I can get them with my price gun," the cashier said as she clicked the gun on the tags connected to the hat and glasses.

"Wow, Malibu, that sounds exciting," the cashier said with a wink to Maggie.

Maggie shook her head with a grin to the cashier as she handed her two fifties from her hand bag.

"You have a good time out there in Malibu," the cashier said as they walked towards the exit.

Chapter Seventeen

Stan found himself speeding the short distance to the Wal-Mart. It was still early in the morning, but he was overwhelmed with the feeling that time was running out.

There was no sight of Maggie or Kylee. He drove through the parking lot looking for Maggie's car. They had agreed she'd wait out front for him to pick them up, but he had taken longer than expected.

Maggie's car was parked across from the gardening area. He parked the truck out in the parking lot away from the rest of the cars. He made his way to her car. As he approached, he saw the red suitcase in the backseat. He was surprised to see the car unlocked. He opened the driver side door and hit the hood release switch under the dash. Stepping back out of the car, Stan looked around to see if anyone was watching before he finally lowered himself to the ground on the passenger side and looked underneath Maggie's car.

He needed time, and the longer he could keep whoever was tracking them off of their trail, the better.

He saw nothing in the engine area, but continued to search the wheel wells, and chassis. Maggie was still nowhere in sight as he looked towards the entrance to Wal-Mart.

Stan wiped the dirt and sand off of his jeans when a carload of teens pulled up next to Maggie's car. The loud music was thumping to a heavy bass line. It was an older SUV sporting new rims that were popular with the kids these days. The teens rolled out of the car. The driver had one of those cockeyed baseball hats that had some NBA team's emblem on it. His pants were halfway down with his boxers clearly visible.

"Mister, you having car troubles?" the youth asked.

"Nah, just heard a strange ticking when I was driving. Thought I would look under the hood."

The Chain

"Cool. Good luck, dude."

Stan watched as the driver and his posse headed to the entrance of Wal-Mart. It was then he saw Maggie and Kylee walking out. Hopefully, they hadn't been waiting too long. He went to the back of the car and looked around the tailpipe. The transmitter stood out with its black case against the chassis. It was situated next to the tailpipe. He pulled it away from the chassis. His arm brushed against the tailpipe. He gritted his teeth, reminded that the car was still very hot. He was sure he would have a heck of a blister on his arm from that mistake. As he rolled out from under the car he saw Maggie standing over him.

She didn't say a word, but put her finger over her mouth. Stan pointed at the device.

Maggie's eyes showed her fear. He got up and pointed at the suitcase. She opened the door, and grabbed it. She handed the suitcase to Kylee. Stan pointed to the truck, and she and Kylee made their way down the row of cars over to the truck.

As he got up from behind her car, he read the words that adorned the back window of the SUV "Florida or Bust Dawg!" Stan grinned as he reached under the back wheel well of the SUV and attached the magnetic transmitter. He made a hand gesture at the vehicle and said "Word!"

He headed to the truck at a quick pace. Maggie had already loaded the bags and was sitting in the front seat. Kylee was in the back sitting quietly.

Stan hopped into the truck and headed west.

Chapter Eighteen

Thirty minutes later, Stan was on Highway 94 heading west. The cab was quiet as no one spoke. Stan's nerves started to calm. He made a hand signal to Maggie, indicating he wanted a pen and paper.

Maggie pulled out a notepad and pen and handed it to him. She noticed a large blister on his arm and gasped.

Stan waved off her concern and wrote, "I found one of those on my truck as well. It looks to be some kind of tracking device. Probably some type of GPS transmitter. It appears like they were recently attached, maybe last night while we were asleep. I suspect Kylee did see someone in the window last night. Can you look around the cab for anything suspicious?"

Maggie read the note with concern, and then showed it to Kylee. She pointed at her eyes then around the cab.

Kylee nodded.

Finally, Maggie wrote on the paper, "Kylee, are there any ears in here that you know of?"

Kylee wrote, "No, Mommy. I don't think so, but the Big Man didn't say anything about Daddy's truck."

Maggie nodded.

Stan grabbed the pad and started to scribble, then handed it to Maggie.

She read the note.

"Here are the rules. If we discuss where we are going, we are going to Florida, even though we aren't. There could still be something in here, but I doubt it."

Maggie showed the note to Kylee, and she nodded.

The Chain

Though Stan gave them the okay to talk, the cab remained silent. The fear of being heard by someone unknown made everyone a bit uncomfortable. Stan eventually put on the radio to calm everyone's nerves.

It didn't take Maggie long to pull out the radio guide and change the station to hits of the 80's.

"You should hear how she talks about you,
You should hear what she says.."

Stan's mind rolled through all the events that lead up to now. He needed answers. He needed help. Some things didn't add up in his mind. Why had Kylee come back now? Who was watching them? What was this all about?

Maggie reached across and took Stan's hand. Her eyes widened as the large blister that was on his hand was gone. Stan had forgotten all about it.

Maggie grabbed the notepad and wrote, "What is happening? Your blister is gone!"

Stan looked in the back of the cab at Kylee. She was sleeping.

Maggie crawled in the back, dug out a small blanket and covered Kylee. She hugged Stan from behind the seat and whispered into his ear, "I'm scared Stan."

"I know, honey. I know," he said with very somber eyes, nodding his head.

Chapter Nineteen

"Water! I need water!" Agent Ross writhed on the medical table.

"Please stay still, Agent Ross. You have multiple fractures here." The doctor ignored his request and continued the examination.

Ross reached out and grabbed the doctor's hand.

"Give me some God damn water now!" he growled through grinding teeth.

The doctor was shocked and said to the nurse, "Okay… bring him some water."

"Now, please, let go of my hand," the doctor requested as he pretended not to feel Ross's crushing strength.

The nurse brought a pitcher of water. She started to poor into a paper cup, but Ross grabbed the pitcher and brought it to his mouth. He gulped down most of the pitcher, but had spilled quite a bit. He was soaked.

Agent Ross held the pitcher out to the nurse.

"More... now!"

She moved away quickly, clearly frightened by his manner.

The doctor was preparing to give him a shot when Ross said, "No pain meds. Do you hear me? None! I need to be coherent."

"Agent Ross, I have to move your arm. It is going to be excruciatingly painful. This will allow you to feel no pain." The doctor proceeded.

Agent Ross grabbed his hand again and said, "I said no meds!"

The doctor shook his head, and then said, "Okay, this is going to hurt. Please don't take this out on me," the doctor said as Ross released his hand.

The nurse came back with another pitcher of water as the doctor moved Ross's arm.

The Chain

Agent Ross screamed for a moment, breaking out in a sweat and going very pale. Then he laid there breathing hard. The nurse went to his good arm and held his hand.

His eyes were bloodshot and he said to her. "Water, please."

She brought a different pitcher this time that would be easier to drink from. She helped him sit up as he drank the entire pitcher and asked for another.

"You appear to be dehydrated, agent Ross. When is the last time you had something to drink prior to arriving here?"

"I had coffee this morning around 7:00AM."

Ross continued drinking water.

The door to the room swung open as Conrad Jenkins and Agent Foster crossed the room. Jenkins wore a black suit and white shirt.

"We are going to need to speak to Agent Ross alone, Doc. Can you give us a few minutes?" Jenkins asked.

"We haven't done x-rays yet," the doctor protested.

"Doc!" Jenkins stared at the doctor in a threatening manner.

"What the hell is going on here today? Come on," he said to the nurse.

"How are you?" Jenkins asked Ross.

"I've been better," Ross said as he continued drinking water.

"What the hell happened in there?" Jenkins asked.

"There were two of them. They looked like us. Well, more like someone from Archie Bunker's neighborhood," Ross said as he grimaced from shifting his weight.

"Did you talk to them?" Jenkins asked.

"A little. They did most of the talking. I wasn't in control of myself or the situation. We are compromised. They knew my call name. They know yours as well. They gave me a warning message for you."

He continued to relay the message and all that he could remember.

The doctor had made his way down the hall to the restroom. The nurse had followed his lead and went to the ladies' room.

He stood at the urinal, pulled down his zipper and breathed out as he urinated. Completing with a shake, he pulled up his zipper. He had the feeling like someone was behind him. Turning, he faced a being unlike any he had seen before. He was a very tall man with eyes that glimmered. The doctor was frozen, but not in fear. His life moved in slow motion. He saw the tall man's hand reach up and touch the doctor's forehead. The last thing he heard was, "Sleep now." The voice was like a pure stream of flowing water.

The tall man gently laid the doctor down on the floor. As he turned, his appearance morphed into that of the doctor and he made his way out of the restroom.

The nurse appeared at the same time. They greeted each other with a nod and made their way back to agent Ross.

They entered the room as Jenkins and Foster were saying their goodbyes.

"Doc, sorry about earlier. I hope you can get our man back on his feet soon." Jenkins patted the doctor on the shoulder as he and Agent Foster left the room.

The nurse approached Ross on one side while the doctor approached him on the other side.

They placed their hands on him and closed their eyes.

"Umm… what's this about?" Ross asked.

They opened their eyes and he could see bright light coming from behind their eyelids. It ignited the room in pure white light. Agent Ross felt himself relaxing and drifting off to another place.

Chapter Twenty

Keeper's phone rang
"Jenkins," he said into the cell phone.
"Is this line secure, Sir?"
"Yes," Jenkins sighed.
"Sir, we have activity."
"Where, and how many?"
"We show two at your location now, Sir"

Jenkins stopped walking and faced Agent Foster with his eyes wide open.

"Ross," he hissed at her as they started to run back down the series of hallways to his room.

Beth Foster was faster and more agile than Conrad Jenkins. She quickly pulled away. By the time they had reached the third hallway, he could only hear her shoes running ahead of him. He reached for his gun, but opted to focus on his pace. He entered the last hallway still running, but completely out of breath. He saw a body fall out of a doorway ahead of him. It was the doctor. He was crawling on the floor, but finally fell, exhausted. The smell of ozone was very strong in the hallway. Jenkins continued past the doctor on to Ross's room.

Jenkins came through and discovered Agent Foster helping Ross put on his gear. He looked amazingly good, almost too good.

"What the hell is going on here?" Jenkins said as he panted and holding his side from running.

Ross stood up and looked directly at Jenkins' face and said, "We were hoping you could tell us."

"What do you mean?"

"You know damn well what I mean."

Ross continued, "We are outmanned, outsmarted, and uninformed! How the hell do you expect us to do our job without knowing what the hell is going on?"

Jenkins knew Ross was right. He heard the cell phone clipped to his belt ringing but couldn't take his eyes off of Agent Ross and Foster. They were his handpicked team leaders. Both exhibited incredible abilities in leadership, marksmanship, but more importantly friendship. In the end, Jenkins was the leader, and for now he still had to lead, but maybe it was time to share what he did, or didn't know.

He pulled the cell phone from his hip.

"Jenkins. Yes it is. And where are they now?" He said.

"Upload what you have NOW!" he closed the cell phone and looked at Ross.

"Are you able to work?" Jenkins asked him.

"Yes. I need to change clothes," Ross replied.

"Foster, what is the status of our temporary Control Center?" Jenkins asked.

"Good to go. Uplink and live wire are already established. We are setup in hanger eight."

"Good!" Jenkins said. He was happy that they weren't completely disorganized.

"Agent Foster, the doctor is down the hall outside of the restroom. Check on him, find that nurse, and try to do some damage control. I do NOT want them talking."

Agent Foster spoke into the headset, "Weasel, I need CC and squelch. Have Gopher make his way to me."

"Affirmative, Chameleon," Weasel spoke into the headset as he re-directed nosey hospital staff away from the corridor. He pointed to Gopher, but Gopher was already on the move after hearing the conversation on the headset.

The Chameleon nodded at Jenkins as she left the room.

"Ross, I will see you and your people at 1100 hours. Have one of your guys get sandwiches and drinks. We have some things to discuss. I don't want you alone, so choose a member from your team to be your shadow."

Ross nodded as he felt his arm and shoulder with his good hand. He expected to find pain or evidence of his previous injuries. Yet, he found none. He was sure his arm was broken in at least two places. His shoulder was definitely dislocated. He knew Agent Foster was correct about breaking his clavicle. Yet, here he was with no breaks, bruises or scratches.

"So, what happened?" Jenkins asked.

"It was the doctor and nurse, or at least they looked like them," Ross said, his eyes full of bewilderment.

"They placed their hands on me, then their eyes. My God, it was like the whitest light. I couldn't see a thing, but I felt great warmth cross my body. I remember not being afraid, actually having no feelings at all." Ross said as if remembering an event that took place years ago.

"Did they say anything?" Jenkins asked.

"Yes."

Ross turned to face Jenkins and stared at his face.

"What is the gift?" Ross asked searching Conrad Jenkins face for signs of the truth.

"The gift?" Jenkins asked.

"Yes, please level with me here, Conrad."

"I will give a complete debriefing at 1100. In the meanwhile, tell me what they said," Jenkins demanded

Ross looked at Jenkins and said, "Protect the gift."

"Protect the gift?" Jenkins said as his eyes searched for answers.

The door to the room opened as Gopher and the Chameleon rolled the doctor and nurse into the room via wheelchairs.

Agent Ross made his way to the nurse. He held her hand and noticed it was very cold. He knew immediately what was wrong. They needed water.

He motioned to Agent Foster.

"They need water and lots of it," Ross said as he went to fill the pitcher.

Ross watched as the doctor and nurse ravenously drank from the pitchers.

"Little thirsty, Doc?" Jenkins asked.

The doctor nodded as he gulped down more water.

"Your arm?" the doctor said as he looked at Ross with a loss for words.

"All better. Thanks, Doc," Ross smiled.

"Sir, we have a meeting." Agent Foster looked at Jenkins, tapping her watch.

Jenkins looked at Ross, who nodded.

"I've got this taken care of," Gopher said as waved to Jenkins and the team leaders to go on ahead of him, 'Just save me a sandwich."

Agent foster smiled as she followed Panther and Keeper out of the room. Things were chaotic. She didn't like chaos.

A car waited for them outside of the hospital. The driver was Agent Joseph McCafferty, code named Clepto. The team teased him about his Irish heritage calling him McClepto, and McAgent, but they were in awe of him and showed him great respect. If not for his work, he would clearly be part of the upper echelon within the Mensa community. He was the proud son of an Irish Catholic family from Boston, but his Asian features assured that he was adopted. He would lead his own team one day, but was happy serving under Panther.

"Where to, Sir?" Agent McCafferty asked.

"The command center at the airport, hanger eight"

"Yes, Sir."

"Get us there quickly please."

Keeper looked out the window searching for answers to the questions he and the others had. Some he knew, others he speculated, and some he had no idea. What was the gift, and how could he and his group protect it?

Chapter Twenty-One

"Daddy, I gotta pee," Kylee said from behind him.

Maggie had fallen asleep an hour ago, but stirred to the sound of Kylee's voice.

All of this wasn't fair. Why had this happened to him, to Maggie, and even Kylee? Why did this have to happen to his family? He lost a daughter and a wife. He lost everything he lived for, yet here in front of him was something that resembled hope. He never had a chance of fighting before. It was all taken from him, like a wrestler taking a bottle from a baby. He had no defense, or understanding of how to defend these things he loved. Stan was ready to fight, but he found himself running.

"Daddy?" Kylee tapped his shoulder.

"Of course, honey. There is a rest stop coming. We will be there shortly."

He smiled, but was far away in thought.

Maggie cuddled under her light jacket, watching out the window. "It's so sad," she said as she looked over the dried up corn fields.

"Very," Stan said shaking his head.

"It's sad because I have to pee?" Kylee asked, confused by the conversation.

Stan and Maggie laughed.

"No, honey, the corn fields. See?" she pointed out the window to the dried up corn fields and parched land.

Kylee looked at the fields as if she recognized the place.

"We are in a drought," Stan said.

"The corn died because it didn't get enough water," Maggie explained.

"Oh, Mommy, it's not dead. It's sleeping," Kylee told them.

"Well, I hope it wakes up soon or a lot of cattle are going to go hungry," Maggie said as she stared forlornly out the window.

Stan pulled up to the rest area. There were a few trucks in the back. He pulled up away from everyone, towards the back of the lot.

"Could we park any further from the door?" Maggie asked, clearly not appreciating the distance she and Kylee would have to walk.

Stan gave Maggie a look that reminded her it was probably for the best. They made their way to the restrooms. Maggie was anxious, as bathrooms meant trouble in their past. It was a clean place, and fortunately for her, no one else was to be seen.

Maggie had Kylee join her in the stall. Kylee sat first, while Maggie listened for activity.

"Your turn, Mommy."

Maggie sat down, and found herself face to face with Kylee. Maggie tried to relax, and then they both giggled.

Maggie made a facial expression and twirled her finger indicating she needed her privacy.

Kylee turned around and faced the door. Maggie's muscles finally relaxed and she felt her bladder empty.

"Okay, let's wash our hands and get out of here," Maggie said.

They exited the stall and washed their hands.

Stan was waiting outside the door for them, thankful to see they hadn't endured another visit by Rudy and Deloris.

They traversed the parking lot and arrived at the truck.

Maggie said to Kylee, "Let's stretch."

"Like Ballerinas! Yeah!" Kylee said happy to participate.

Maggie watched Stan as he looked over the truck. She was always amazed at his relationship with trucks. He seemed to have some sort of a bond, like a cowboy and his horse. She once teased him that he cared more about his truck than her, but he always assured her there was no competition. He never did say who won that competition.

"Mommy, can I walk over there?" Kylee asked as she pointed to the edge of the corn field.

"You need to stay where I can see you," Maggie said.

"Okay". Kylee nodded as she skipped over toward the edge of the corn.

Maggie walked over to Stan, all the while watching Kylee. She saw Kylee reach over and touch a corn stalk. She saw her skip down a row.

The Chain

Maggie snapped at her, "Kylee, I can't see you!"

"Sorry. Mommy." Kylee made her way back towards the edge of the corn.

As Maggie approached Stan, it was clear he was troubled. He had taken on a look that concerned her. Maggie placed her hand on his back.

"What's wrong?" she asked him.

Stan continued to look over the truck as if he were grooming it looking for the smallest flaw.

"Stan?" she asked.

"I...I don't know Maggie. What's right?" he asked.

He turned to face Kylee as she skipped around the corn stalks.

"Look at her," Stan said as he watched her perform imaginary ballet maneuvers around the corn.

"She is just a child. Not a care in the world, but we have cares. We have big time cares. I'm supposed to be her provider, her protector. Hell, I can't even protect me, much less her. We need help. I feel helpless."

Maggie searched for the right words to say as she heard Kylee singing in the background, "You gotta get up. You gotta wakeup. You gotta get up in the morning!"

Maggie grabbed Stan by the hips and turned him to face her.

"You are a great father, and a great husband. We were dealt a strange hand. I don't know why, but we were. She loves you very much, and so do I Stanley Weaver."

They embraced and Stan wept in her arms. He had done all he could, and though he had made mistakes along the way, he knew he did his best. He just knew it wasn't going to be enough.

Maggie pulled away and wiped his tears.

"Kylee!" she called, waiting to her Kylee respond.

There was no answer. Maggie whipped around and yelled again, "Kylee!"

"Dear God!" Maggie said as she moved toward the corn field.

Stan followed her and called to Kylee as well, but there was no response. Stan grabbed Maggie's arm and said, "Wait! You will never see her like this. Come with me. "

He climbed up on the truck and looked out of the cornfield and said, "Wow!"

"Do you see her, Stan?" Maggie asked impatiently.

Stan was oblivious to her comments and stood there in awe.

"Stan! Do you see her?" Maggie was adamant.

Before him laid a large dead corn field, but he could see a single line of green that led towards the center of the field.

"No, but I have a pretty good idea where she is!" He jumped down from the truck and ran for the field.

Maggie stayed close behind. She noticed that he was running between two rows of corn that didn't look so dead after all. It seemed the further they traveled into the field, the greener the corn became. She also noted the ground being wet. At first, it seemed like wetness of morning dew, but it eventually gave way to puddles of water. By the time they reached Kylee, they were standing in a large puddle of water in the midst of the greenest healthiest corn they had ever seen.

"See, Mommy! It was sleeping!" she yelled as she clapped and continued to sing, "You gotta get up. You gotta wakeup. You gotta get up in the morning!"

Maggie and Stan's faces were covered with huge smiles. Their eyes were filled with awe as they turned completely around to take in what was happening.

"Come on, Daddy," Kylee called to Stan.

They both traipsed across the puddle to Kylee.

"Chain Dance! Chain Dance!" Kylee said as she made an "Oh" shape with her thumb and pointer finger.

Stan tried to hold her hand, but Kylee said, "No, like this, Daddy". She made the same "O" with his thumb and pointer and they joined their O's. Maggie joined them.

"See, a chain!" Kylee said and they all laughed.

They danced in a circle, jumping in the wet puddle, singing, "You gotta get up, you gotta wake up, you gotta get up in the morning!"

The water seemed to spring at Kylee's feet moving outwards. Stan and Maggie were mesmerized at what was happening before them as they saw hill after hill in the distance turn from brown to green.

Maggie wasn't sure what was happening, but she knew it was a good thing. They were laughing together and soaked.

Kylee finally stopped and exclaimed, "That was fun!"

"It sure was, but I think we need to get out of these clothes," Maggie said, laughing at herself and everyone else as they were soaked in muddy water.

The Chain

Stan picked up Kylee and carried her. She giggled in his arms and said in her best actress voice, "My Hero!"

"Daddy, can we get something to eat. I'm starving," Kylee asked.

"Me too!" Stan said.

"Me three!" Maggie added.

"I want a hamburger, with fries, and a milk shake!" Kylee said excitedly

They all laughed as they exited the corn field.

A trucker saw them emerging from the field covered in water and mud. Stan just waved like the scene was normal, but knew in his heart it was far from normal.

"Let's get cleaned up. We can change in the truck," Maggie said as she looked behind to see a completely green perfectly healthy corn field.

Stan said, "Umm... yeah, let's get moving." He was nervous.

Chapter Twenty-Two

"Who are we missing?" Jenkins asked, his eyes sweeping his surroundings.

"Gopher is on the way. He is dealing with the doctor and nurse," Agent Foster answered, looking over her laptop screen,

Clepto was configuring a projector that was attached to Jenkins' laptop.

"Do we have the files uploaded from Schriever?" Jenkins asked.

"They are uploading now, Sir"

"Okay, let's get this thing started."

Ross whispered to Agent Foster, "This should be interesting."

She nodded.

Jenkins stood in front of the group and began to speak. "Let's review what we know, or think we know."

"These apparently are not your typical Extraterrestrial Biological Entities. They are exhibiting technologies not consistent with previous encounters. We do know they aren't of this world, as the eye in the sky caught their arrival." Jenkins rested, concerned with the information he was about to present.

"Clepto, are the uploads complete?" Jenkins asked.

Clepto gave the thumbs up.

"Okay, as you know, the eye in the sky takes lots of, shall we say, 'special' pictures for our government. Let' take a look at what we got."

Jenkins signaled Clepto to start the video presentation.

"This is a video of the encounter that took place at the Weaver home. The camera used infrared technology to capture what you are about to see."

The room was quiet as the video began to play.

The Chain

"You can see from a time lapse that the two entities appear to traverse our atmosphere at incredible speeds. It seems they have created the ability to displace matter as well."

The two teams looked at the screen, watching what appeared to be two beams of light dropping down from the sky and crashing through the roof of the home.

"Keep in mind they are moving at incredible speeds, but we were able to catch this," Jenkins said as he showed what appeared to be the arm of a creature.

"Well, we know it isn't human," Ross said.

"The next sequence is from the hospital. Note the difference in the shape of the objects. Note they are much larger and brighter. They also seem to be exhibiting this same displacement of matter. These two appear to be different from the pair at the Weaver home." Jenkins said.

"I can vouch for that," Ross said, nodding his head.

"Now, for the part you didn't know," Jenkins took a deep breath then continued.

Clepto moved away from the laptop, allowing Jenkins to drive.

"As with all of these matters, this is highly classified. Six years ago in this town, an eight year old girl left this world. She was the daughter of Stan and Maggie Weaver."

"What do you mean she left this world? I thought she just disappeared?" Ross quizzed Jenkins, his brow wrinkled.

"Well... yes and no. Watch this," Jenkins said as he started another video from the laptop.

A time lapse video played. It showed a large glowing ball of light descend to the earth at an incredible speed. The ball landed in a grassy area, and you could see a little girl in a party dress walk over and step inside. The ball then departed and headed straight up.

Everyone in the room gasped.

"Jesus Christ! What the hell was that?" Ross asked.

"I honestly have no idea, but they took one of ours, and we want her back."

Agent Foster fought to hold her tongue, but finally interrupted the conversation.

"I'm a bit confused. First, what makes you think the two at the Weaver house weren't associated with the two at the hospital? And what is the story with this video from six years ago?" she asked

"We all have a lot of questions, but the truth of the matter is I don't know all of the answers. I can only speculate." Jenkins walked away from his laptop, handing control back to Clepto.

"Well, start speculating, please," Ross urged Jenkins with a rolling hand gesture.

"We didn't anticipate another contact situation, but when the Weavers reunited, we called up the teams as a precaution. We had no idea what to expect, but it seems it was the beginning of this new encounter." Jenkins explained.

"Encounter! Is that what you call that? I was mind fucked by Edith Bunker and tossed across the room like a cat that shit on the rug. Encounter my ass!" Ross said as he smacked the table.

"Ross, I'm sorry about what happened out there. I have no idea why they did that to you, but it sure seems that they are the bad guys and these other ones are the good guys."

"Why now? What do they want?" Foster asked.

"Well, let's look at that. Lights, please," Jenkins said.

The lights came on and Jenkins sat on the edge of a desk in the front of the room.

"Clepto, can you play back the audio from the Weaver incident?"

Clepto toyed with the laptop. The sequence played back from the Weaver's home. The dialogue played out with Deloris' voice calling out to Ross as her kitty cat. It was clear that Ross was re-living a bad experience, and Agent Foster put her hand on his shoulder. The tape played along until Rudy spoke.

"Bas Khalas!"

"Wen il ha-deyah?"

"Stop! Rewind that and play it again, louder please." Jenkins instructed.

"Bas Khalas!"

"Wen il ha-deyah?"

"Wow!" Clepto said.

"Wow, what?" Jenkins asked.

"That is Arabic," Clepto responded as he rewound it and played it again, ignoring everyone in the room.

"What is he saying? What's it mean?" Jenkins asked.

Clepto played it over a few more times and finally spoke.

"He tells the woman 'Enough of this foolishness'. Then he says 'Where is the gift?'

The Chain

Everyone looked at Jenkins for some type of explanation.

"And Ross, your encounter. They said 'Protect the gift'," Jenkins said to no one as he searched an empty whiteboard for the answer.

"I guess the real question is 'what is the gift?' "

"I think I know," said Agent Foster.

Surprised, everyone turned to look at her as she made her way to the front of the room. Beth was a confident woman with an affinity for detail. Everyone respected her, and yet feared her. Her ability to shift from one mode to another made those around her nervous. The name Chameleon came easy to her. She had a way of copying personalities and re-using them at a whim.

She started to speak slowly, "I stayed behind at the house after the incident today. I was looking for anything that would make sense of what happened.

Agent Foster paused and looked down at the floor, then back out towards Conrad Jenkins and the two teams.

"I found a few things, "she revealed.

She pulled out a stack of $50 dollar bills and dropped it on the desk.

"I found this stack of money in Mrs. Weaver's closet on the floor."

She pulled out a small juice glass from her bag.

"And this" she said as she held the glass high.

"So the lady drinks juice and has a wad of 50s in her closet?" Ross asked, shrugging and confused as to the relevance.

"I believe they have their child and are on the run," agent Foster said.

"But the eye only reported two entities," Jenkins shot back.

"You're right, but was the eye watching them the day before?" she asked.

"The teams hadn't been assembled in time to tail them." Jenkins trailed off.

The room went quiet.

"Jesus Christ, Beth," Jenkins said in a very excited tone, a smile playing at the corners of his mouth.

"Clepto, give me GPS on both their vehicles. Now!" Jenkins ordered.

Clepto spoke slowly, "Mr. Weaver's truck just passed through Windom, Minnesota and is heading west. Mrs. Weaver's car is south of

Madison, Wisconsin heading south towards…" Clepto paused to check the map again and said, "Chicago, Sir".

"Foster, find Maggie Weaver. Ross, get another bird and track down Stan Weaver. I think it's time we had a talk with these two. Bring them home safe and sound people," Jenkins said as he packed his laptop and gear.

Chapter Twenty-Three

"This milk shake is so good," Kylee said as she sucked on the straw and wiggled a dance in her seat.

"Mine's better," Stan said with a wink to Kylee.

"No, mine is the best! " Maggie teased them both.

Stan paid the bill and they made their way back to the truck. Kylee continued working on her milkshake.

"Any chance you got some cash?" Stan asked as he helped Maggie into the truck.

"Yup. We should be good on money," Maggie nodded.

Stan started the truck and looked over at Maggie. She had a large purse in her hand and was digging through it. Stan threw the truck into the gear and asked, "Everyone ready?"

"Yup," Maggie said as she continued digging through the large handbag.

Stan looked in the mirror and got a "thumbs up" from Kylee as she continued to nurse her milk shake.

"Here we go!" Stan revved the truck and pulled out on to the highway. He heard Maggie counting and finally looked over to see the stacks of money on her lap.

"My God! What did you do? Rob a bank or something?" he asked shocked at the large sum of money sitting beside him. His wide eyes showed his surprise.

"Worse," she said as she dug out more money.

"I inherited it," she said, flashing Stan a smile.

"Who died and left you all of that?"

"Uncle Cecil."

"What? Who is that? I don't remember any Uncle Cecil, he said. Stan gave a perplexing glance and tried to remember that name from their past.

"That's because he was not a real uncle, "she said very confidently, a secretive smile on her face.

"Are you going to come clean?" he asked.

"Remember Mr. Underwood that lived next to my parent's?" she asked.

"Yes, the old man that looked like Cousin Fester from the Adam's Family?" he asked.

She laid out more piles of cash and said, "Well Cousin Fester's real name was Cecil Underwood. He passed away four years ago. The mailman noticed he wasn't retrieving his mail, and went up to the house and found him dead in the backyard. Apparently he had a heart attack. Five, ten, fifteen," she said, counting.

"A month or so later, I get a call from this attorney in Eau Claire asking if I could meet with him to discuss the Estate of Cecil Underwood. I never knew his first name was Cecil, because everyone called him Jeb. I guess Jeb was his nickname or something. So Dad and I went up there together to meet this attorney. Apparently, Mr. Underwood accumulated a small fortune over the years. He left the house to Daddy, and left me $150,000."

"Dear God!" Stan said happy for her.

"Of course Uncle Sam got his share," she said, frowning.

"Yeah, hate that about Sam," Stan said."

"Yeah, me too, but either way most of it is in the bank gaining interest. I don't know why, but I always kept $30,000 aside in case of an emergency, "she said as she continued separating the money.

"Isn't that crazy?" she asked with a giggle. "Like I would really ever have an emergency that requires $30,000, but strangely enough here we are... running. Sixteen, seventeen, eighteen, something is just not right." Maggie said.

"What's wrong?"

"I'm missing a stack," Maggie said puzzled. She looked about the cab as if she expected to see it lying on the floor of down the side of her seat.

"How much are you short?" Stan asked.

"Looks like I'm missing a stack of fifties," she said as she rifled through the bag again.

The Chain

"Well, it looks like we have plenty," Stan said with his eyes opened wide. He stared out the windshield at the traffic moving in front of him and let her financial tale sink in.

"Well, we only have $27,500 left. Oh… and minus the change I got back from the two fifties I gave the gal at Wal-Mart, "she said as she put the money back in the bag.

Kylee hummed as she continued nursing her milk shake.

"Whatcha doing back there, Kylee?" Maggie asked, glancing over her shoulder.

"I'm writing in my diary, Mommy. I have a lot to update."

"You sure do, "Maggie said looking for Stan's reaction.

"Are you putting things in there about me?" Stan teased, glancing at her in the rearview mirror.

"Of course, you are Captain Hook!" Kylee said with a giggle.

"I'm even putting the directions to the pirate's treasure, but you will never find it, Captain Hook." Kylee continued slurping the last of the milk shake.

Maggie searched for a way to get more information out of Kylee. She needed to know what happened to her daughter, what they did to her, and who they were.

"Kylee, remember how you woke up the boy's legs earlier?" Maggie asked.

"Yes, Mommy," Kylee said as she continued writing in her diary.

"And then you woke up the corn?" Maggie asked.

"Yes, Mommy." She continued humming as she wrote in her diary.

"Are you able to wake up everything that is sleeping?" Maggie asked.

"Only some things."

"Are you able to wake up people that die?" Maggie asked.

Stan glanced at Maggie, concerned where she was taking the conversation.

"No one dies, Mommy, they are all just sleeping, "Kylee said, still writing away in her diary. She never lifted her eyes from her diary.

"You didn't answer my question, are you able to wake up someone that is sleeping like the corn?"

"I don't know, Mommy," Kylee replied, shrugging. "If we see someone sleeping, I can try, "she said clearly, focused on finishing her diary entry.

"No, no, honey, that is okay. I was just curious, "Maggie said, clearly concerned and her eyes showed her fear.

"Curiosity killed the cat," Kylee said as she wrote more in her diary.

"Yes it did," Maggie nodded.

"Mommy, is a panther a cat?" Kylee kept on writing, but tilted her head a little to hear Maggie's response.

"I believe a panther is considered a type of cat. So, yes. Are you writing about cats in your diary?" Maggie asked with a questioning look on her face.

"Oh, no, Mommy. I was just being curious too."

Stan continued down the highway heading west on highway 90. Maggie and Kylee had both dozed off. He used the time to plan. His plan was to make it to California, ditch the truck, and finally make his way to Mexico. The money should keep them going long enough for them to re-establish themselves and create new identities, but it would eventually run out. He and Maggie would have to work and start over.

What have they done to my daughter? His mind could only wonder. *Did he dare ask? Clearly Kylee did not like talking about it.* Stan put the radio on and hit the preset channel for classic rock.

Roger Daltrey sang, *"We won't be fooled again..."*

Stan played the steering wheel along with The Who, chiming in "We don't get fooled again..."

Chapter Twenty-Four

Beth's team was airborne and flying south towards Chicago. The modified Blackhawk moved at over 200 miles an hour, but she knew it would be tough to catch up to Maggie Weaver before they reached Chicago. What she needed was traffic to stop, but that would take a miracle.

"Keeper, can you check traffic conditions north of Chicago? Any delays?" she shouted over the radio.

Jenkins responded after a long delay, "There are no delays at this time."

"Okay, listen up, people. 2005 White Ford Escort. Have weapons ready. Don't fire on the man, woman or child. We are protecting and escorting them. Understood?"

The team members nodded.

Beth tapped Gopher. He was piloting today, but it could have been any of them. Holding the map out, Beth pointed at Beloit, Wisconsin.

"Get us there as quick as possible!" she directed him.

Chapter Twenty-Five

Ross piloted his helicopter on a south westerly route. He knew his team would have an easier task than Beth's. Highway 90 wouldn't have the traffic congestion that her team would have to weed through.

"Clepto, what are we looking for?" Ross asked into the headset. The noise of the helicopter was intense, as the jet engines raced them across the sky.

"Sounds like your basic black Peterbilt truck pulling a trailer, but GPS will help us narrow it down quickly." Clepto shot back.

"Let's hope," Ross said as he steered the Huey and followed Highway 90 west.

"How long until we intercept Weaver's truck?" Ross asked Clepto.

"At this speed, I anticipate we will over take him in eighteen minutes," Clepto said as he looked at his laptop.

Ross announced, "Okay, people. Get your colors up!"

The team put on their FBI marked jackets and hats. They weren't FBI agents, but that didn't matter. They were beyond FBI, CIA or any other identifiable group. As far as they were concerned, they were ghosts in a mind numbed world. A world told what to see and believe, never knowing the truth about life, death, and everything in between. They were black, and covert. They didn't exist.

"We're five minutes out, Sir," Clepto said into the headset.

"Okay, folks, we don't have time for games. I'm landing hard and fast. Taco, you take the truck and drop it at the next exit. Keeper will arrange for your pick up," Ross said.

Taco nodded.

Hector Delorentis was of Mexican descent. The team gave him the nickname Taco. He grew up on the rough streets of east LA, but could

The Chain

wear a tuxedo with the class of a dignitary. He had a swagger that ensured him the confidence to easily walk a runway in Milan or Paris. He balanced this team with his many skills and had more than once helped the team out of a bad situation.

"Two minutes. Should get a visual soon," Clepto said into the headset.

Air splashed into the helicopter as Taco pulled back the door. The team readied themselves for the coming landing.

"That him?" Ross shouted.

"Affirmative," Clepto responded.

Ross passed the truck and went about a half a mile down the highway. After seeing there was no traffic he descended quickly and placed the helicopter on the highway.

Three agents got out quickly with their weapons drawn as the semi approached.

Tony Conlin slammed on the breaks as he saw the helicopter drop down to the highway in front of him. He slowly pulled over to the side of the road as the three agents sporting FBI hats pointed their guns directly at him. He stopped the truck and raised his hands to surrender.

Taco opened the truck door and told him to get out. Another agent opened the passenger door and got in. There was no one else in the cab. He gave the all clear sign.

Clepto handcuffed Tony Conlin and lead him to the helicopter.

"What the hell is this all about?" Tony asked his face adorned with a scowl.

"Hey! That's my truck. What the hell is going on here? I did nothing wrong. What do you people want?" He asked.

"Where is your wife, Sir?" Clepto asked.

"Home canning tomatoes I believe?" Tony said with an odd expression on his face. "Did something happen to her?" Tony asked, worry clouding his brown eyes.

"What about your daughter? Where is she?"

"I don't have any daughters. I have two sons, Kevin and Tony Jr., "Tony said the worry in his eyes quickly being replaced by confusion.

"Is it possible you are mistaking me for someone else?" Tony asked.

Clepto reached into Tony's back pocket and pulled out his wallet. He found his license and saw that it read Anthony Conlin.

Clepto spoke into the headset, "We got a problem, Panther"

"What kind of problem?" Ross asked.

"This isn't our guy. Weaver must have switched the tracker on us."

"Oh, you thought I was Stan Weaver?" Tony asked. "Stan is on a fishing trip," Tony freely volunteered; then thought to ask, "Is he in some kind of trouble?"

"Son of a bitch! Clepto, find the tracker. Taco, give him back his truck and let's get out of here pronto!" Ross yelled into the headset.

Clepto unlocked the handcuffs on Tony's wrists and ran back to the truck. He searched for the transmitter. He located it in the wheel well. He and Taco ran back to the helicopter.

"What the hell? You people make a mistake and that's it? You leave me here in the middle of the road with no explanation!" Tony yelled as the helicopter lifted off and flew away. As they flew away they saw a few cars backed up on the highway. It didn't matter though, because they were never there, and this never happened.

"Keeper, you get all of that? The guy was a decoy. I repeat a decoy. Warn Chameleon," Ross said.

"10-4. Panther, come home," Jenkins said as he stared off into the horizon.

"Chameleon, target one was a decoy. I repeat target one was a decoy".

Beth responded, "10-4."

The Chameleon gathered her thoughts. Obviously, the Weavers realized they were under surveillance, but how? Someone had to be helping them. She had to reach them before they reached Chicago.

"The target is stationary, Sir," the agent said to Agent Foster.

"How do you mean?" She asked.

"As in it isn't moving."

"How far out?" she asked.

"Five minutes"

"Okay, colors up, people. Think public appearance. Sunglasses and lots of smiles." She said as adrenaline started to course through her veins.

"Should have visual now," the agent said as they approached a field behind a gas station. The tall grass billowed from the rotating blades that allowed the helicopter to move across the field.

The Chain

"Put us down in the field next to the gas station," Agent Foster said.

The doors slid open, and she and two other agents started running towards the gas station. There were no white cars to be seen. Beth looked at the agent with the tracker and he nodded and pointed at the gas pumps. Her facial expression changed.

"Shit! Come on." She said and made a gesture to put the guns away.

Beth approached the SUV that was thumping. The driver was paying for the gas with a credit card when she approached him.

"Hey, did you just come from Eau Claire?" she asked, still breathing heavy from the run.

"Yeah, what's it to you?" he asked as he walked away to get back into the vehicle.

She grabbed him by the arm and twisted it behind his back and slammed him against the car.

He cried out, "What the hell is wrong with you! You whacky bitch!"

She pulled her gun out and put it against his head and said, "Do you want to see how wacky I can get?"

"Nn nn no, Ma'am," he said.

She saw movement in the SUV and pointed the gun in the vehicle.

"Put your hands on the roof now! I will pop a cap in you so fast your momma will think she birthed a cyclops!" The young man in the passenger seat put his hands on the ceiling, petrified.

She pointed to the boy in the front seat and said, "Shut that shit you call music off now!" There was silence all at once as he quickly hit the off switch to the radio.

She moved back to the driver and asked, "Did you see a strange man around your car today?"

"Uhh nnn noo, well wait, yeah. At Wal-Mart in Eau Clare. He was working on his car. He was looking all over his car. He said it was making a strange sound," the young man said.

"What kind of car?" she asked.

"Hmm… some white thing… ugly"

Another agent reached into the wheel well and pulled out the tracking device. He showed it to Beth.

She shook her head, clearly disappointed.

"Okay, here is what I want you to do. I want you to get in this car and get back on your way, but if I hear one more complaint about that shit you call music being too loud, I will take you in. You understand, boi?" she said in her best street slang.

"yy yes, Ma'am," he stuttered.

Beth looked at the other two agents and let the young man go.

"Let's get out of here," she said.

She was clearly pissed, but thankful she didn't have to play that scene on the highway.

"Keeper, they knew. Someone has to be helping them. I sincerely doubt that an over the road truck driver could have figured out we had trackers on them," Beth said as the helicopter lifted off.

"Panther is on his way here now. Come home, Chameleon and let's figure this out," Jenkins said into the headset.

"Permission to stop at Wally World first, Sir?" she asked.

"Good idea," Jenkins said as his phone rang. He looked down and saw that the call was marked private.

"Is this line secure?" the voice asked.

"Yes, Sir," Jenkins responded, recognizing the voice.

"I would like a progress report," the voice said.

Jenkins paused and finally spoke, "I have nothing to report yet. We have had limited activity, but I'm curious. What is the gift you are expecting?"

The phone was quiet for some time. Then the voice responded, "Just be sure to secure it, and deliver it to me."

Jenkins heard the phone hang up and wondered what was really going on.

Chapter Twenty-Six

Maggie yawned as she watched the sun set in the Western Sky. The purples and pinks glimmered off of the clouds. It was picturesque. Stan caught the yawn and continued it on to Kylee.

Maggie chuckled.

"Daddy, I think we should call it a day; don't you?" Maggie asked Stan.

Stan heard her words, but everything inside him told him to run and not stop till they reached California. He had to find a safe place. It wouldn't take long for the people who placed the GPS transmitters to learn he had found and moved them.

"Daddy? Earth to Daddy?" Maggie asked, leaning toward him.

"Yeah, I heard you the first time," Stan shot back in a negative tone, squeezing hard on the steering wheel.

Maggie reached over to touch his arm, and Stan's facial expression softened a little.

"Okay," he begrudgingly agreed, nodding his head. "There isn't much around here. We can stay in Murdo. I saw a sign for a Days Inn. It's about twenty miles from here. You are going to have to pay cash, and decide now on a new identity." Stan said.

Stan was right. Maggie really hadn't considered the depth of their issues. They were going to have to come up with new names, new identities, new everything.

"New names?" Kylee piped in.

"Yeah, it will be fun, honey," Maggie said, forcing a smile.

"This is your chance to be anyone you want to be Kylee," Maggie said with a smile.

"But I like being Kylee," She said with a sad face.

"Well, if you could have been someone else, what name would you have liked?" Maggie asked.

"Abbey," Kylee said as she looked out the window.

"Now your turn," Maggie said to Stan.

"Whatever you want," he said with a smirk, barely giving her a glance.

"Hmmm… Cindy and Bob?" she asked.

"Okay, Cindy," Stan grinned.

"Cool, Bob," Maggie smiled.

"I will grab us some food after we get in the room," Stan said.

The truck rolled into the parking lot, and Stan went out of his way to park away from the building. They tumbled out of the truck and made their way to the check-in counter. There was an Indian girl behind the check-in desk. She stood as Maggie approached.

"Welcome. Do you have a reservation?" she asked. Maggie was surprised to hear her perfect English. She wore black slacks, and a white floral top, and a tiny red vest.

"No, I'm so sorry we don't. Is there any chance you have some rooms open?" Maggie asked.

"I don't think it will be a problem tonight. Two adults and one child?" she asked, her eyes making a quick sweep of them all.

"Yes." Maggie plastered on a smile in response.

"Just for one night?" the woman asked.

"Yes."

"It will be $59.00. The room has two queen size beds. Will that be okay?" the woman asked.

"That would be wonderful."

"Okay what type of credit card would you like to put this on?" the clerk asked.

"Would it be okay if we paid cash?" Maggie asked.

The receptionist looked surprised.

"I just hate to use those things," Maggie tried to cover.

The woman behind the counter smiled and said, "Sure. I will need a name though for the computer."

"Oh, of course. Cindy," Maggie said.

"Last name, please?" the receptionist asked, glancing back up from her computer screen.

"Oh, so sorry. Brady," Maggie said.

The Chain

"I see. I guess he is Bobby and that is Jan?" The receptionist said with a grin.

Kylee burst out laughing along with Maggie.

"Oh, ha-ha, yeah, we get that all the time," Maggie said as Stan kicked her shoe.

Maggie paid and handed Stan the key.

"Let's go Abbey, "Maggie said with a smile to Kylee.

Their room wasn't very far and Stan brought the rest of their things in.

"I'll be back in a few minutes with some food. Alice had a date with Sam the Butcher," Stan said with a wink.

"Oh, wait. Here, take this," Maggie said as she handed him several twenty dollar bills.

"Thanks," he said as he walked out the door.

"Mommy, can I take a bath?" Kylee asked.

"Why sure you can, honey. Are you not feeling well?" Maggie asked her eyes full of concern as she looked over her daughter.

"I feel fine, I just wanted to sit in it and relax," Kylee said.

They both chuckled.

Maggie checked the tub to make sure it was clean. She was satisfied and started the water for the bath.

She called out, "Do you want it warm, very warm, or hot?"

Kylee startled Maggie when she said, "Hot, please," from behind her.

"Gosh, honey, you scared Mommy," Maggie said.

"Sorry, Mommy," she said as she started to undress.

"Okay, I'm going to give you your privacy, but can you not lock the door please?" Maggie asked.

"Yes, Mommy," Kylee said.

Maggie took Kylee's clothes and left the room, closing the door behind her. She proceeded to take off her clothes as well and found something more comfy to wear. She pulled out the tie-died pajamas and held them to her face and breathed deeply. It was a smell she would never forget. Kylee sang from the bathroom the theme song to the Brady Bunch.

"Here's the story of a lovely lady. Who was bringing up three very lovely girls… ," she sang.

"Kylee, your jammies are outside of the door with your toothbrush. Be sure to brush your teeth," Maggie said.

"Okay, Cindy" Kylee said.

Maggie heard the knock at the door. She couldn't see who it was and asked, "Who is it?"

"It's Bobby Brady, and if you don't let me in I'm going to tell Jan and Marcia how you stole their hair brush!" Stan teased.

Kylee burst out in laughter from the bathroom.

Maggie opened the door and let Stan in.

Stan walked in to find Maggie in an oversized T-shirt and sweatpants.

"Well, Cindy, does mom know you are wearing that outfit?" Stan teased

"Hey, I'm a big girl now Bobby! So bug out!" she teased.

Kylee yelled from the bathroom, "Marcia! Marcia! Marcia!"

Stan and Maggie laughed and embraced in a long kiss.

"Mommy, can you come help me, please?" Kylee yelled.

"Sure, honey," Maggie said, making her way to the bathroom.

Stan started unpacking bags and placing food on the table. Maggie helped Kylee dry off and get in her pajamas.

"Do you think the Brady kids had pajamas like this, Mommy?" Kylee asked.

"I'm sure they did. They were very hip."

"How about we brush our teeth after dinner?" Maggie asked.

"Yay!" Kylee said as Maggie helped Kylee dry her hair.

"Something smells good," Kylee said.

"No peeking!" Stan said.

Maggie knew by the smell that it had to be fast food.

She combed Kylee's hair a few times, and finally said, "Okay, let's see what Daddy's surprise is!"

He had covered the plates with large paper napkins. They edged closer till finally Stan said, "Okay, open your eyes."

Kylee saw the emblem on the napkins and screamed, "Taco Bell! I love Mexican! I wanna be Mexican!"

Kylee tore into her soft taco and asked Stan if he had brought some fire sauce.

"Of course, Senorita," he said with a smile and handed her a few packets.

"Gracias, Bobby!" she teased.

Maggie was looking for the right time to quiz Kylee further, and felt it was better now than never.

The Chain

She decided to take a different approach. "Miss Kylee, I have a question for you."

Kylee leaned over and whispered into Maggie's ear, "Its Abbey, Mommy."

"Oh," Maggie said with a nod.

"Miss Abbey, I have a question for you."

"What is your question, Cindy," Kylee responded

"Are the Seevers and the Watchers the same people?" Maggie asked.

"No, the Watchers are people. The Seevers are… The Seevers," Kylee said as she prepared her next soft taco.

"And what about the Big Man," Maggie asked.

"What about him?" Kylee asked, sticking her taco in her mouth and taking a big bite.

"Is he like the Seevers?" Maggie asked.

"No, he is nothing like them. They are afraid of him," Kylee said.

"Why are the Seevers after you?" Maggie said.

"Because they want what the Big Man gave me," Kylee said.

"And what did he give you?" Maggie asked.

"A gift," Kylee said, drinking from her cup.

Maggie was speechless.

"Can I see it," Maggie asked.

"No, Mommy. Only I can see it," Kylee said.

Stan listened quietly and let the two of them talk.

"Kylee, I mean, Abbey, is the gift the Big Man gave you what allowed that boy to walk and the corn to wake up?" Maggie asked.

"Mommy, I don't want to talk anymore," she said with a frown on her face.

Maggie kneeled down in front of Kylee so she could see her face to face. She looked into her eyes and said, "Kylee, you can tell me. I'm your Mommy."

"Is this the last question, Mommy?" Kylee asked.

Stan finally got Maggie's attention and gave her a look that said, "Stop!"

"Yes, honey. Cross my heart," she said to Kylee, running her fingers across her heart.

Kylee's countenance changed and became emotionless. She looked directly into Maggie's eyes and Maggie felt her hair stand up on her arms.

Kylee said, "Yes, that is the gift."

Maggie was shaking. Kylee reached out and hugged her. Maggie cried and Stan came to hold both of them.

"Now you two. If we keep this up much longer we won't be able to have banana splits!" Stan said.

"Yay!" Kylee screamed!

Maggie rolled her eyes at Stan as he unpacked whipped cream, chocolate syrup, ice cream, plastic bowls and spoons.

"Stan…you are going to make me fat," Maggie complained with a big smile.

"It was Bobby's idea," Stan said as he shrugged his shoulders with a look on his face like he had no idea how this happened.

After they had finished their desserts, Kylee quickly got over her sugar rush and fell asleep on the bed. Maggie covered her with a blanket and propped her head under a pillow.

She and Stan brushed their teeth, and climbed into bed.

"I have missed her so much," Maggie said to Stan, her eyes welling.

Stan pulled her close and said, "I have missed you both so much." They kissed and he whispered into her ear, "About that rain check?"

"Oh, Bobby!" she whispered into his ear, her eyes loving.

They made quiet love. Maggie waited for Stan to start snoring before she went to the bathroom to clean up. She looked in the mirror and thought she never remembered looking or feeling so good. She felt a tug on the button down shirt she had borrowed from Stan.

Kylee whispered, "Mommy, I'm thirsty"

Maggie removed the plastic wrap surrounding the cup and filled the cup with cold water. She handed it to Kylee.

She drank a few sips and said, "Thank you, Mommy"

Kylee just stood there half awake in the light of the vanity area.

"What's wrong, honey?" Maggie asked her.

"Mommy, could you sleep with me tonight?" Kylee asked.

"Of course, honey," Maggie said with a big smile.

Maggie shut off the light, opened the door, and led her daughter back to the bed. She helped Kylee get settled and then climbed in behind her. Maggie stroked Kylee's hair till she finally drifted off to sleep. She wasn't far behind her.

Chapter Twenty-Seven

"Okay, that's two number eight's with coffees, the scrambled egg platter, and three bottles of water. Will that complete your order?" the young pimple faced teenager behind the counter said to Stan.

"Yes," Stan said as he paid him.

Stan looked like a circus performer trying to balance the waters and coffees along with the bags of food. He stopped at the condiment counter and picked up several napkins, straws, and the pink stuff for the coffee.

Back at the hotel, Maggie and Kylee woke together. Stan's bed was empty.

Kylee said, "Oh look! The logger left us."

Maggie smiled and said, "Oh, he'll be back. You will learn that about men. They always come back. Let's just hope they come back with breakfast."

"Oh, yeah!" Kylee said very excited.

Stan kicked the door a few times. Maggie opened the door and saw Stan performing his balancing act. She immediately took the cup holder full of drinks, and they made their way toward the small table.

"Kylee, it looks like we are eating Irish again," Maggie said as she unpacked the bags.

"Irish? What kind of food is Irish?" she asked, scrunching up her face.

"This kind," she said as Kylee saw the full spread on the table.

"McDonalds! YAY! I love Irish food. I want to be Irish. McPlease!" Kylee asked.

"McSure," Stan said.

"McYay! This is so McGood!" Kylee said.

"McDelicious," Stan smiled.

"McStop already," Maggie said as she rolled her eyes at Stan.

"Okay, McCindy," Stan teased.

It was an uneventful morning. Maggie pulled out fresh clothes for everyone after they showered, and packed up the rest of their things.

"Sorry, this is all I had for you, Stan" Maggie said as she offered him a Bruce Springsteen concert T-shirt and a pair of old black jeans.

"Wow. Where did you find these?" he asked.

"They were in the wash. You left them there. I conveniently forgot to return them to you," she said as she looked at him, a sad expression crossed her face as she remembered the day he left.

Maggie had tried so hard to put that day out of her mind. Stan had been drinking once again, and he was being ugly. They were on a collision course and she knew someone was going to get hurt. It was the last thing she wanted, but her survival instincts finally won out. They blamed each other for losing Kylee. That day pain and anguish took over, and the words that were spoken were like an oak tree after a hail storm. Their lives were shredded and broken, and all because of a merciless freak storm that came from nowhere. She knew they had to go their separate ways. Yet here they were together again, as if that storm never happened. Yet something had happened. Something traumatic and it followed them. They were on the run because of it. They had unseen enemies that wanted to do... what? She had no idea, but knew it wasn't a good thing.

They gathered the rest of their things and got back into the truck. Kylee sat in the back reviewing her diary and making changes and additions. Maggie sat quietly watching the morning traffic fill the highway as Stan directed the truck toward safety. He hoped.

"Maggie?" Stan asked.

"Yes?"

"Do you?" He asked.

"Do I what?" she asked with a look of confusion.

"Do you smell it?" he said as he looked in the rearview mirrors.

Maggie instantly realized what he was saying. The smell of ozone was all over the cabin of the truck. She looked at Kylee who was writing in her diary and humming, oblivious to everything.

Maggie's heart raced as panic began to overcome her being. She placed a hand over here mouth and looked nervously out the windows of the truck.

"I don't see anything, Stan," she said as she looked out the window towards the back of the truck.

The Chain

"I do…" Stan said.

Stan's truck came over the top of a small hill. Maggie felt the truck slow as the brakes were applied.

"Oh, my, God!" Maggie said as she saw the two people standing in the road.

Rudy and Deloris stood there like a scene from an old western movie. The truck started sliding on the pavement as Stan kept the brakes applied. The front end started to turn right.

Maggie screamed, "Go! Don't stop!"

But it was too late. As the truck slid sideways, Stan's horrified eyes never left Rudy and Deloris. The moment seemed surreal. The truck finally came to a halt, and Stan reached for his crowbar.

Maggie reached behind her to grab Kylee, but she was gone.

"Oh, my God! Stan! Kylee is gone!" she said.

"Son of a bitch! I'm going to deal with these two!" Stan said, his hand clenching his makeshift weapon as he reached for the door handle.

"I'm coming with you."

"No stay here," he yelled.

"No!" Maggie yelled as she jerked open her door and leaped from the truck. Stan jumped out to stop her.

Rudy and Deloris stood before them like two frail grandparents in their retirement age. Rudy had on a button down shirt that should have been thrown away in the seventies, with stretchy polyester brown slacks. Deloris clutched her purse and wore the same pale yellow dress that looked to be something found at a goodwill store from the early seventies. This odd couple stood thirty feet in front of them and Maggie started to yell.

"I don't know who you people are, but I want my daughter back!" Maggie said as she continued to approach them, shaking her finger in front of her.

"Well, of course you do, Mrs. Weaver. Maybe it is time for us to introduce ourselves," Rudy said.

"Oh, I know damn well who you are. You are Rudy and Deloris Seever. I know that much. I want to know what the hell is going on here! Where is my daughter?" Maggie said, struggling to keep her composure.

Rudy gave Deloris a look of surprise.

"There is much you don't know and understand. We can help you, but you are going to have to trust us," Rudy said.

"Trust you!" Maggie screamed at him.

"I don't trust anyone right now!" Maggie said.

"Now, honey, you are stressed and obviously upset. Please give us a chance to explain," Deloris interrupted.

Stan held the crowbar tighter waiting for his chance to use it.

"Come with us, we will explain everything once we get there," Rudy said.

"To where?" Stan asked in an untrusting tone.

"To the laboratory of course," Deloris said in her kindest grandmotherly tone.

"Laboratory?" Maggie asked.

"Just follow us in your truck. I promise you will have the answer to all of your questions," Rudy explained.

"No, we want answers now. We want our daughter," Stan said.

"You want answers now?" Rudy asked in a sarcastic tone. "Okay, how about your daughter Kylee vanished years ago from a birthday party, and six years later she re-appears in the same birthday dress. She looks and sounds like your daughter, but Mr. Weaver she most definitely is NOT your daughter." Rudy waited to hear their response.

"What? How? What are you saying? She isn't my daughter?" Stan asked with an agonized expression on his face.

Maggie just stood there unsure what to say. *Not her daughter? How could that be? She was sure it was Kylee. How could it not be? They are lying. They had to be lying.*

"You are lying! I know you are lying! Where is she?" Maggie demanded.

"Lying? Me? Could it be that it is you that is the liar?" Rudy asked.

"What are you talking about?" Maggie asked her mouth hung open and her eye brows creased.

"You are both lying to yourself. You want her to be your daughter so much that you have been fooled. Have you ever considered that she hadn't aged a day, Mrs. Weaver? Have you?" Rudy pushed.

"You did something to her! What did you do to my daughter," Maggie screamed as she collapsed into Stan's chest.

"She is our daughter. How could she look, act, and smell so much like my daughter and not be her?" Stan asked rubbing Maggie's shoulders but keeping his eyes planted firmly on their nemesis.

"It's called genetics, Mr. Weaver," Rudy responded.

The Chain

Stan and Maggie shared a bewildered glance, standing there in awe. Rudy's words weren't what they were expecting to hear. Their world was crashing and they had no way of stopping it.

"Why don't you folks come with us? The lab isn't far from here. It will explain many things for both of you," Deloris said.

Stan looked at Maggie and back at Rudy and finally responded.

"We will follow you in the truck," Stan agreed.

Turning with his arm still around Maggie, Stan walked her back to the truck, helping her inside. She was trying to regain her composure.

"Don't you trust them, Stan!" She whispered.

"Don't worry. I don't." he told her.

Stan put on his sunglasses and put the truck into gear as he followed the yellow Honda Accord. His mind was reeling. *Genetics? How could that be? What had they done to his daughter?*

"If she isn't our daughter, then where is our daughter?" Maggie asked, forlornly staring out the windshield.

"I don't know, but if they cloned her or something, then they must still have her," Stan said as he followed the Seever's car.

They turned off of Highway 90 and headed south on Highway 83. There were signs for the Rosebud Indian Reservation. The highway traffic dwindled rapidly as they ventured further from the interstate.

Rudy put on his right turn signal and turned onto a gravel road. Stan was focused and taking in everything, as the truck jarred them along. They followed the road for some time till they finally came to what appeared to be an old Radar facility.

"What is this?" Maggie asked Stan, her eyes narrowed.

"I'm not sure, but I think we're about to find out."

Rudy parked the car and got out. Deloris wasn't far behind him.

Stan parked the truck.

"I don't like this, Stan," Maggie said, her face tense with concern.

"Just stay close."

Stan and Maggie got out of the truck and made their way over to Rudy and Deloris.

"This doesn't look like any laboratory," Stan protested, his eyes hard.

"Good. That is what people are supposed to think," Rudy said pointing to a building and leading the group.

Deloris rambled as they walked, "Oh this? Oh my. No no. The laboratory is deep underground. This is just a ghost town." At that, she and Rudy chuckled.

Maggie gave Stan a glance showing her concern.

"Okay, everyone in," Rudy directed them.

Deloris went first. Maggie and Stan followed. They were in a metal building. It appeared that no one had been in there for years. The room was an empty dusty skeleton. Whatever equipment occupied this space had been long gone.

"Okay, show them where to stand please, Deloris," Rudy said.

"Oh, over here please. I know it seems odd. It was strange for me the first time. Now you stand here," she said to Stan as she picked his spot. "And you stand here, honey," she said to Maggie as she guided her to a spot on the floor.

"I remember you from the restroom," Maggie said, staring at her face with no hint of a smile.

"Oh, yes," she smiled at Maggie.

"Okay, Deloris, take your spot," Rudy said.

Deloris instantly appeared across the room next to Rudy at the door.

"You all enjoy," she said as she gave a grandmother's best smile with a hand wave.

She and Rudy left the room and closed the door. Stan realized the trap when he saw her wave, but knew it was too late. The steel door closed with a loud clink.

"No!" Maggie screamed. "You can't leave us in here. We will die!" She yelled.

"Oh, now you be quiet in there," Deloris responded.

"We are Americans!" Maggie yelled as tears rolled from her eyes.

Stan held Maggie as she repeated over and over in a soft whisper, "They can't leave us in here. They can't leave us in here."

Chapter Twenty-Eight

The helicopter landed in a field behind Wal-Mart.

"Okay, you know the drill, folks, we had a mechanical failure and are waiting on parts." Agent Foster said as she exited the helicopter.

She traded her FBI hat and jacket for a dark blue non-descript windbreaker as she made her way to the Wal-Mart. It was going to be more difficult to track down the Weavers now. They had already staged two decoys, and she had no clue as to where they might be headed. Logic told her they weren't heading south, and the Great Lakes were to their east, so that left north to Canada or west towards California. There were many roads that went south along the way, but the real question is "where would she run if she were in Stan Weaver's shoes?"

She made her way to the customer service counter and asked to speak to the manager.

Evan Barnes wasn't the stealthiest man in the world standing six foot six inches tall with a broad linebacker build. Agent foster looked pleased with what she saw. He had blue eyes and a nice smile with dimples. He wasn't your typical Wal-Mart manager, or was he, she wondered? She used her fake FBI ID and asked if she could talk to the cashiers that were on duty that morning.

There were only three, and one stayed in the customer service area that morning. That left two, an elderly lady with grey hair, and a woman in her mid fifties.

The chameleon changed her colors and spoke with the cashier.

"Hello," Agent Foster said with a strong southern accent. Her smile was contagious as the woman reached out to shake her hand.

"I'm Beth Duncan. I'm on official business with the FBI," Beth said as she withdrew her hand.

"Oh, hello. I'm Lisa Trump, and sorry to say no relation to Donald." She laughed nervously.

Beth laughed as well and thought to herself, *"How many times has this lady said that?"*

Beth continued, "I know you are busy, but I'm curious if you might have seen this woman this morning?" she asked, holding out a picture of Maggie.

"Why, yes, I did. Is she in some kind of trouble?"

"Can you tell me about your encounter with her? Did you notice anything suspicious?" Beth asked.

"No, it was just her and… oh, this is one of those kidnapping things isn't it. Did the husband beat the mom or something, and she took the kid and is on the run?" The cashier asked, looking troubled.

"Just answer her questions please," the store manager reminded Mrs. Trump.

"Oh yes, sorry." She smiled.

"Did she have a little girl with her ma'am?" Beth asked.

"Yes, she did," the cashier said, nodding her head.

"Any chance you might have a tape of that, sir?" Agent foster asked directing her attention to the store manager.

"Definitely. Come with me," he said, motioning with his hand.

Beth's intuition paid off, and she was excited. She followed the manager to the security area.

He asked for the picture of Maggie, and Beth handed it to him. She watched over his shoulder as he rewound the video tape from that morning. He then ran the tape at a faster than normal play speed. Then they both saw her and Kylee on the tape, and he stopped the tape.

"Stop! Could you rewind it again and replay it?" Beth asked, wide-eyed.

"Sure," he said, doing as she asked.

Beth stepped out of the room and used her phone.

"Keeper, she has the girl. I have video tape here at Wally world."

"Wow! Get that tape and get back here," Jenkins said with a sense of urgency in his voice.

Beth got a copy of the tape from the store manager and thanked him for his assistance. She offered him a copy of her fake FBI card and asked him to please call that number if they should see Maggie and the girl again.

The Chain

He looked over the card. It read "Special Agent, Beth Duncan". It had the FBI headquarters address, and a phone number. Beth could tell the store manager was getting curious about things, but she wasn't worried. She didn't exist. She never existed. She was a ghost. The phone number on the card re-routed to Keeper. He would handle any cleanup required.

Beth was making her way towards the store's front door when Lisa Trump stopped her.

"I remembered a few things," she said.

"I asked the little girl where she was going because she was wearing a baseball cap that said 'surf's up', and star shaped sunglasses. She told me they were going to Malibu, California."

"Malibu? Hmm, that is odd. Was there anything else?" Beth asked.

"Well, maybe this is me just being nosey, but I thought it was odd that the mother paid with two fifty dollar bills. Who pays in cash anymore?" she said, shrugging.

Beth's hunch was right.

"You're right, Mrs. Trump. You never know. Thanks again for all your help."

Beth gave the woman a polite handshake as she headed out of the building and back towards the helicopter.

Chapter Twenty-Nine

Jenkins' phone rang.

"Federal Bureau of Investigations, Agent Jenkins speaking," he spoke in a perfect southern accent.

"Hello, this is Evan Barnes. I'm the manager of the Wal-Mart located in Eau Claire, Wisconsin, and I was wondering…"

Conrad Jenkins interrupted him, "Hello Mr. Barnes, has Special Agent Duncan visited with you yet?"

"Oh… well, yes," Mr. Barnes said not sure how to continue.

"Is there a problem, sir that I need to be aware of?" Jenkins asked in a stern voice.

"Oh. No, sir. I just wanted to let you all know that I can make additional copies of the video if needed," Evan Barnes said realizing how stupid he must sound.

"We appreciate your full cooperation, Mr. Barnes. It has been greatly appreciated. I will send one of my team out to see you if we need more information, and thanks again."

Jenkins winked at Ross across the table.

"Anytime, sir," Evan Barnes said as he adjusted his shirt and made his way back to the Customer Service area.

Chapter Thirty

They had both looked around the room for some time. There seemed to be no way out. Stan used his pocket knife in an attempt to dig, but quickly found a solid concrete floor below the dirt covering. The sun had gone down and the room was getting cooler. He was in survival mode and knew they needed protection from the elements, but more so, they needed water. Stan listened for movement outside the door, but it was very quiet. He couldn't tell if Rudy and Deloris had left. He didn't recall hearing their car leave.

He felt around the door for some type of latch or release, but had no luck. Though the building was old, it was still quite sturdy. He made his way back to Maggie who was huddled in the center of the room.

"They are going to leave us to die here," she whispered to him, her eyes full of fear.

"I don't plan on staying around long enough to find out." He assured her.

"Do you know something I don't? Because from what I see we're on concrete and surrounded by metal walls," she whispered in a sarcastic tone.

He pointed up, but it was too dark for her to see. He whispered into her ear,

"There is a vent or something up there. I think you can squeeze through it. I won't be able to fit through it," he said.

"And then what? You want me to fight those two? Run for help?" She was clearly exhausted with it all.

"Well, we will decide that once we figure out how to get up there."

"Stan, that has to be fifteen feet tall. There is no way you can reach that."

"Come here," he said as he drew her close and she sobbed into his chest. He did his best to keep them both warm, and prayed for help.

Chapter Thirty-One

"Okay, play the video," Jenkins said as sat on the desk.

The room was made up of two rows of tables converted into makeshift desks. A projection screen hung from the wall in the front center adjacent to a large map of the United States and Canada. Jenkins' laptop sat on a desk adjacent to a projector in the front of the room. Clepto sat with the equipment and with a click of the mouse started the video as Jenkins watched and walked slowly around the room.

"As you can see, she is with her mother, but being that the transmitters were both setup on decoys, we should believe that the father has joined them. We need to think, people," he said, tapping his temples. "Where would you go if you were in their shoes?"

Ross said, "That would depend on how much money I had and who or what I was trying to get away from."

Ross's eyes were full of irritation as he stared at Jenkins, confirming he was dissatisfied with the fact that Jenkins was clearly holding back some information.

"Well, it is doubtful they went east, unless they have a boat or were planning on swimming. But my guess is North or West." Beth said.

"They didn't go north," Ross shot back.

"Why's that?" Beth asked.

"I spoke with his boss. Apparently, Mr. Weaver took off for a last minute fishing trip to Canada. I contacted border patrol. They will be watching for him, but I doubt he is headed that way. He would know we were looking for him," Ross answered.

"Okay, so they fooled us, and made their getaway for now. Let's go with what we have," he said, leaning on a nearby desk. "Mrs. Weaver's car has been accounted for, so I'm assuming they are in his truck. We have a description of the vehicle. Let's start there and assume they are traveling west," Jenkins said.

"Actually, we might have a bit of a break here. The foreman at Weaver's company indicated that he left without a trailer." Ross said.

"How is that a break?" Jenkins asked.

"Well, you don't see many truckers driving cross country without a trailer behind them. I suggest we place an APB out for this guy, play it up as a kidnapping and let the local law enforcement help us?"

"Excellent. Get your team on that," Jenkins told Ross, with a smile for the first time in several moments.

Jenkins faced Beth.

"Beth, I want to move your team."

"Move us? To where?" she asked with a surprised look.

Jenkins moved to a large map on the wall ten feet in front of the table where Agent Ross and Agent Foster sat. He paused for a moment, and said, tapping his finger on a specific spot, "Here."

His finger rested on Denver.

"Hmm... what's in Denver?" she asked, her eyes fixated to that spot.

"A hunch," he replied.

"Strategically, it will place you in a position to intercept them," he said, circling his finger on the map face. "There aren't too many corridors to the west, and if I were going west, this is the way I would go."

"Assuming you know where he is going." Beth searched him for an explanation.

Ross lightly kicked her foot under the table. She pretended not to notice.

"I don't. Do either of you have a more logical intercept point?" Jenkins asked with a sincere look on his face.

The room was silent. Beth bought into the logic, but knew he was withholding something. It wasn't like him, and she was concerned.

"There is a plane on the tarmac waiting for your team, Beth. Get your people on it and prepped. Cars will be waiting for you in Denver. Try and get some rest on the flight, I suspect you are going to need it." Jenkins said as he folded up his laptop and briefcase.

"And what about my team?" Ross asked.

"I want you to take two cars and split up and make your way west. Start asking questions at truck stops, hotels etc. See if you can dig up anything." Jenkins rolled the cord to his laptop's power supply.

The Chain

Something wasn't right, and Ross new it. As he and Beth made their way out of the building, Ross escorted her to the plane. As her team entered, he grabbed her shoulder and said, "We have to talk Beth."

Beth turned, clearly troubled.

She looked at him and finally said, "What the hell is going on here?"

"How do you mean?" Ross asked.

"Since when do we operate like this? Keeper seems troubled," she said.

"Or in trouble," Ross said as he looked back towards the hangar. They seemed oblivious to the activities around them as aircraft were taxied to and fro along with the various vehicles delivering fuel and equipment.

"Keep an eye on him, Ross. I'm worried." Beth said.

"I will. I will keep an 'extra eye' on him." He said with a stern look.

"Good. Talk to you after we get settled," Beth said, turning and disappearing into the plane.

Jenkins was quiet as he gathered the last of his things and went to a black sedan. Ross trusted Jenkins but lately he wasn't sure if the feeling was mutual.

"Keeper, will you be joining us?" Ross asked.

"No, I have a few things to tidy up here, but then I'm flying to Denver."

"Hey, what's wrong with you?" Ross asked with a sincere but stern face.

"I… I just have a lot on my mind," he replied, looking down at the asphalt. "This case has been dead for so long, and now it is alive, and I feel like we're always ten steps behind."

"And?" Ross pushed.

"And what?" Jenkins asked in a grumble.

"And what else are you not telling me?" Ross titled his head waited for the truth.

"We have worked together for a long time, Ross. I hand picked you because I trust you, and respect your abilities. There are very few of you out there. Your team and Beth's are the best in the world. I would hate to lose any of you. I know you think that I'm keeping some dark secret from you about this mission, but I'm not. I honestly feel the same way you do," Jenkins said.

"And how is it that you think I feel?" Ross asked.

"Like someone isn't telling you everything you need to know to get the job done," Jenkins said.

There was a short moment of silence between the two of them. Ross searched Jenkins' face for the truth.

"Look. Are we on the level here?" Ross asked.

"As far as I'm concerned we are."

"So what the hell is out in Denver?" Ross asked.

"Not *what*, Ross. *Who* is the question?" Jenkins said as he fumbled with entirely too many things in his hand.

"Let me help," Ross said as he took the tumbling laptop bag from Jenkins.

Ross helped Jenkins load up the rest of his gear. His laptop, jacket, and briefcase were proving to be a challenge this morning with the added suitcase. Agent Ross was careful about planting the tracker in Jenkins trench coat. It would cost him his job if caught, but he didn't inherit the name Panther by chance.

"So, who is out there?" Ross finally asked.

"Maggie Weaver's cousin, though the little girl referred to him as an uncle. They were close. When the disappearance took place the local detectives convinced Stan Weaver that the cousin abducted the child. Weaver got drunk and broke the man's nose. It was ugly," Jenkins said.

"So, why haven't we been watching him," Ross asked, looking perturbed.

"Oh, we have." Jenkins said as he stared off and spoke to himself again "We have…"

Their conversation ended as Ross's team pulled up in two black sedans.

"Looks like your 'posse' is here," Jenkins said with a smile.

"Yeah, we better get moving. You sure you don't want to come with us?" Ross asked again.

"No, I have a flight in the morning back to Denver. I will call you before the plane takes off."

Ross jumped in the car with Clepto.

"Where to, homeboi?" Clepto asked in his best street accent.

"Let's start with some grub," Ross said.

"Sounds good," Clepto said.

Jenkins waved as they drove away. The wind had kicked up, as he looked at the building behind him. He could see clouds in the distance,

The Chain

and wondered if weather was approaching, but then it wouldn't matter. He had a little time. He hoped. He had to make some decisions, and they had to be the right ones.

Chapter Thirty-Two

Jenkins pulled the black sedan into Beverly Clayton's driveway. She'd be waiting for him with a nicely prepared meal and a bottle of wine. Their relationship was professional and yet they shared a closeness that surpassed a married couple. Their affections were sincere and loving, but not passionate or sexual. They had mutual respect for one another, but Beverly always showed Conrad Jenkins respect around his staff.

Jenkins entered the house and hung his jacket on the coat rack.

"Hello there, Mister," Beverly said as she approached him and kissed him on the cheek.

"Something smells delicious," he said as he placed his car keys on the small table by the door.

"I made a roast with potatoes, carrots and onions. If I recall that was one of your favorites," she teased.

"It absolutely is my favorite."

They enjoyed a bottle of wine together over the great meal Beverly had prepared. Afterwards, she led Conrad to the den and returned to the kitchen to clean up.

"Let me help you with those," he called after her.

"No, no. I'm fine. How about a cup of coffee?"

"Yeah, can I get it leaded?" he asked.

"Sure," she said from the kitchen.

She returned a few minutes later with his coffee and a piece of Dutch Apple Pie. Conrad smiled and said, "I'm in heaven."

"Well, you look like you have been through hell," she said as she left the room again.

He thought for a moment about what she had said. It had surely been a strange ride so far. So much of what had happened was just not right, and yet he still needed to perform his job, and perform it well.

The Chain

Beverly Clayton giggled as she returned with her coffee cup in one hand and a small piece of pie in her other hand.

"So, may I ask how things are going?"

She was trustworthy, and another one of his hand picked personnel, but she also in no way had security clearance to know what had taken place. He had assigned her to this position due to her age and lifestyle. She needed the work, and it required nothing more than… watching. Though she could shoot a gun, it didn't mean she used it very often. She had definitely not been in a situation where she was required to use it.

"It's hard for me to say. I honestly am not sure how it is going. I feel like we're always ten steps behind the bad guys."

"And do we know 'who' the bad guys are?" she asked.

"Now that is another problem," he said as he sipped his coffee and ran the events through his mind.

Beverly could see he was troubled and kept the conversation light for the rest of the evening which eventually led to them both yawning and saying their good nights.

Jenkins stood up and kissed her cheek then headed off to bed.

Beverly put the coffee cups in the dishwasher. She proceeded to rinse off the small serving plates from the pie when she thought she saw something outside. She turned on the outside floodlights and searched the yard through the window. Living in the country meant all kinds of animals came around at night. Being from the city, she never really got used to it.

"Stupid cats," she said as she shut off the lights and locked the doors. She walked by Conrad's room and he was already fast asleep. She wasn't far behind him.

Chapter Thirty-Three

Ross was breathing hard. He was sure Beverly Clayton didn't see him, but when the lights came on he almost panicked. Fortunately for him, he was behind the shadow of a tree. The revelation that Conrad Jenkins and Beverly Clayton had something going on was a new twist he hadn't expected. He stayed low to the ground and made his way behind the house, slithering to the back yard where he could 'watch'. By now, his team was heading west, with the exception of Clepto. The car was parked one mile down the road, hidden behind brush and trees. It was there that Clepto waited for Ross's return. The transmitter had worked well, and allowed them to track Jenkins after their departure from the airport.

Ross adjusted his night vision goggles and watched the house for any signs of movement. He wondered if this was just a waste of time.

He thought to himself, *so Jenkins and Mrs. Clayton are secret lovers...* Though she did appear a bit older than Jenkins, Ross had seen crazier things.

It was then that he saw Jenkins exit the house. Ross saw him heading towards the Weaver's house. That was a bit unexpected. Ross's stomach knotted up at the idea of going in there again. His last experience in that place was frightful, and he didn't want to endure those events again.

He followed from behind making sure to stay low.

Chapter Thirty-Four

Jenkins went directly to the front door of the Weaver's home. After all, no one was home. He wasn't sure what he would find, but he hoped to find anything that would help him locate the Weavers. He picked the lock easily and made his way inside. He found the hallway light and flipped the switch up. The room lit, exposing the coat rack and a wall of family photos. Jenkins moved further in, looking for anything out of the ordinary. The kitchen and living room seemed ordinary and inviting. Everything had its place in this home as nothing was out of place. He found the light switch for the stairway that lead to the second floor. He expected someone or something to jump out at him, but once again there was nothing. Climbing the steps, he found Kylee's room. A small light on her dresser was still on. He was saddened for this family. They were involved with something that they had no control of. They were people in the wrong place at the wrong time. They endured great loss and suffering. They were victims.

Jenkins left the room and made his way to Maggie's room. She was a very orderly lady. The bed was made with an old folded quilt folded at the bottom. A small lamp sat on a nightstand adjacent to an alarm clock. He turned off the lights as he followed the family's steps in his mind, and decided to look in the bathroom. A hand soap dispenser sat next to the sink, and a small cup that held a toothbrush. Again, everything looked in order. Usually in such an orderly place, the unusual would stand out, but nothing seemed odd.

He realized he hadn't brushed his teeth during his exaggerated bedtime departure from Beverly's coffee and pie visit. He paused to think while pulling out a piece of gum from his pocket. He toyed with the wrapper deciding to go back to the room with the fireplace. He searched for a trash can in the bathroom to throw his wrapper. He tossed the wrapper, and turned to leave shutting off the light switch. He made one step and stopped. His subconscious mind saw it. It knew something was out of place. In nanoseconds the brain sent alerts down the various neurological paths alerting him to go back and look in the trash can. He turned around and flipped the light switch back on. He noticed two pieces of crumpled tablet paper. He unfolded the papers and flattened them against the bathroom sink. There were two pen colors on the paper. One was blue, but most of the blue was scribbled out with a black ink. Jenkins folded the papers and placed them in his pocket. He shut off the light switch again and started back along the hall when all of a sudden the lights in the house went out. Conrad Jenkins froze. He could smell the ozone in the air. His phone vibrated in his slacks. He was thankful he had shut the ringer off.

"What is it that man fears more, Keeper? The darkness? Or that which he can't see?" a deep raspy voice spoke

"We mean you no harm," Jenkins said, his eyes wide as he stared into the darkness, waiting for his vision to adjust in hope of seeing the unexpected guest.

"Of course you don't," the voice said.

"Your technology is so advanced. We only wish to learn from you." Jenkins said as he took a step closer to the voice.

"Learn from me?" the voice said in a booming laugh. Then becoming somber again, the voice said, "You know what we want, Keeper. Where is it?"

"My guess is that you want the gift," Keeper said.

"Yes, the gift. Where is it?"

"I don't know. They evaded us. They used decoys."

"Stupid humans!" the voice said.

"Is the girl the gift?" Keeper asked.

"Yes, haven't you already figured that out? You are an amazing race. You have eyes that don't see, and ears that don't hear. Yet everything has been made plain to you. This war will end, and the gift will be ours!" the voice said sternly.

"Who are you? Are you at war with your own kind? How can such an advanced race still be at war with each other?" Jenkins said taking a fearless stance.

"Wouldn't a caveman say the same to you today?" the voice said.

Jenkins heard movement in front of him. This being was massive. He estimated it stood eight feet tall and weighed close to five hundred pounds.

The Chain

Suddenly, he felt the presence of the voice behind him. Somehow this being had moved his massive body, in the blink of an eye, behind Jenkins.

The voice whispered in Jenkins' ear, "Keeper, deliver the child to us, and we will share technology that far exceeds your wildest dreams."

Jenkins hair crawled on his skin. He knew the voice couldn't be trusted. There was no way he could negotiate with this being.

"And what about your enemies?" Jenkins asked.

The voice hissed, "They are weak. They only seek to do their master's bidding. They are misguided and have lost their ability to think for themselves."

"And who is your master?" Jenkins pressed on.

The voice spoke as if describing a great wonder, "He is a king, and the true leader of our kind. He led us away from a life of senselessness. We were like cattle in a pasture before he led us to a place of consciousness. Before that, we were meaningless, senseless. We were a dying breed."

The voice stopped for a moment in thought, then continued. "But tell me, Jenkins. Who is *your* Master? Who is pulling *your* puppet strings? Isn't that what you are? A puppet? When will you learn to think and break away? How long will you continue this senseless journey you have been placed on? You don't even know your master. You have never met him. He is a voice at the end of a phone. You are nothing more than a puppet, senseless, non-thinking. Do you really want to be cattle? Is that what you want for yourself?' The voice spoke like a spider spinning a web.

"What do you want from me?" Jenkins was clearly perturbed.

"I want the gift, Keeper," the voice said.

Jenkins swung around to face the voice and said, "I don't have the damn gift!"

But the room was empty. He gasped as the lights came back on. His phone continually vibrated in his slacks, but he opted not to answer it. He left the house, making certain to turn off all the lights, and went back to Beverly Clayton's home. The house was lit up like a Christmas tree. It was clear that Beverly was awake as he saw her looking out the window.

He made his way inside, and she hugged him.

"You had me worried, Conrad," she said.

"Sorry, I couldn't sleep and thought I would check out the house. What are you doing up?" he asked.

"I got a call from Shriever. Apparently you weren't answering your phone, and when you weren't in your room...," she said.

"Yeah, well I was a little tied up," he said, looking down at his hands.

There was a knock at the door. They both turned to see Ross in a dark outfit. Jenkins looked a little surprised as he let Ross in.

"What are you doing here?" Jenkins asked.

"I was going to ask you the same thing, but I see you and Mrs. Clayton are more than friends. Look! I could care less 'who's sleeping with whom' here, Keeper, but I want some answers, and I want them now!" Ross yelled.

Beverly Clayton and Jenkins laughed out loud. Ross looked confused and obviously still irritated.

Jenkins chuckled and said, "Ross, come with me."

"I will put on some fresh coffee," Beverly said, heading away to the kitchen.

Chapter Thirty-Five

"So what's going on?" Ross asked.

"Have a seat, Ross," Jenkins said as he sat down in a lazy boy chair.

Beverly arrived with a rolling cart complete with coffee, cream, sugar, and pie.

"How would you like your coffee?" she asked Ross.

"Just cream please."

She gave them both a cup of coffee and cut them both a piece of apple pie.

Jenkins pulled out the papers from his pocket. He laid them flat, pulled out a pair of reading glasses from his pocket and attempted to read the scribbled mess.

"Let me see your night vision goggles please," Jenkins said to Ross.

Ross pulled the goggles out of a pocket in the side of his pants and handed Jenkins the goggles.

"Ross, you are right. There is something I have been keeping from you. I didn't share this with you because it wasn't relevant to this mission, but being that your curiosity is aroused. I would like you meet my sister, Beverly Clayton," Jenkins said as he looked over his reading glasses to see the dumbstruck look on Ross's face.

"Sister. Uhh. Oh my," Ross said and they all chuckled.

"Oh, boss, I'm so sorry. That was really rude of me back there in the kitchen."

"No worries," he said waving his hand and shaking his head. "Forget about it. Beverly, could you cut the lights for me, please?" Jenkins asked.

"Sure," she answered as the lights went out.

"What are you doing, Keeper?" Ross whispered with concern in his tone.

"Using a trick I learned. I found these papers in the bathroom trashcan at the Weaver's house. I'm guessing they used this as a way to communicate in the house, fortunately for us they used one ink to communicate and another to scribble it all out." Jenkins put on the goggles.

"How does that benefit us?" Ross asked.

"Ahha! Perfect. Here, take a look, Jenkins said, taking the night vision glasses back off. He arose from his chair, walked the few paces to Ross and handed him the goggles and the papers.

As Ross slipped on the glasses and looked at the papers, he commented with a widening smile, "Wow. Neat trick. Where did you learn that?"

"On the internet. Ever heard of YouTube?"

"No shit. That is awesome," Ross said amazed at the bag of tricks Keeper still had.

Jenkins took the goggles and papers back and read the hand scribbled notes. It was apparent that the Weavers became aware of what was happening the night they stayed in the house. Apparently Kylee had some type of communication with one of the entities in the middle of the night warning them that they were being watched and telling of the bugs that Ross had hidden in the house. But why were they helping the Weavers? He was troubled, as it was clear to him that there were two factions to these entities, and they were clearly at odds. They obviously knew all about his team and their purpose. His team's purpose… was really not clear even to Jenkins. *The voice at the end of the phone wants the gift delivered to him. The entity in the house wants the gift, and the Weavers just want their little girl back, and yet one faction of the entities delivers the message through Ross telling him to protect the gift. From what? And who? And how was he to do that?*

"You can turn the lights back on," Jenkins said to Beverly, slipping off the goggles.

"There is nothing there very telling, but at least we know that they are aware." Jenkins handed the goggles back to Ross.

"Aware of what?" Ross asked.

"Aware that we were watching and listening."

"Where's your escort?" Jenkins asked.

"Down the road. Parked and waiting for my return."

The Chain

"Call him in. I'm going to travel with you two tomorrow. We will move west and see what we can dig up together. I'm off to bed," he said, moving toward the hallway. Before he disappeared, he asked his sister, "Beverly, can you ready a room for Ross and Clepto?"

"Surely," she said as she passed her brother, making her way to the guest rooms.

"Oh, I found something of yours," Jenkins said as he tossed the transmitter to Ross.

Ross blushed and said nothing. Jenkins smiled and made his way off to bed.

Chapter Thirty-Six

Stan woke to the sound of voices. It was a guttural language that he didn't recognize. Maggie was still asleep covered in his denim jacket. He shivered as he got up to examine the walls. The eastern wall of the building was warming from the morning sun. He rested his back against it, and looked up to examine the vent in the roof of the building. He would never be able to fit through it, but Maggie could, as he suspected.

He looked around the room for anything that could help them. There was nothing to be seen. No tools, no chairs, nothing. It was an empty metal windowless room, and quickly appearing to be an unsolvable puzzle. The concrete floor offered no exit as well. He moved towards the door where the conversation outside had stopped. After examination, he saw nothing that would aid him in their hopeful escape. He pushed very lightly on the door to get a feel for its weight. It moved slightly. He let it rest and tried again. This time it moved a little farther and he let it rest again. Stan realized it wasn't locked and was about to start pushing harder when a loud thud on the other side of the door reminded him that his captors were outside waiting for him.

"Stan?" Maggie whispered, shaking off sleep.

He returned to Maggie's side and held her. He could see her lips were dry, and already knew that they were going to require water soon.

"Stan, we have to get out of here. We need water, and food. We won't last long like this." She reminded him in a pitiful whine.

"I know. I have an idea. You are going to have to trust me though."

Stan proceeded to lay out a plan. It would require a diversion by Maggie so that Stan could escape and get help. His hope was that she could lure Deloris and Rudy to the backside of the building. He would then attempt to get the doors open and make a run for his truck.

The Chain

They were desperate and Maggie knew they had to start trying something. She pulled a hairbrush out of her purse and moved toward the back of the metal room. The air was already getting hot as the sun moved high in the sky.

Stan moved closer to the doors preparing for his run.

Maggie banged on the back wall with the brush. The clang vibrated through the metal building. She continued her commotion, calling out for help. Stan heard Rudy and Deloris both move away from the door and he prepared for his run.

Maggie increased her activities and called out louder and more forceful. Rudy banged the wall from the outside hard enough to put a large arm dent into the metal.

Deloris yelled, "Now you be quiet in there!"

"Or what, Deloris? Are you going to come beat me with your purse? You old lying hag!" Maggie yelled.

Rudy once again hit the wall. His strength was incredible.

"You have no idea what I can do?" Deloris said.

"I know you are a liar. I know you want my daughter, but you will NEVER have her!"

At that, Rudy and Deloris both started slamming the outside walls. The rumbling was amazing and Maggie covered her ears and screamed.

Stan saw his chance and ran for the door, slamming his arms and chest into it as hard as possible. He expected it not to budge, but instead it flew open as if nothing was holding it back. He stumbled to the ground, but quickly got to his feet and ran for the truck.

Maggie increased her commotion, taunting her captors.

Rudy yelled at her through the walls, "Be quiet, you annoying bug. You will never see your daughter again!"

Maggie laughed at him, "You fooled me once with your lies, but you will not fool me now."

That is when it hit Maggie. She now understood what Kylee had said to her.

"You are both liars. Kylee named you correctly. You aren't the Seevers. She meant you are Deceivers! Nothing like the truth, Rudy, is there?"

Stan unlocked the door and started the truck. Maggie heard the growl of the engine. She turned to run for the door, but came face to face with Deloris.

"Who's the deceiver now, missy?" Deloris said as she threw Maggie across the room.

Maggie landed hard on her back against the rough concrete floor. The impact temporarily winded her. Maggie stood back up and regained her breath. She wouldn't relent and continued her verbal attack on Deloris.

"What are you going to do when the Big Man comes?" Maggie asked, pointing directly at her.

"The Big Man?" Deloris said with a hint of fear in her eyes.

"Who are you talking about?"

She appeared behind Maggie. She once again threw Maggie through the air.

Maggie's lip was bleeding, and parts of her body throbbed, but she wouldn't stop her tirade.

"Oh, you know damn well who he is, and when he gets here there will be a price to pay." Maggie hissed at her.

Stan jumped when he realized Rudy was in the passenger seat next to him.

"Leaving so soon, Stan?" Rudy said as he slammed Stan against the door, knocking the wind out of him and hurting Stan's arm.

"You bastards!" Stan said, swinging his fist at Rudy.

Stan's fist passed through Rudy and slammed into the passenger seat.

Rudy re-appeared outside of Stan's door. The door unlocked and opened. Rudy pulled Stan out of the truck and threw him to the ground. He reached inside the truck and took out the keys and threw them to the ground.

"You humans and your technology." He shook his head.

Rudy grabbed Stan by the legs and drug him back into the room where Deloris and Maggie were still having their verbal battle.

"Look what I found, honey?" Rudy said as he tossed Stan into the room and against the metal wall. There was a loud thud, and crack. Stan felt ribs break as he grimaced, grabbed his side, and gasped for air.

"Leave him alone," Maggie screamed at Rudy with a raised fist and defiance in her eyes.

"Or what?" Rudy said with a smug smile on his face.

Maggie stood her ground and stared defiantly into Rudy's face.

"When the Big Man comes you will pay a dear price for all of this!" Maggie stared at him.

The Chain

"Oh, the Big Man!" Rudy said as he walked towards Deloris. "Is that what he calls himself these days?" Rudy asked.

"And what name do you have for him?" Maggie asked. She realized she was hitting a nerve with both of them.

Deloris again appeared directly in front of Maggie. She had the poise of a teacher with her purse under her arm.

"He has many names, but his real name is never to be spoken," Deloris said as her voice trailed off and she looked away.

"We were once together. All of us. Before the war, but… that was so long ago now…" Deloris continued.

Maggie saw Rudy transform into a little girl with Downs Syndrome. She had on a white top and a little blue dress with suspenders. She had dark hair and small bow on the top of her head. She gave the appearance of innocence, but Maggie didn't trust anyone. She realized he was the child in the bathroom that had accompanied Deloris.

The child spoke to Deloris, "Mother, that is enough. We must wait for the gift. Come now," the child insisted with an outstretched hand.

Deloris gave Maggie a saddened smile and took the hand of the child. They instantly re-appeared at the door.

Maggie cried out to Deloris, "We need water. We will die in here."

Deloris stared at Maggie as the child closed the door on them.

Chapter Thirty-Seven

Ross and Jenkins stood in front of the corn field amazed.

"What the hell happened here?" Ross asked.

"I don't know, but it is nothing short of a miracle," Jenkins said.

"The reporter said it goes on for miles," Ross added.

"Well, we have to assume this is related to the Weavers. The reporter indicated that it happened yesterday near the lunch hour."

Jenkins shook his head hardly believing what he saw.

"That has to put them pretty far in front of us," Ross said.

"Yeah, let's hope Beth's team can come up with something," Jenkins said, kicking at the gravel.

Ross got back into the car and waited for Jenkins.

Clepto looked out the windshield, amazed. He spoke to no one, "That is pretty wild."

Ross stared out the window, having no response. Jenkins got back into the car and dialed Beth's cell phone.

Chapter Thirty-Eight

Stan woke to a chill in the dark room. Maggie was asleep next to him cuddled close. He tried to move, but the pain was incredible. He gritted his teeth to keep from screaming and waking Maggie.

When Maggie stirred, he whispered, "Maggie."

She moaned and finally came to.

"Stan, I'm so sorry for everything."

"Shhh… You didn't do this. This is no one's fault. This is out of our hands."

After a long pause, she turned to Stan to speak.

"I believe I have figured something out."

"What's that?" He asked.

"Their weakness." She continued.

"Their weakness? How do you mean?"

"They fear the Big Man. I could see it in their eyes. They actually looked frightened."

"He's just another one of them," Stan said as he carefully moved himself into a sitting position. The pain was excruciating, but he knew it was better to sit up. He didn't want to drown from the fluids in his lungs.

"Also, remember Kylee calling them the Seevers. Well, I figured out she meant deceivers, as in liars." She said.

"Well, that doesn't sound right. Kylee doesn't use those kinds of words."

"No, *she* doesn't, but maybe the Big Man does?" Maggie asked.

Stan said, "No matter what, I want you to live through this, Maggie. That means you may have to…."

Maggie placed her hand over Stan's mouth.

"Don't you even think it, much less stay it, Stan Weaver. We're going to come through this together. Do you hear me?"

"Well, I'm not much of a help right now, and I don't hear the cavalry close."

"Well, let's pray," she said.

Stan held her hands in the darkness, searching for the right words to say. He had needed nothing but help from the beginning. Yet, he continued to feel helpless, and now he was at the end of his rope.

He prayed quietly, "God, if ever we have needed you… it is now, Lord. You have witnessed what has happened. I know nothing escapes your eyes. Please send help and rescue us."

Maggie ended the prayer with, "Amen."

Stan stared into the darkness still searching for a way to fix this problem.

Maggie huddled close to Stan trying to hide her shivers. It was going to be a cold night, and tomorrow would make a third day without water. She was worried. Stan's condition was going to worsen. How could Deloris let them suffer like this? Deloris' eyes showed that she had once been caring, but there was a darkness about her.

* * *

Stan woke to the sound of a low rumble. He placed his hand over Maggie's mouth. She sat up and looked around. The room was still quite dark, but according to her watch it was early morning. The rumble increased.

She whispered, "What is that?"

"Not sure, a vehicle? A helicopter?" he said.

They heard Rudy and Deloris up and about. They were speaking in some language that neither Stan nor Maggie understood.

Maggie cried out, "Looks like we have company!"

"You shut up!" Rudy screamed as he leaped high in the air and landed on the roof. He walked around the roof denting it where he walked. He obviously weighed much more than his appearance.

"He's coming, Rudy!" Deloris said, clearly nervous.

"No, it's…" Rudy started to say when the rumble increased.

It sounded like a freight train was adjacent to the building. The foundations shook, and a large flash of light shined around the edges of the door that served as the Weaver's only exit. Stan and Maggie heard two tortured screams and finally the door exploded away from the build-

The Chain

ing. The last thing either of them recalled was a bright light flooding the room.

Chapter Thirty-Nine

Beth listened to Jenkins' voice detail how one of their operatives had been watching Michael Stewart since the event six years prior. She wondered how many other teams were operating like this, and what else Keeper had kept from her. She smiled at her pun on words. They said their goodbyes and she placed the cell phone back in the clip on her waist.

Maybe it is time to move on from this job, she thought as she drove with her team towards Steamboat Springs, Colorado. Things had gotten weird, and Beth Foster didn't like "weird".

Chapter Forty

Stan struggled to open his eyes. He could hear the faint sound of music as he tried to focus. The melody was hypnotic and comforting. He closed his eyes and tried to take in what had happened. It was hard for him to focus on anything. He had lost track of time and events.

He opened his eyes again and a young woman with long dark hair stood over him. She placed her hand behind his head and brought a cup to his lips. He was too weak to deny her offering as he started to drink the warm liquid. He drank too quickly and was greeted by a spasm of coughs. Stan closed his eyes, anticipating the sharp pain he knew his broken ribs would send, but instead, there was no pain. He tried to move a little, but a very large hand held his shoulder in place.

A deep voice spoke to him, "Rest now, my friend, and regain your strength."

Stan turned to face the voice. Leaning over him was a very large man. He had a long face with deeply set dark eyes. His hair was long and white and hung down into his chest. He was dressed in white garb and was ominous in appearance. Stan's eyes went into focus as he realized this must be the Big Man.

Stan said, "Big Man."

The large figure smiled at him and said, "Get your rest, friend."

The large man spoke to the young woman, "Bring her."

The young woman said nothing, as she turned and left the room.

Maggie entered the room and sat at Stan's side. He had been unconscious for over twenty four hours. The young woman returned and brought a pitcher and two cups to Maggie.

"Thank you, Chenoa," Maggie said.

"You're welcome. Can I get you anything else?" the young woman asked.

"No, honey, but thanks again," Maggie said.

The young woman placed her hand on Maggie's shoulder in a comforting gesture and made her way out of the room.

Maggie combed Stan's hair to the side with her fingertips. Caressing him like a small child fighting his first fever. The room was dimly lit by candlelight. It was warmed by a fire that cast an orange aura all about. Maggie stayed by Stan's side for a long while. He drifted in and out of sleep. Each time he woke, he sipped the warm tea.

Stan finally opened his eyes long enough to make extended eye contact with Maggie. His smile told her that he was clearly pleased to see her.

"Well, hello, Mr. Weaver. I'm Maggie Franklin," she said with tears rolling down her cheeks.

"No, you are Maggie Franklin Weaver." He grinned as he moved to sit up.

"Nice and slow, friend, you have endured much," the tall man said.

"I assume you are the Big Man?" Stan said in a defeated tone.

The tall man and Maggie both chuckled.

"No, I am not the Big Man you two speak of. My name is White Eagle."

"White Eagle is a friend," Maggie assured Stan.

With a defeated look, Stan said, "He is one of them."

Again, Maggie and the man laughed.

"I can assure you I am not one of them. I am an American just like you, I am a Native American," the man said.

Stan shook his head and said, "What next? Ghost Busters?"

White Eagle gave Stan a look of confusion, "I shall leave you two alone to reacquaint. Chenoa has prepared dinner and we will be eating soon."

Maggie stood and hugged White Eagle. She was like a child in his arms.

"Thank you," she said to him.

He smiled at Maggie and said to both of them, "Gather your energies. We have much to discuss."

He was an incredibly large man standing well over six feet tall. Stan watched as the Indian turned to leave the room. His immense shadow traveled along the walls from the candlelight until he finally left.

"What is going on?" Stan asked Maggie

The Chain

Maggie stared at the fire and started to speak, "I remember being in that metal room. There was a very bright light and a huge explosion of force. I woke up in White Eagle's arms. I remember him carrying me to the truck. He laid me in the front seat. I saw you lying in the back of the truck. I woke up this afternoon *here*," she said, looking about the room. It was a simple guest room with off-white walls, and a stenciled border where the walls met the ceiling. A small antique desk sat off to the side. Candlelight lit the room giving it a soft glow.

"Who are these people? And where are we?" Stan asked.

"White Eagle brought us here in your truck. We're at some Indian Reservation called "Rose Bud"?" she said, unsure where or what that was.

Chenoa entered the room with fresh towels and wash cloths.

"Chenoa, this is my husband Stan."

"Hello, Mr. Weaver. I brought you some fresh towels and wash-cloths. I thought you might want to shower before dinner."

Chenoa handed them towels.

"Thank You. You can call me Stan."

Chenoa smiled and left the room. The smell of a freshly cooked meal began to fill the air. Stan's stomach growled with anticipation. He needed food and answers.

Maggie helped Stan to his feet. He was amazed that he had no pain in his ribs. It was as if they were never broken. Stan hoped that the shower would give him renewed energy. Maggie led him to the bathroom. He was still thirsty, and brought his tea along.

"Will you be okay?" Maggie inquired.

"Yes, I will be fine."

"Here are your clothes. Chenoa washed them for you. I'm going to go help her with dinner."

She placed them beside the sink.

"And where exactly is the kitchen?" he asked.

"Follow your nose. You will find it," she teased with a smile.

Stan closed the door to the shower and made his way to the sink. He saw himself in the mirror then and realized he was wearing something odd. He had on some type of long shirt looking thing. He chuckled and said to himself as he removed the clothing, "Hi ho, Silver... away".

The shower was incredible and Stan stood in the warm water falling over his head and shoulders. It was revitalizing, and he was pleased that his energy was returning. He finished his shower and drank the rest of his tea. He was happy to see his shaving kit next to the sink and thankful that Maggie had retrieved it from the truck. It has been several days since he last shaved, and he wondered who the old man was staring at him in the mirror.

He finished dressing and realized he had lost a few pounds. Food would be good.

Stan followed Maggie's instructions and followed the smell of the food. He passed through the room where he awoke and down a long hall. The smell was coming from a room off to the right. He turned and found Maggie and Chenoa setting a table.

"Is there anything I can do?" Stan asked.

"No, food is ready. Have a seat," Maggie said.

Chenoa left to retrieve White Eagle.

They both returned a few minutes later. White Eagle had changed his clothes. He was wearing cowboy boots, blue jeans, and a denim shirt. He was a handsome man with eyes that seemed to see through you. He took the head seat at the table.

"It is good to see you up and about. I hope you are feeling better," White Eagle asked.

"Yes, thank you for your hospitality. Thanks for rescuing us, but how did you..." Stan started to ask.

White Eagle held up a hand and said, "Let's enjoy a good meal, and fine drink. Afterwards, we will both tell our stories. I also have many questions. But for now, what can I get you to drink?"

Stan was leery of this man, but realized White Eagle had helped them, and that is what they needed most right now.

"Just water please."

Maggie and Chenoa brought food to the table. It was decorated for a feast. Chenoa removed the lid of a large oval pot revealing a large roast adorned with potatoes, and carrots. Maggie brought a large bowl of freshly baked corn bread. Chenoa dished out food for everyone, but no one touched their food. She finally took her seat and White Eagle spoke aloud, "Let us pray."

Stan and Maggie were both nervous. They had never dined with Native American Indians and had no idea of their customs.

White Eagle and Chenoa bowed their heads. Maggie smiled at Stan as they followed suit.

The Chain

"Lord, I thank you that you are with us. I thank you for our guests, and ask for your incredible blessing on this food and our time together. Amen"

Maggie and Stan seemed relieved as they replied in unison, "Amen."

Chenoa sat across from White Eagle. The food was delicious, and the quiet dinner table attested to its quality. The conversation was limited to Maggie asking Stan to pass the pepper.

Stan finally spoke to Chenoa and said, "The food is delicious."

Chenoa smiled and said, "Thank you."

Stan looked at White Eagle and said, "How long have you two been together?"

White Eagle looked confused; then everyone looked at Chenoa, who rolled her eyes and laughed.

"Chenoa is my daughter. So, we have been together twenty one years now," White Eagle explained.

There was a silence at the table and all of a sudden everyone burst out in loud laughter. Stan was relieved as the tension finally left the air.

Chenoa offered second helpings to everyone. Stan passed on the food in favor of the corn bread. He buttered the bread and hummed as he took a big bite. It was still warm, and was clearly made from scratch.

White Eagle looked at Stan and said, "Let us move to the living room. I will add some logs to the fire. I believe Chenoa has prepared something sweet for all of us."

Maggie shooed them on as she and Chenoa cleared the table. The girls giggled and laughed between themselves as the men left the kitchen for the living room.

White Eagle directed Stan to a large chair that sat to one side of the fire. He left Stan to gather some firewood from outside. A small table separated the chair from a large couch. A beautiful country quilt blanketed the back of the couch.

Maggie came to the room with a tray holding a large pitcher, cups, cream, and sugar.

"I'm going to leave you two be and spend some time with Chenoa. If that's okay?" Maggie asked.

"Sure," Stan said, nodding.

White Eagle came back into the house with a few logs in his arms. He placed two of the logs in the large open fireplace. He added some old newspaper under the logs to encourage their ignition.

Stan asked, "Can I pour you some coffee?"

"I believe that is tea actually. Would you prefer coffee?" White Eagle said.

"Actually, no."

Stan poured them both a cup of tea.

Stan added sugar and cream, and stirred his cup. White Eagle continued to tend the fire. He was an interesting man to watch as he seemed to flow with his surroundings in a very unique way. He displayed an incredible confidence in every move that he made, and it was what he didn't say that assured Stan of his wisdom.

Stan sipped his tea and said, "This tea you have is incredible. Is it some Native American Indian blend?"

"It is something that many Americans have not experienced it seems," White Eagle said in a serious tone.

"What kind of tea is it?" Stan asked.

White Eagle sipped the tea and closed his eyes. He appeared to be a much focused man. A deep sense of spirituality emitted from him in silent waves. He finally opened his eyes and looked at Stan with a grin and said, "Tetley. British Blend."

Stan was dumbfounded. Then they both laughed. The laughter finally wound down and they found themselves staring at the fire.

Finally gathering his thoughts, Stan chose the most direct method.

"How did you find us?" Stan asked.

"I was led to you."

"Led to us? By who?" Stan asked.

"One of them."

"What are they?" Stan asked.

"They are aliens to this world."

"That is obvious," Stan said.

White Eagle sipped his tea, and turned to look at Stan. It was as if the Indian could see through him. Stan felt naked, but sensed he was safe. He didn't know what this man knew, but he was sure he had information that would aid him in finding Kylee.

"Where is the gift?" White Eagle asked him.

Stan looked into his eyes before finally turning away from White Eagle and staring at the fire.

The Chain

"What gift are you referring to?"

"I know you and your wife were given a gift. I will not lie to you and pretend that I know what the gift is or where it is, but I have given an oath to protect you and the gift. There is just one problem though," White Eagle said.

"What's that?" Stan asked.

"I do not know what this gift is." White Eagle moved to the fire to move the logs around.

"I do," Stan said, never taking his attention from the flames in the fire.

"The gift is my daughter Kylee," he told him. Then Stan shared the story of her disappearance and all that had happened up to now.

White Eagle was silent for a long time. He stared off into the distance as if he could see through walls. Chenoa came into the room with a plate filled with sliced coffee cake. It had a nice pumpkin spice smell. She set the plate on the table for the men.

"Daddy? Are you okay?" she asked.

"Yes. Where is Mrs. Weaver," White Eagle asked.

"She is taking a bath. She shouldn't be much longer."

"Could you ask her to join us in the living room?"

"Yes, Daddy."

"Thank you for your help today, Chenoa."

"No problem, Daddy" Chenoa said as she leaned over and kissed White Eagle's cheek.

Chenoa left the room quietly. Stan helped himself to a piece of the coffee cake. It was full of wonderful flavors. The cinnamon and nutmeg complimented the pumpkin flavor, and it was full of chunks of English Walnuts throughout.

"I know you have questions, and I would like to share my story as well, but I ask that you wait till your wife can join us."

"Good idea. I'm sure she has questions as well."

In the bathroom, Maggie dried her hair and was thankful to finally be clean. She wouldn't let herself shower until Stan recovered. Not that it would have impacted his recovery, but at the time in her mind she felt like she needed to wait. She was glad the waiting was over.

Maggie looked in the mirror and said, "Kylee, where are you?"

So much had happened. The last few days felt like months. Yet she still felt like she hardly had a moment to enjoy Kylee. Life was not fair, but this was torturous for her and Stan. Stan was right from the beginning. They needed a plan, and had to stay a step ahead of those seeking Kylee.

Chenoa knocked on the door and spoke, "Maggie, they have asked you to join them in the living room. Is there anything else I can get for you?"

"No, honey." Maggie opened the door.

"Thanks so much for everything," Maggie said as she gave Chenoa a hug.

Maggie held both of Chenoa's hands and said, "Chenoa, your hair is so beautiful. You must have gotten this from your mother, because your father's is white as snow."

"My mother passed when I was born, but my father tells me we had the same hair. His hair was once very similar they tell me, but that changed one day when he went through the rites of passage that shaman endure."

"Oh, he is a shaman? Well, he does seem very spiritual, but well... I wasn't sure."

Chenoa nodded and smiled as they said their good byes.

Maggie went to the living room. She felt good in her jeans. They actually fit a little looser than she remembered.

But then a few days without food will do that to you, she thought.

"Hi guys. Can I join the powwow?" she asked as she entered the living room.

Stan poured her some tea, and she thanked him. She could see they had been in deep conversation.

"Your husband has shared your story with me, and the difficult journey you have traveled. I wanted to wait for you to join us, so that I could share my story as well. It is my hope we can make sense of this."

White Eagle stood up in front of the two of them, pacing.

"I, too, have much to tell, and I ask for you both to be patient with me as I try to explain my journey this far."

There was a long pause and then the tall Indian sat down across from them both with his back to the fire. It was an amazing picture as he was a tall man even when sitting on the floor. The flames of the fire seemed to decorate the outline of his head adding more to his mystique and silent power.

"I am White Eagle. I am a shaman by birth. I am also a Christian. It is important to know there are places where those two ideologies collide, but regardless I am what I am. As you can imagine, my faith in God

The Chain

isn't always well received here in the Indian Nation by the older and wise, but they fear me, and thus respect me," he said.

"Why do they fear you?" Stan asked.

"When I was a young man I had an... experience."

"I was with other young men my age. We were preparing for a ceremony that all shamans go through. I was born into this role. It was not something I chose, but that does not mean I would not have sought it out."

White Eagle stared straight ahead not focused on any particular thing in the room, and continued to speak.

"We were racing to the top of a ridge. I was the fastest runner and much more agile than them. I reached the top of the ridge and looked down. I waved my hands in triumph as I looked down the hill toward them. I could see fear in their eyes, and some of them began to run." He paused.

"I faced the sun, but realized that a bright light shone from behind me. It was calming and peaceful. I sensed the presence of a great being and fell to my knees and cried, 'Please do not hurt me!'"

The voice responded, "Take off your shoes."

"I removed my sandals and pushed them aside."

"I was frightened, but in a strange way. "

"The voice then told me, 'From this day forward, you will be known as White Eagle and will no longer be known as Hethonton. Fear not, for I will be with you always. Learn my ways, and walk my path, and you will be with me, and I will be with you. Do not fear your enemies for they are my enemies, and I will quickly put them under your feet.'"

"I am speechless and in fear of you, my Lord," I said."

"Thus, your wisdom begins," the voice said.

I asked, "May I turn and face you?"

"Yes, you may, but do not look at my face or you will reach your end."

I turned to face the voice on the ridge and looked down at the ground. It glowed, and I saw he had feet. He was very large, and I kept my head low in fear of my end. He placed his hand on my head and said to me, "I have left my mark upon you so that every living thing will know you are mine."

"A great wind blew around me from all directions. I was in fear and felt the winds rise up and away from me. I found myself face down on the ground. I was afraid to rise, but finally gained my courage. I lifted myself from the ground and found my sandals. When I leaned over to slip them on, I discovered that my hair had turned white as snow. I made my way down from the ridge, and three of the young men were there. They laid prostate at the ground trembling. I called to them, but they wouldn't move. I helped each of them to their feet. They screamed and ran from me back to our home."

"Alone, I made my way home. The village was assembled and watched my approach. My father stood in front and fell to his knees when he saw me. A Shaman approached to ask me what had happened, but before I could answer one of the young men said, 'The Great White Eagle descended upon him and spoke to him!'"

"The shaman asked me if this was true, and I told him it was. From that day on, they have called me White Eagle."

He looked at Stan.

"That is a pretty incredible story, but what does that have to do with our daughter," Stan asked.

White Eagle stared at them with a concerned look in his eyes. He actually looked frightened.

He began to speak, "Two nights ago I had a dream. In my dream, the same being spoke to me. He instructed me to meet him at the ridge where we had first met. I tried to go back to sleep, but I couldn't. I dressed and went there in the dark of the night. There was no sign of him when I approached. I climbed to the highpoint on the ridge, but no one was there. I faced out towards our village and sat and meditated. A slight wind blew upon me, and I sensed the presence of someone behind me. I spoke aloud and said, 'Did you summon me?'"

The voice responded, "Yes, White Eagle. Come and walk with me. We have much to discuss."

"Let me cover my head so I will not come to an early end." I said.

"Fear not, I am not him, but only his advocate. You may look upon me safely."

"I stood and turned to face him. He was a very tall being, standing nearly eight feet in height."

"It is nice to meet you," I said to the being.

"And you my friend," he answered.

"You are not of this world, are you?"

"No more than you are of this world," he said.

The Chain

I walked with him through fields and over hills. We seemed to be able to cover a great distance in such a short time. My stamina was incredible, and I felt no fatigue while we walked. We traveled a long time before he finally spoke to me.

"Do you understand that there are no coincidences in life?" he said.

I nodded and listened.

He continued, "Everything happens for a reason. There is nothing new under the sun. You think of things in reference to your time, but time is relative. You are going to witness something incredible this day in your time."

"How so?" I asked.

We stood on a hill and down below us was an abandoned radar facility. There were two tall beings standing by one of the buildings. He pointed to them and said to me, "Captives are about to be set free. They have been given a very important gift. Will you make an oath to protect them and the gift they bear?"

"I was surprised at his request, but turned to him and swore an oath to protect those held captive and whatever gift they bore."

I said to him, "How can I protect them if they are captives? Must I set them free?"

"Surely not. One much greater than you will set them free. Behold!"

He pointed to the Northern Sky.

"A great rumbling shook the earth as a flash of light shone in the sky and streaked towards the building. The ground heaved and moaned as the foundations of the earth trembled below us. I feared for my life as it felt like a great earthquake. The light was as bright as the sun. As it reached its destination, I heard screaming and wailing. The impact sent a great concussion shock, and threw me to the ground."

"I rose to my feet, unable to see immediately as the darkness of the night once again surrounded me. I said, 'How could anyone survive that?'"

"There was no response. I turned and realized I was alone. I ran down the hill and searched the buildings. That was when I found you."

White Eagle rose again and sat on the couch beside Maggie. Tears rolled down her cheeks as she stared into the fire.

"Why is this happening to us? None of this makes sense. What are these things?" she asked.

"It is a mystery to me," White Eagle said.

"As a shaman, we deal with spiritual things. We have an understanding of the spirit world based on our old traditions and practices. I can tell you that these are good spirits, but it sounds as if there are others involved here that are not so good. It also sounds as if they are in a struggle of some sorts. Unfortunately, your daughter is a point of contention, and it is because of her we are here today. We must find her. How can I protect her if I do not know where she is?" he said speaking into the air hoping that the voice in the ridge could hear him.

Stan jumped up from his chair and said, "Where is my truck?"

"It is parked outside the house?" White Eagle said.

Stan walked to the door. White Eagle reached up on the mantle and gathered something in his hands. When Stan turned back to face him, he tossed this item toward him.

"You may need these."

Stan caught the keys to his truck and proceeded outside. It was a cool night, and he felt a light breeze blowing across the yard. He unlocked the driver door and made his way to the back of the cab. He found a small red bag that Kylee carried and brought it with him as he returned to the house.

He placed the bag on the table next to the coffee pot and opened it. In the middle of Kylee's clothes was Kylee's Diary.

He quickly thumbed through the diary till he found the last entry.

We had fun today. We played in the cornfields and they woke up. We were all wet and muddy. It was great fun! We danced and sang. I wish Michael could have been with us. I want to go see him and have a tea party. Bad things are coming. I'm sad because I will have to go soon.

"Bad things are coming," Stan said in a mumble.

"She knew!" Maggie gasped.

"Who is this Michael?" White Eagle asked.

"He is my cousin," Maggie said as she retold the story his relationship with Kylee. She also told of the confrontation Stan had with Michael and how Michael had moved out west.

"Do you think she could have gone to him," White Eagle asked.

"Well, she has asked about him quite a bit since her return," Maggie said.

"Then it sounds like that is where you need to go," White Eagle said.

The Chain

"But we don't know where he is. He dropped off the face of the earth. Even his parents don't know where he is. They don't speak to him," Maggie said hiding the truth.

"Why would they not speak to him?" White Eagle asked.

"Because he is gay, and I don't want to hear one negative thing about it!" Maggie scolded Stan and White Eagle.

"It is not my place to judge this man or any man," White Eagle said.

"We must figure out how to find him," Stan said, fighting off a yawn.

"Get your rest this night. Maybe our helpers will show us the way by morning." White Eagle ended the conversation.

Stan yawned again while Maggie gathered up the coffee tray and took it into the kitchen. Stan followed her with the empty plate that once held coffee cake.

"Are you ready to go to bed, Mr. Weaver?" she asked.

"I am, but let me get Kylee's suitcase," he said as he left the kitchen.

Maggie took the tray from the table and went to the kitchen. She placed the dirty utensils and cups in the dishwasher. She paused for a moment to plan her next move. Nodding to herself she made her way to the bedroom. She got undressed and slipped under the covers of the bed.

Stan joined Maggie a few minutes later in the bedroom, with the red suitcase and placed it beside the dresser. He undressed and climbed into the bed.

He snuggled close to her, but Maggie whispered, "Just a minute" as she fiddled with her watch.

"Whatcha doing?" Stan asked.

"Shutting off the alarm on my watch. I didn't want it to wake us up at dark thirty tomorrow morning". She had lied, but she would explain tomorrow.

After another minute of fidgeting, she whispered, "Okay all set."

She turned to hold Stan, but he was already fast asleep. Tomorrow couldn't come soon enough. She knew what they would have to do.

Chapter Forty-One

Maggie woke before her alarm went off. She had been up for an hour. She hated lying to Stan, but he needed his rest, and she didn't want to tell him what she knew. The truth was she knew exactly where Michael was, and even though his parents had disowned him, Maggie hadn't. She got out of bed and quietly slipped on her jeans and a shirt. Stan continued to snore each time he inhaled. She could watch him for a long time like that. She loved the way he looked when he was asleep, but her time was precious and they needed to move. She leaned over him and woke him slowly. She rubbed his back till his snoring stopped and became long slow breaths. Leaning over him she whispered into his ear, "Stan, I need you to quietly wake up and get out of bed."

He didn't move for a moment, and then turned to face her. She placed her hand over his mouth and whispered into his hear, "Stan, you must trust me on this. Get dressed quietly. We're leaving."

He leaned into her ear and asked, "Where are we going?"

She whispered, "To get Kylee."

"You know where she is?"

"No, I know where Michael is. I will explain later. Just get your stuff so we can get out of here," she said.

"What about the Indian?" he asked.

"Stan, please!"

She carried Kylee's suitcase while Stan brought two other bags out to the truck.

Stan's heart was racing as he turned the ignition. He was sure everyone in the house would hear the engine rumble. He didn't give the rig time to warm up, and threw it into gear.

"I have no idea where the hell I am," he said to her as they headed on down a desolate country road.

The Chain

"Where are we headed?" he asked.

"Steamboat Springs, Colorado."

"Steamboat Springs... Okay, one second. Let's see what Sally has to say about that."

"Sally? Who is Sally?" she asked, her eyes a mask of confusion.

Stan pulled down the visor and punched in the destination address on a small keyboard and a female voice spoke from the GPS system.

"Maggie, I want you to meet the 'other' woman," Stan said with a wink.

Sally spoke, "Continue on US 18 for one mile.

"Nice!" Maggie said. "But can she cook as well as me?" she asked with a chuckle.

Stan said, "No one can cook like you, Maggie."

"So, did you have a revelation in your sleep about where to find Michael?"

"Well, no. I have always known where he was," She admitted, slowly meeting his eyes.

"So you kept in touch with him?" Stan asked, staring out the front windshield.

"Yes, but...," she paused, searching for what to say. "We haven't talked in a year," she said.

"Why's that?" Stan asked, giving her another glance.

"Because he got sick, Stan, very sick. I used to visit him, but he asked me to stop coming, and finally he wouldn't take my calls anymore."

"Sick? What is wrong with him," he asked, his eyes questioning.

"He has HIV," she said in a quiet voice, as tears rolled down her cheeks.

"Oh, my God," Stan said as he ran his hands through his hair.

"How do you know if he is still alive?" he asked.

"Because his partner calls me and gives me updates."

"His partner? Who is that?" he asked.

"His name is Bill. You would like him."

Maggie opened her "Christy Love" purse and moved the stacks of money aside. She found her phone and turned it on to check for messages. There was a message from her dentist's office, reminding her of a cleaning she was scheduled for next week. She closed the phone and heard Stan yell, "Oh shit, hang on!"

170

She dropped the phone into the purse as Stan swerved the truck around a dead deer on the road.

"Nice move, Mario Andretti, she teased him, trying to calm her racing heart.

"So any messages on your phone from boyfriends?" he teased, giving her another glance.

"Oh, Dr. Randal's office called to remind me of a teeth cleaning I have scheduled next week."

Stan didn't respond as the truck rolled down the highway, making its way to Steamboat Springs.

Chapter Forty-Two

Jenkins felt his phone vibrate.

"Jenkins," he said. "Where? When? Call me if there is any change" he said, very excited.

"Well, folks, we have the break we needed."

"How so," Ross asked, momentarily looking away from the road.

"Mrs. Weaver used her cell phone. It appears she left it on as well. We show them on Highway 20 going south into Nebraska. Ross, can you catch them in this thing?"

"Definitely."

"Can you get the other half of your team to intercept as well?"

"On it!"

Ross threw the flashing blue and red lights on and raced west on Highway 90.

"Clepto, any idea how far ahead of us they are?"

"I'm working on it." Clepto said as he connected with Shriever via his uplink cell modem.

"They are about an hour ahead of us."

"Should we call in the locals for help?" Ross asked Jenkins.

"No," Jenkins replied.

"Well, should we get Beth's team in the air?" Ross asked, confused at Jenkins' last response.

"No, I think we can handle this without a lot of commotion. Have the rest of your team intercept from Denver."

Ross wasn't sure what Jenkins was up to, but it almost seemed like he wanted them to get away. It was a logical solution to have Beth's team in the air for recovery. This wasn't the way Ross would have handled this, but he knew Keeper had his reasons.

Chapter Forty-Three

White Eagle was up long before Stan and Maggie left the house. It was clear to him that they were frightened. It was also clear to him that one of them knew where the gift was. The woman seemed anxious at first, but after Stan read the child's diary, it was clear to White Eagle that Maggie's demeanor changed.

He thought about their conversation the night before, and wondered why Maggie had withheld what she knew. He nodded to himself that he also hadn't shared all he knew. The being did say that the parents would lead him to the gift.

He finally pulled the Blue 1972 Chevy Nova onto the road, hoping to give Stan and Maggie the comfortable feeling they had left unnoticed. White Eagle's whole persona changed in this car. He was an ominous figure with his hair in a pony tail, and a black leather vest over his white shirt. Soon, the sun would rise, and he would complete his look with dark sunglasses.

He left off the headlights and watched from a distance to see if this journey would take him north or south. As he guessed, they headed south.

He gave them a long lead and finally turned on his headlights. Following at a slow pace, he settled in for a long ride. The rebuilt engine purred like a kitten, but knew how to roar like a lion on demand. He turned on the radio. The Police sang to him about a canary in a coal mine. He chuckled, knowing how crazy the idea sounded, but more so realizing how crazy his life had become in the last three days. His life would never be the same from this point forward. He didn't care. It was his destiny.

Chapter Forty-Four

Ross headed south, traveling down the highway at an incredible speed. Fortunately, there weren't many vehicles on the road this early in the morning.

"Clepto, have you determined an intercept point?"

"I'm guessing somewhere near North Platte, but I suspect it will be past there unless they get slowed down."

"Get Taco on the phone and see how close they are to intercept," Ross said.

Jenkins stared out the window, listening to the conversation, and wondered where this road was really leading them. How could the Weavers not be farther ahead than they were already? Where had they gone for so long? Had something happened? Or was this just another diversion?

"Taco's car should intercept just after we overtake them. I'm estimating just outside of North Platte. Not knowing which way they will go makes it difficult," Clepto said.

"Let's hope she leaves that cell phone on," Ross sighed.

* * * *

Maggie rummaged around the back of the truck cab for drinks. She returned with two bottles of water. She handed Stan his bottle and said, "We're going to need supplies soon."

"Yeah, I figured. What was your take on White Eagle?"

"I really don't know. He is such a kind soul, and his daughter was wonderful. I feel awful leaving them like that, but there is no need to put them in danger."

"So you think we're heading into danger?" he asked.

"It seems we have been since this journey started."

"And what did you think of White Eagle?" she asked.

"I liked him. He has been through quite a bit. I was thinking what it would have been like to have his experiences and share them with others. Imagine the people that laughed at him and scorned him. That had to be awful."

"What about the hair thing?" she asked.

"What about it?"

"Well, I have heard of that happening to people who go through extreme stress or fear. Do you think that is what happened to him?"

"Well, I know something happened to him, and if it hadn't, you and I would probably have died in that metal room by now." He took a swig from his water bottle and looked at her briefly then checked his mirrors.

Maggie shivered at the thought of that place. It was something she didn't want to think about right now. Stan was right. There was no denying that White Eagle's timing was perfect. She wondered what had happened to Rudy and Deloris, and then her mind returned to Kylee.

"What did you think of Kylee's last diary entry?"

Stan was quiet for some time. He had thoughts about it, but wasn't sure Maggie was ready to hear them. Stan and Maggie both wanted their daughter back, and it seemed there were other factions that also wanted her. More and more, he just wanted to know the truth.

"It bothered me to be honest," he finally said.

"Why?" she asked.

"The way she said things, the way she expressed herself. If I hadn't known better, I would have suspected someone else had written it."

"What are you saying, Stan? You think someone else wrote that?"

"I don't know," he said adjusting his feet to a more comfortable position. He shook his head.

"What the hell do you mean you don't know, Stan? What aren't you telling me?"

Maggie was clearly getting upset.

"Well, what makes you so sure that she is our daughter," he asked.

"Well she... is... She must be... She has to be." Maggie stared out the large windshield, clearly having a private conversation in her mind.

She finally broke from it and asked, "Why would you think she isn't our daughter?"

The Chain

"Lately, she isn't the little girl I remembered. She is and she isn't. She uses bigger words now, and talks about things in a different perspective."

"Well, don't you think she has been forced to grow up a lot recently," Maggie asked.

"What if she is something like that boy from that AI movie?"

"AI? Artificial Intelligence? You think she is a robot now? Oh Christ, Stan!"

She looked at him with a smirk on her face. He turned to look at her, and they both laughed till the tears ran down their cheeks.

Maggie took a tissue from her purse and wiped away his tears. She kissed his cheek and said, "Don't worry, one way or another, this is going to get resolved."

Stan nodded as he passed the highway sign that read "10 miles to North Platte."

Chapter Forty-Five

The black sedan appeared in White Eagle's mirror with flashing lights in the grill. It was approaching at a very high speed. He pulled over to the side of the highway anticipating a ticket, but the vehicle passed him, traveling in excess of eighty miles per hour. He was thankful for being overlooked, but was now more concerned that the Weavers were in trouble.

He accelerated the car staying far behind the black sedan. His mind raced knowing that it was unlikely a State Police or highway patrol vehicle.

He pushed down farther on the accelerator, hoping that he could shadow the black Sedan without standing out too much in the background.

It wasn't too hard to keep up with the Sedan, but as it closed in on Stan Weaver's truck, White Eagle backed off.

He watched as Stan pulled the truck off to the side of the road. The sedan raced passed Stan's truck as if it were oblivious. White Eagle also pulled over and slowed, waiting for Stan to pull back on the road.

He followed Stan's truck as it rolled back onto the road, careful to stay back as far as possible. He watched the truck come over a rise and saw the truck's brake lights illuminate. White Eagle couldn't see what was happening, but guessed they had set up a road block of some sort.

Chapter Forty-Six

Stan moved over to the side of the road to allow the speeding black sedan to pass. The sirens flashed and raced ahead of him out of the distance.

"Hmm, think there was a wreck?" she asked.

"Not sure."

Stan moved back onto the highway and settled back into cruising speed. He brought the truck up a long hill, and as they crossed over the top, Maggie gasped, "Oh my God, Stan. Stop!"

Two black sedans stood before them blocking traffic in both directions. Men in dark clothing stood with their guns drawn. Stan had to make a split second decision. He could ram them and keep going, or even attempt to drive around them, but he knew it would be in vain. He stood on the brakes and stopped in the middle of the road.

The agents approached with their weapons ready.

"Mr. Weaver, please get out of the car," Jenkins said.

"What's this about?" Stan said as he got out.

Agent Ross opened Maggie's door and helped her out of the truck.

Jenkins intercepted Stan and escorted him to the first car. Ross directed Maggie to the other car. Taco climbed into the truck and closed the door.

Neither Maggie nor Stan said a thing. They were both tired. Tired of running, tired of the battle, tired of the unknown.

The cars moved out of the road and headed west on Highway 76. White Eagle shadowed the convoy.

Stan finally asked, "What is this about?"

Jenkins answered him with a question, "Mr. Weaver. Where is your daughter?"

"I don't know."

"Where were you and Mrs. Weaver going?" he asked.

"Road Trip to California."

"California is nice this time of the year," Jenkins said as he looked out the window.

"Is that where your daughter is?"

"I honestly don't know where she is. Where are you taking us?"

"Oh, I thought we would ride around for a while and talk," Jenkins said.

"I have rights. You can't take me hostage like this!"

"So you feel like you are a hostage?"

"When is the last time you saw your daughter?" Jenkins asked.

Stan just stared out the window and said nothing. He recently wondered the same thing. Was she actually his daughter? She looked like Kylee, even smelled like her, but was it really her? In his heart, that was what he wanted, but she wasn't the same person that vanished six years ago. Maybe Maggie was right. Maybe all of this had taken a toll on his daughter, or maybe Maggie was wrong.

* * * *

Ross sat quietly next to Maggie Weaver. She said nothing as she stared at the other black sedan in front of them, concerned for Stan. Ross felt guilty. This was all wrong, and he knew it. These people had been through enough.

"Mrs. Weaver, is there anything I can get you to make you more comfortable?"

Tears rolled down her cheeks as she watched the roadway pass by. Exhaustion and the never ending battle had weakened her will.

Ross reached out for her, and she turned and screamed at him, "Don't you touch me! You people disgust me! You are to blame for all of this! Aren't you? What the hell have you done with my daughter? Where the hell is she? Is this one of your experiments? How could you do this to us?"

She continued to weep, keeping her face turned away so Ross couldn't see her. She didn't want to be seen. She wanted to drift off and be forgotten. Maybe she died in the metal room, and this was her personal hell, a never-ending search for her missing daughter who is constantly taken from her over and over again.

The Chain

The convoy took the first exit off of the highway and headed for a truck stop. Taco parked the truck in the back of the lot and got into Keeper's vehicle.

White Eagle parked on the other side of the truck stop to keep an eye on the occupants of the sedans.

Jenkins asked Stan, "Would you like anything while we're stopped?"

Stan was quiet and finally said, "I could really use something to drink and a visit to the restroom."

"Sure," Jenkins said, nodding to Taco to escort him.

Jenkins spoke into his headset, "Mr. Weaver needs to use the restroom. Could you check on Mrs. Weaver as well please?"

Ross said to Maggie, "I know you are upset. Your husband is using the restroom. Do you need to use the ladies' room?"

She was angry, and it took everything for her to acknowledge what he was saying. She was going to ignore him, but then she realized that bathrooms always meant trouble. She was worried for Stan. She wasn't sure what she could accomplish, but she had enough and was ready to fight. She nodded to Ross, and he accompanied her to the building.

* * * *

White Eagle watched as he saw Stan and Maggie escorted inside the truck stop. He stayed low in the car, avoiding eye contact. How was he supposed to protect these people? These men obviously had guns, and he was outnumbered. That was when he realized he wasn't alone in the car. A very large being sat in the passenger seat next to him and said, "Do not be afraid. We are here to aid you."

"We?" White Eagle asked.

Another sat up in the back seat and startled White Eagle.

"Man, you people can scare a man" White Eagle said.

"Let your ears hear my words, and your mind understand what I am about to say. Watch for the husband and wife. Do not be deceived by what your eyes see. For it will not be them that departs with these men," the being in the passenger seat said as he continued to stare directly ahead.

In the blink of an eye, they were outside his vehicle and moving towards the front entrance.

Taco followed Stan inside the restroom. Stan went into a stall, dropped his pants, and sat on the toilet. Stan needed to think. His mind was still searching for a way to solve this puzzle. He needed to escape. *Why was he always running? Should he attempt to fight his way out?* He looked down at the ground, searching for an answer when he realized a large man was in the stall looking at him. The man was dressed in a white robe and placed his hand on Stan's head and whispered, "Sleep."

Stan instantly fell asleep. The being caught him and rested him carefully against the wall of the stall. The entity turned and transformed into an identical replica of Stan. He exited the stall and closed the door behind him.

Taco nodded at him and said, "You ready?"

Stan's twin nodded and followed Taco out of the bathroom.

In the ladies' room, Maggie entered the bathroom with the hope of being alone. She knew Stan would be looking for a way to escape, but her hopes were dashed when Ross followed her into the bathroom.

"Were you going to hold my hand?" she asked in a sarcastic tone.

Ross rolled his eyes and turned his back to her, in an attempt to give her privacy.

Maggie entered the stall, clearly upset. She didn't have to use the bathroom, but sat on the toilet, searching for a way to escape.

A large figure appeared in front of her. He placed his pointer finger over his lips signaling her to be quiet. She looked into his eyes. They were the purist blue she had ever seen, and his white robes appeared to glow. He placed his hand on her cheek and whispered, "Sleep." He caught her as she fell into a slump against the stall wall. He instantly transformed into Maggie Weaver. He opened the door and closed it behind him.

Ross asked, "Are you ready?"

She didn't respond, but instead headed for the exit. He followed her as she moved towards the counter in the front of the store. He saw her stop as Taco and Stan Weaver stood in front of them. The two captives looked at each other, and then went outside. Ross directed Maggie to the vehicle, while Taco led Stan Weaver to Jenkins's car.

White Eagle watched and wondered what was going on. Something wasn't right about the Weavers. Their faces were expressionless, and they moved funny. As Stan turned to get into the car, White Eagle noticed he looked directly at him from across the parking lot. White Eagle felt exposed, and he froze. He wanted to duck, but it happened so quickly.

The Chain

He saw a glimmer in Stan's eyes like a reflection of the sun off of a beachgoer's sunglasses. White Eagle knew then he wasn't looking at Stan Weaver. He then understood what the being said in the car.

As soon as the Sedans drove away, White Eagle ran into the building. He was in a panic and asked the young man at the register where the men's room was located. The store clerk pointed to the back. White Eagle raced away as the store clerk made a joke to a patron about how that guy really had to go.

There was a man standing in front of one of the urinals. White Eagle checked the first stall, but there was no one. He opened the second stall, and there was Stan Weaver asleep with his pants at his ankles.

He entered the stall and said, "Stan! Stan, wake up!"

He ran to the sink and got a paper towel and soaked it. He brought it back and soaked Stan's face. Stan's eyes opened in a startled fashion and finally focused on White Eagle standing before him.

"Water! I need water!" Stan cried.

"Stan, hurry, we don't have much time," White Eagle said.

"Get yourself together and meet me at the front counter, I need to get Maggie."

White Eagle exited the stall and ran for the ladies' room.

The man at the urinal turned to leave and saw White Eagle exiting the stall of a half naked man whose face was soaked. The man shook his head in disgust completely misunderstanding the situation. Stan shook his head and put himself back together.

White Eagle burst into the ladies' room. There were two stalls and both had occupants. He finally said, "Maggie? Maggie where are you?"

He looked below the stall and could see the one she occupied. He could tell her body was slumped up against the stall. He grabbed a wet paper towel and opened the door. He woke her gently.

"Maggie, honey. We have to go. Maggie?"

"White Eagle. Thank you. I need water," she whispered.

White Eagle helped Maggie to her feet and escorted her to the front of the store. Stan waited for them with food and drinks. The clerk rang up the total and White Eagle intervened and said, "I will pay for that."

Stan didn't argue, but instead moved to Maggie, handing her a large bottle of water.

"Are you okay?"

"Yes, but I'm so thirsty," she said as she swigged down the bottle's contents.

She took a big breath and said, "We must get moving, Stan. I feel like time is running out."

White Eagle led them to his car, carrying two bags of groceries. Stan followed with a case of plastic water bottles in his arms.

As they all climbed inside White Eagle's car, Stan asked, "Wow, pimp my ride much?"

White Eagle chided back at him, "What? An Indian can't have a little bling?"

"Bling? Ughh, men and their toys," Maggie said from the back seat.

White Eagle started the car and began to pull away when Maggie yelled, "No. Stop. Wait. I have things in the truck I need."

White Eagle raced to the truck. The door was locked, but Stan had a backup set of keys hidden behind the large gas tank. They grabbed their bags and were about to throw them into the trunk of the car when they heard Maggie's Cell phone ring. Everyone froze.

"Holy Shit!" Maggie said as she frantically dug through her purse looking for the phone. The call went to voice mail before she could answer it.

"That is how they found us. Put the phone in the truck and leave it on," Stan insisted.

Maggie nodded and placed the phone in the back of the cab. She ran back to the car, hopped inside, and White Eagle sped away.

"Where to?" he asked them.

"Steamboat Springs, Colorado," Maggie said.

"And how does one get there?" White Eagle asked.

"My girlfriend will tell you," Stan said as he pulled out the travel GPS system.

"Sweet. I need to get one of those!"

The GPS guided them back onto the road and finally west onto Highway 76.

"Who called?" Stan asked Maggie.

"Bill," she said.

"Bill who?" Stan asked.

"Michael's partner," she said, looking at Stan concerned.

The Chain

Maggie opened her third bottle of water and offered one to Stan and White Eagle. Stan eagerly accepted the water, but White Eagle declined as he hadn't finished his first.

"You're thirsty, it seems," White Eagle said.

"Yeah, this explains a lot." Stan said.

"Definitely," Maggie agreed.

Chapter Forty-Seven

Maggie opened the bag from the truck stop. She sorted through the goodies and distributed them.

"We have Ham and Cheese, Ham and cheese, and finally another Ham and Cheese."

"There weren't a lot of options in there, and they looked to be the freshest," Stan replied.

"Do you believe your daughter is in Steamboat Springs?" White Eagle asked.

"I do," Maggie said.

"You knew this at my house. Did you not?"

"Yes, I suspected," Maggie replied.

The car was quiet as everyone ate their sandwiches. Maggie delved out more snacks and offered apples.

Maggie curled up in the backseat and closed her eyes. She wanted to sleep and wake up to find this all to be some strange dream, but she knew that would never happen.

Stan's mind raced. He needed to find his daughter. He needed answers, he needed help.

"I'm sorry we left like that. We wanted to say goodbye and thanks, but we didn't want to wake you and trouble you."

"You are no trouble, and I was awake long before you left."

"Did you see us leave?" Stan asked.

White Eagle acknowledged he had with a nod, but his face stared ahead. He was a well defined man. His body seemed younger than his years, yet his face often appeared chiseled from stone. He was indeed a special man. Stan liked him, but was afraid of what secrets this man held.

"Mr. Weaver, what happened in there?"

The Chain

"I was sitting on the john and one of them appeared in the stall with me. He put his hand on my head and said the word 'sleep'. That is the last thing I remember."

"Where are the agents?" Stan asked.

"What makes you so sure they are agents?" White Eagle finally responded.

"Well, they had guns, black suits, unmarked cars. I just assumed…"

White Eagle quietly nodded and turned to look at Stan.

"You have to learn to see with your eyes, and hear with your ears."

Stan looked perplexed.

"What the hell is that supposed to mean?"

"It means you watch too much TV. You let too much around you influence your thought process. You believe what you have been trained to believe. You believe every Mexican is a migrant worker, every black youth wants to rob you, and every Indian is a teepee living, pipe smoking, alcoholic, but the truth is the Mexican man is a lawyer and prefers to rake his own yard, and that the black man is a scientist."

Stan was shocked.

"Are you calling me a racist?"

"Not at all, I am trying to wake you up. I am trying to show you that everything is not as it appears to be, and the man that sees with his eyes and hears with his ears is more aware of the truth. You seek the truth, but I tell you that it can not be found unless you open your eyes to see and your ears to hear."

"So what am I missing?" Stan looked at White Eagle, perplexed.

"That, my friend, we shall see. We need to be better prepared. Our 'friends' have bought us some time, but I suspect we're coming to a place where time is running out. We will have to make quick decisions. We must establish some type of plan.

"What are these things?" Maggie asked from the back seat.

White Eagle looked at Stan again.

"I don't know. Tell us what you saw, White Eagle."

White Eagle recounted the beings appearing in his car, and going inside. He retold what they said, and how they departed in the cars with the men. He told the Weavers how the beings took on their appearances.

Stan had to think about it. None of it really made any sense. Were they aliens? Angels? Could this be some kind of super race?

Maybe genetically altered beings? They definitely could perform some supernatural tasks.

"You are a spiritual man. Do you think this is spiritual?" Stan asked.

"Yes, but I don't understand it all."

"Well, I have been thinking about everything. They are aliens, angels, or genetically altered beings. Unless there is some other explanation either of you have?" Stan asked, glad he finally said it.

White Eagle looked in the mirror, waiting to see Maggie's reaction.

She looked back at him, then down at her hands. She finally broke the silence and said, "Or all of the above."

"All of the above?" Stan asked

"Christ, I don't know Stan, but let's face the facts. They can put people to sleep at will. They can appear out of thin air, and can change their appearance at will. I'm not sure I know of anything in my world that can do that. Do you?"

She was clearly upset.

Chapter Forty-Eight

Jenkins stared out the window of the black sedan. His eyes traveled over the landscape, searching for an answer, searching for the truth. But the view before him held no answers, and he was blind to the truth that sat beside him. He needed to know what Stan Weaver knew, and he was sure Mr. Weaver wasn't going to cooperate. Turning his view back towards Stan, he watched as Stan stared out the window.

"I know you have endured quite a bit, Mr. Weaver, and I know that you have spent time with your daughter in the last few days. We have video of your wife and Kylee from the Wal-Mart back in Eau Claire."

Stan just nodded while looking out the window, but not really responding.

"I know you and Mrs. Weaver both have to be exhausted, but we really wish to help. Do you have any idea where your daughter is?"

Jenkins got no response as the man next to him continued to stare out the window. Jenkins decided to not speak and allow Stan Weaver to talk when he was ready.

"Take some time; I know you have been through a great deal. We can talk when you are ready."

Again, Stan nodded, but continued to look outside.

* * * *

Ross was never the great orator, but he knew that he would have to make some kind of breakthrough to Maggie Weaver.

"Is there anything I can get you?"

She shook her head with a definitive "no", all the while looking outside. He assumed she was still quite angry, but then she should be. He didn't have children, but he wanted them one day, and if he were in the Weaver's shoes, he would have made a run for it as well. The difference is he would have gotten away.

"Maggie, well, may I call you Maggie?" he asked.

She nodded but continued not to look at him.

"We want to help you find your daughter. We know you have seen her. I'm sure you want her back as well. Do you know where she is?"

Maggie shook her head no, and continued to look out the window as if the window, the car, and even Ross never existed.

Chapter Forty-Nine

White Eagle adjusted his position as he listened to the voice on the GPS continually updating their journey. Stan and Maggie had been quiet for some time, and he could tell they were both walking on pins and needles.

"I would like to hear more about Kylee. Would you mind if I asked you a few questions?"

"Of course," Maggie responded from the back seat.

"I would like to hear what life was like before her disappearance. Was there anything out of the ordinary?" White Eagle looked in the mirror to see Maggie's facial expression.

Maggie searched for anything that stood out and finally started talking.

"Kylee was just a fun, up beat, little girl. She was doing fine in school. She was well liked. She liked what most girls liked. Barbies, dress-up, etc. I don't think there was ever anything out of the ordinary."

Stan chimed in, "I have to agree. I never noticed anything that stood out."

"What about spiritual activity. Has she or either of you ever had any strange spiritual encounters?"

Maggie asked, "How do you mean?"

White Eagle took a minute to assemble his response.

"Have any of you ever had an experience with spirits? Ghosts? Poltergeists? Demons? Etc."

Maggie gasped, "Oh goodness, no."

White Eagle pressed on, "Did she have imaginary friends? Or ever tell you there were people talking to her in the house that you all could not see?"

"No, nothing like that ever happened," Stan said.

"Were you all active in a church? And if so, could you tell me a little about it?"

"We went to the local Methodist church. Nothing crazy went on there. No snake handling or anything excessive. Pastor Dean was a solid balanced man. We all went together, including my cousin Michael. Though he often said the place needed a remodel," Maggie reminisced.

"Did a visiting minister ever prophesy over you or your child?" White Eagle asked.

"Prophesy? Like Hell fire and brimstone?" Maggie asked.

"Not all prophesies are as you have been lead to believe, Mrs. Weaver," White Eagle said as he eyed her in the backseat.

It was evident that Stan had been quiet for some time. There was that one little incident, but he was sure it meant nothing. *After all, she was little. It was a fluke, and it didn't apply.*

"Mr. Weaver?" White Eagle asked turning to look at Stan.

"Yes?" Stan replied far away in though.

"What are you contemplating? Is there something you have thought of that might be relevant?"

"Well... ummm... Nah, it's not relevant." Stan waved it away as he looked out the window.

"Would you mind sharing it either way?" White Eagle pressed him.

"Oh, it's silly. But sure, why not."

"Maggie, remember the time in St. Louis at that black church?" Stan Asked.

Maggie sighed. "Stan, first of all, it wasn't a black church. They were African Americans, and I believe Kylee corrected you about that back then as well. "

"Yes. Yes. Why does everyone think I'm a racist? I honestly am not. It is just what we called African Americans. I hate this whole politically correct crap. It's not like I used the 'N' word. Which I would never use," Stan said, looking for sympathy.

Maggie tilted her head and raised her eyebrows, waiting for Stan to tell the story.

"His name was Reverend Logan Winslett..."

Stan recounted the story of traveling to Memphis, Tennessee and passing through St. Louis, Missouri. Maggie had reserved a room for the three of them just outside of St. Louis. They were on their way to visit Graceland, and spend some time at Mud Island. They left late Saturday

The Chain

morning, and arrived at the hotel in St. Louis, Missouri in the early evening, after a quick bite to eat at some local dive.

"I wish Michael could have come with us," Kylee said as she played with her Barbie doll.

"Well, he has his garden shop to take care of," Maggie reminded her.

Stan turned on the TV. A rerun of Andy Griffith was playing. Kylee didn't seem to notice the show. She was preparing a tea party. Barbie was dressed in her finest, and Maggie was helping her heat up water in the single cup coffee pot provided by the hotel.

Stan was finally pried away from the TV when Kylee said, "Daddy, I said one lump or two?"

"Yeah, Daddy! Are you listening?" Maggie teased.

"Oh, one lump for me." He smiled.

Being that it was getting late, Maggie ensured that they used decaffeinated tea bags. Everyone sat around the small table, and Barbie sat off to the side with her Stepford wife smile eager to please.

The TV show cut to a commercial for some hair care product.

Kylee sipped her tea and said, "Let's see. Today is Saturday. Tomorrow is Sunday, and we're going to The King's house on Monday."

"That's right. It will be fun," Maggie said as she sipped her tea. Stan nodded in agreement.

"I have never been to a King's house. Will there be guards and a princess there too? Or what about the Queen? Will she be there?"

"Oh, no, Kylee, the Queen had to stay home to tend to the flower beds..." Stan started to say, but was quickly kicked under the table by Maggie. Kylee didn't get the reference to Maggie's cousin, Michael.

"What Daddy meant to say was that Elvis wasn't a real king. Well he was, but not like in the old days with castles and chariots and stuff like that. It was a title given to him. His wife never took on a title of queen, but she is a lovely lady and beautiful to behold."

"Does that mean there is no princess?" Kylee looked deflated.

"Well, they did have a daughter, and I guess she would be considered a princess, but..." Maggie was interrupted by Stan.

"But there is going to be a lovely princess there. She stands about as tall as you, and has pretty blonde hair, and she will be escorted by a knight in shining armor, her maidservant, and Barbie! Right Barbie?" Stan looked at Barbie's enthusiastic smile.

Everyone giggled and sipped more of their tea.

"Well, I guess we better get this tea party over with and get ready for bed time." Maggie said.

Kylee stopped her. "Wait a minute. We have a problem. Where are we going to go to church tomorrow?"

'Church... uhh" Stan said, tapping his finger to his lower lip.

At that moment, the Television boomed out a commercial for the River of Life church with Reverend Logan Winslett. The Gospel music and choir belted out, "I got a river of life flowing out of me..."

Kylee said, "Oh, let's go there! Can we? Can we?"

Stan looked at Maggie. Maggie had an awkward smile on her face that said, "Help!"

Stan then said to Kylee, "Let's ask your good friend." He turned to look at Barbie.

Barbie had that same elated and ecstatic smile.

"Looks like Barbie says it's a go!"

* * * *

The River of Life church was in an old building. Just as Stan had expected, it was mostly populated by people of color. Kylee looked stunning in her little white sun dress. She and Michael had picked it out. Maggie had put a pink ribbon in Kylee's hair. She was radiant.

The music was very upbeat, and the musicians and choir set the stage for what Stan imagined would be quite an animated sermon. The air was electric. Kylee clapped and sang along when she could catch the repeated phrases. She was having the time of her life, and Stan actually let his shoulders relax and clapped along too. He watched Maggie as she also participated.

As the choir and music reached its crescendo, the Reverend Logan Winslett approached the pulpit. He was a young man probably in his thirties. He had a round face and dimples. He was portly, but not fat. His eyes were considerate and kind. He had a serious, yet humbled, demeanor.

He brought the length of his pointer finger to his mouth and turned to face the choir and musicians. Complete silence filled the stage. He then turned to face the people of the congregation and did the same thing. Complete silence filled the room.

He waited a minute and looked over the congregation. He searched among the people as a shepherd counting his sheep.

The Chain

For what seemed like eternity, he didn't speak.

In a quiet tone, he asked to no one specifically, "Do you feel it?"

"It is all around you."

He turned to the choir, "Do you feel it choir?"

A few people raised their hands in praise to the Lord, nodding and confirming the Reverend's question.

He then turned to the congregation and asked them, "Do you feel it?"

One woman shook her white handkerchief over her head and nodded her head vehemently. Most of the congregation nodded.

The Reverend began to speak, "Close your eyes, everyone. Everyone, please. Close your eyes. You need to feel this."

Maggie and Stan both closed their eyes. You could feel electricity in the air.

With his eyes closed, Reverend Winslett spoke, "This thing you feel is the peace of God."

"Do you feel it?" he asked again.

Whispered voices answered, "Yes."

Reverend Winslett spoke again, "And the peace of God, which transcends all understanding, will guard your hearts and your minds in Christ Jesus."

"Keep your eyes closed, and let the Lord minister to you, because this is a special day. Some of you came here expecting to have church. Well, I got news for you, this is Church!"

"Amen," voices in the choir and congregation responded.

This lasted for a few minutes and then finally Stan heard Maggie gasp as she grabbed his arm. He opened his eyes and saw what startled Maggie. There on the stage standing in front of Reverend Logan Winslett was their six year old daughter Kylee.

Maggie's gasp startled everyone, and the room was filled with gasps. Revered Winslett opened his eyes and looked down to see Kylee in front of him.

In a loving manner, he brought the length of his pointer finger to his lips again, with a gesture for all to be quiet, all the while never taking his eyes off of Kylee.

"What a beautiful gift from the Lord that stands before me." He squatted down and in a quiet voice asked her, "What is your name?"

She said, "My name is Kylee."

Maggie stood up in an attempt to retrieve Kylee, but Reverend Winslett indicated with a gentle hand gesture everything was okay. Maggie slowly sat back down, all the while leaning forward in her pew.

"Well, hello, Kylee. It is very nice to meet you. May I ask what made you come up here to visit with me?"

Kylee smiled and said, "God told me to give you something."

Maggie squeezed Stan's hand. He reassured her with a gentle nudge.

Reverend Winslett responded in a loving fatherly way, speaking to the child, 'He did! The Lord spoke to you and told you to come up here and give me something? That is exciting. What is it that He gave you to give me?"

Kylee moved closer to him. She wrapped her arms around him and gave him a huge hug. He returned the embrace as tears streamed down his face. He was overcome and held her very close. The entire congregation wept, and the choir praised the Lord as their faces reflected the same flood of tears.

Kylee and the Reverend eventually slowly let go, and Reverend Winslett praised the Lord. His wife, Rosalyn came forward and she hugged him. They finally let go, and Rosalyn made her way to the Choir director and gave him a hug. Reverend Winslett made his way down to the first pew and gave a hug to the first person. The hug traveled around the room.

Maggie was hugged by a short elderly lady. They smiled and wept together. She finally turned to Stan, and laughed and hugged. Stan finally released Maggie and turned to hug the person behind him. The man stood six-foot-eight and had to weigh close to 400 lbs. Stan reached for him, and dissolved into the man's chest. The hug continued through the entire congregation.

When the last person was hugged Reverend Winslett said, "Today, we had church, people! Real church! Take this thing that God has showed you and share it with your friends and family. Today, God touched us all!"

Maggie's mind was whirling. She came back to focus when she saw Stan approaching with Kylee in his arms. She gave them both a hug.

"I think we need to get on the road. What do you two think?" Stan asked.

"I think so," Maggie replied.

"Can we go to IHOP?" Kylee asked?

The Chain

"Definitely!" Stan said.

Stan lowered Kylee to the floor. They headed towards the exit, all three of them holding hands. As they reached the doors, Reverend Winslett and his wife were there to greet them and say good bye.

"Thank you so much for visiting with us today. Do you live in the area?" Rosalyn Winslett asked.

"Oh no, "Maggie replied. "We are on our way to Graceland from Wisconsin."

"Yeah, we're going to go see the King!" Kylee announced in an exciting tone.

"The King!" Reverend Winslett said, as he stooped down to see Kylee.

"I think you had a nice visit with the King here today." He smiled brightly.

"Yes, we did. It was very nice."

"Give me a hug, child and thanks for visiting." Reverend Winslett picked her up, and whispered in her ear. Kylee cupped her hand and whispered back.

He put her down, and the couples hugged and said their goodbyes.

Reverend Winslett yelled after Kylee, "Umma hold you to that, little miss!"

Kylee giggled as the three of them made their way to the car.

Maggie asked, "And what secrets were you and Reverend Winslett telling?"

"That is a secret, Mommy." Kylee cupped her mouth with her hand.

They both giggled.

"International House of Pancakes, here we come!" Stan said as they pulled away from the church.

"Mommy, I want to be international!" Kylee cheered.

As Stan finished telling White Eagle his story about Kylee and Reverend Winslett, the car was silent, minus the tires rolling down the highway. Maggie could see White Eagle's face from the backseat through the rear view mirror. He had a single tear rolling down his cheek. Maggie dug through her purse and reached forward from the back and handed him a tissue. She then saw Stan's face and offered him one as well. That was when it appeared to her that they all had been crying. These weren't tears of sadness or loss, but of joy and hope.

Stan finally asked, "Does any of what I told you mean anything to you?"

White Eagle quietly shook his head and said, "It means everything, though to some it would mean nothing. You have ears and you heard it, you have eyes and you saw it. What stands out the most about that event? Think about all of it."

"Well, it was a beautiful day with God. If that is what you are referring to?" Stan continued, "It was odd in that it was a different church experience for us, but it was a good experience."

"And what about you, Maggie? Does anything stand out to you?" White Eagle asked.

Maggie sat there and went through all of it again. Honestly, she had forgotten all about it, but now it came back to her memory very clearly. She even remembered the little white sun dress Kylee wore that day. She remembered her up on the stage and gasping in fear. It was just then, when the right neurological connections did their magic. Her brain performed its miraculous ability to logically sort and select information, analyzing and scrutinizing the data until she arrived at a solution.

"Oh, dear God," she said, bringing her hand to her mouth.

"Yes, I think you are putting pieces together now, aren't you?" White Eagle inquired, his astute eyes studying her in the rearview mirror.

"Reverend Winslett. I feel so stupid. I can't believe I didn't think about this before. I was so focused on the relevance of here and now, that I didn't put two-and-two together," Maggie said as she hit the seat in front of her.

"How about someone clue me in on this?" Stan asked, looking from Maggie to White Eagle with utmost confusion written all over his face.

Maggie looked into Stan's eyes and said, "Reverend Winslett referred to Kylee as a gift from God."

"A gift from God? I don't see the point…Oh, my God!" Stan gasped, his jaw hanging open.

"White Eagle, are you saying my child is some kind of prophet or something. What are you saying?"

"No, not Kylee, because there is no evidence that she is exhibiting the gift of prophecy, but whether he knows it or not this Reverend may very well be a real prophet. I do know that he declared her as a gift from God, and I was told to protect the Gift. I think it is very relevant." White Eagle never stopped watching the road.

The Chain

The GPS interrupted the quiet confines with the announcement that they were thirty-two miles from their destination.

"When this episode took place at the church in St. Louis, did the reverend refer to her as "a gift from God, or a beautiful gift from God" White Eagle asked.

Stan and Maggie both answered in unison, "a beautiful gift from God."

White Eagle's eyebrows rose at their answer. He nodded to himself while driving, as if having acknowledged an internal conversation that no one else could hear. After a moment, he smiled and said, "Well, we're almost there."

"Is there significance to whether it was a gift or a beautiful gift?" Stan asked.

"Yes, what God calls beautiful is beautiful, and so much more than what the eye can behold." White Eagle stopped mid sentence and drove quietly the rest of the way.

Chapter Fifty

Jenkins was amazed that Stan Weaver was able to sleep as long as he had. Ross's confirmation that Mrs. Weaver was still not up unnerved him a little. Keeper wondered what these two had been through the last couple of days. To fall off the radar so long and yet not progress in their travels seemed odd. He assumed their destination was Steamboat Springs, and his team had been ready for their arrival. When the Weavers hadn't arrived, he was concerned that he had overlooked something obvious. And maybe he had.

The drive through Denver was uneventful. Of course, as they headed west, the terrain would become more mountainous. He was thankful to be heading to Shriever, but also concerned what would happen once they arrived. The facility was laden with many secrets, some he wasn't privy to, but people whispered things.

Jenkins turned from the mountain views out his window to look at Stan Weaver once again. He was startled to see Stan looking right at him.

"Welcome back, Mr. Weaver," Jenkins said with a nervous smile.

Jenkins heard Ross over the headset, "Mrs. Weaver is awake."

"10-4," he responded.

"Are you hungry? Would you like some food?" Jenkins asked in a sincere tone.

Stan looked up at the ceiling of the car as if he saw or sensed something. His facial expression changed.

"Conrad Jenkins, you are in danger."

"I am. Am I? Well, why do you think that?" Jenkins responded, confident in his safety.

"Stop this vehicle now!" Stan's twin demanded continuing to look through the roof of the car.

The Chain

"Oh, Mr. Weaver. I'm the one that gives orders here." Jenkins grinned.

Like the scene from slow motion car wreck, Jenkins felt the vehicle's brakes being applied at full force. The car started to turn so slightly before coming to a complete stop.

"What the..." Jenkins started to say.

In the road before them stood an older couple.

Stan grabbed Jenkins' arm as he reached for his weapon, "Your weapons are useless here Keeper! Protect the gift!"

Stan Weaver shimmered for a brief second and immediately his appearance changed. Unbeknownst to Keeper, in Ross' car, Maggie Weaver's appearance had changed at the exact same moment. In unison, the beings jumped out of the cars, passing through the roofs and landing in the roadway. The earth gave slightly when they both landed.

Jenkins team exited their vehicles with weapons drawn.

"Well, well, well. Look what we have here. It looks like we have been deceived. Imagine that Deloris?" Rudy said, adjusting his belt like a school boy about to get into a fight.

"Oh, this won't do. This won't do at all," Deloris said as she took a step forward. She resembled one of those grumpy women who would stand on her front porch and yell at the kids running through her grass.

"Now where could she be?" Deloris asked no one.

"Oh, and look who it is! My favorite Kitty." Deloris smiled as she looked at Ross.

Ross was shaking as his stomach turned. His anger and fear overcame him, and his finger squeezed off two rounds. His aim was true. Deloris placed her hand over her chest, and blood dripped down between her fingers. She slowly fell to the ground and landed in a sitting position.

"Kitty! Why!" she cried out to him.

"Why, Kitty?" She asked again, followed by a deep and dark laughter. Her demeanor changed, and she transformed into a hideous beast. She was very tall, but she appeared battered and disfigured. She stood eight feet tall with dark bloodshot eyes. She had no hair, she had no gender. The skin of the creature looked burned and blistered.

Her laughter continued as she pointed at Ross and said in a dark and ominous voice, "Why, Kitty... don't you come over..." She waved her hand and screamed at him, "Here!"

Ross flew across the roadway and landed at her feet. The air left his body as he heaved and breathed in deeply.

"Aww, you have been a bad kitty. Very naughty indeed." Her appearance shifted back into her yellow dressed meek and mild persona. There was no blood, and Jenkins realized there never was.

"Enough of this! Where is it?" Rudy yelled, pointing directly at the taller of the two beings.

"It does not concern you," the tall one responded. His voice was amazing. It sounded like a voice one would expect from a tall tree if it could speak. It was full of wisdom, humble yet full of authority. The shorter being kept his eyes on Deloris.

"Concern me!" Rudy laughed louder than a freight train passing by. The gift is here in our place. Thus, the gift is ours!"

"Does your deception run so deep that you have even deceived yourself?" The tall one asked.

At that instance, the shorter one moved his hand in a reaching motion and pulled Ross to his side. Ross landed on his two feet with his jaw wide open. Deloris was in shock and acted as if someone had insulted her.

"How dare you. Well I never..." She started to say with squinted eyes.

It was then that the tall one pulled out what appeared to be a great illuminated sword. It shone like the mid day sun. The alloy of the sword appeared to be covered with moving text of a language Jenkins didn't recognize. Keeper finally covered his eyes as it was too brilliant to look at. The rest of the team followed his lead.

Deloris rolled her eyes as if she had enough of the foolishness of the moment. In unison, she and Rudy's images transformed into two very tall hideous beings. They were massive creatures, but disfigured. Their blistered skin seemed to barely cover their large limbs and skeletal system. Their limbs seemed to be bent in abnormal shapes giving them a deformed appearance. Their eyes were dark and full of hate.

The short being appeared next to Jenkins and spoke," Leave here. This is not your battle. Protect the gift!"

At that, Jenkins spoke into the headsets, "Retreat to the vehicles now."

Everything moved slowly in Jenkins' mind. There were several flashes of light and screams. The last thing he remembered was running toward the car, but before he could reach it, it was thrown by an unseen force over the mountainside.

Chapter Fifty-One

White Eagle pulled over to the side of the road as the female voice of the Global Positioning System announced their arrival. They were in the middle of nowhere on a road with a large lake in the valley far below. Mountains could be seen in every direction.

"Looks like the GPS took us as close as we could go?" White Eagle turned to look at Maggie.

"Yes. Keep going for about a quarter mile. You should see a gravel road on the right. Take that road for a bit and we should be there."

Maggie could tell Stan was getting edgy. She, too, was feeling the pressure. She reached her hand up and touched his shoulder. He turned to see her concerned face.

"What is it?" he asked.

"We have to plan a little. What if Kylee isn't here? What if this was for nothing?" Maggie searched Stan's face for the answer.

"If she isn't here, then we will wait a few days. You believed she was coming here. Trust your intuition, but let's not panic either way. If she is here, then we will rest for a day and move on. If not, we will wait around a few days, and see if she comes. I don't know why, but this feels right to me. I believe she is going to come." Stan said, displaying an air of confidence.

White Eagle found the road and traveled deeper into the surrounding woods. The trees here were tall and it seemed one could quickly get lost if it weren't for the constant reflection of the sun off of the large lake below. Eventually, the vegetation cleared, and they arrived at a large two-story log cabin. The cabin had a vaulted roof with large windows across the front of the home. The house was adorned with stunning plants and trees. There was a garden area with herbs, and an abundance of flowers.

White Eagle parked the car, and Maggie began to speak, "There is something you need to know, Stan. Michael's significant other is someone you know. Please be sure to be respectful to him."

"Why wouldn't I be respectful?" Stan asked, moving his hand in a questioning manner. He looked at White Eagle for support.

As they left the car, Maggie responded, "Well, because you might be a bit surprised."

Just then, a tall older man stepped out of the front door. He had on a tank top and a pair of jeans. He was slightly overweight, and touted a white beard, offsetting his baldness. Stan looked at him, perplexed, and then realized it was Bill Brandt.

Maggie ran up to Bill and gave him a hug. She turned to face Stan and said, "You remember my husband Stan?"

Stan shook his hand and said, "It's good to see you, Bill. It's been a long time." Stan was shocked to see his old mailman.

Bill greeted Stan, clearly not suspecting this visit.

Maggie then introduced White Eagle. "And this is White Eagle."

They shook hands, and Maggie asked, "Is Michael inside?"

Bill looked down and said, "Yes, he's resting. He isn't doing very well."

Maggie turned to Bill with a concerned look, "Bill, we need a place to stay for a couple of days. I know I should have called, but... Well... My cell phone broke and..."

Bill Brandt waved away her concerns, "No problem. I'll help the guys with your things. Go and visit with Michael."

He grabbed her arm, "But Maggie, you need to prepare yourself. He's very ill."

She nodded, gave a thankful smile and trotted off behind Bill through the front door of the cabin.

The place was immaculate. She entered into a large open area. There was a large kitchen with a granite topped peninsula surrounded by bar stools. The peninsula served as a divider separating the kitchen and living room. A stunning stained glass table lamp with a geometric design pattern sat on one of the larger end tables. Two large leather chairs and a couch filled the area. A massive fireplace served as a focal point to the living room. Art Nouveau candlesticks topped with iridescent shades adorned the mantle on each side of a portrait of a little girl in a dress.

Maggie was taken back when she realized that it was a portrait of Kylee. The portrait showed Kylee in the same dress she wore the day she

The Chain

disappeared at the birthday party. Her blonde hair flowed down over her shoulders and her blue eyes were focused on a flower in her hand. As with most portraits, the image resembled Kylee closely, but not perfectly. It was eerie, and yet touching.

She heard a cough from the other side of the house and made her way past the kitchen and down a short hall. She passed a staircase to the left, and made her way through the open door to the right.

Nothing could have prepared Maggie for that moment. Lying in a large sleigh bed against the back wall of the room was Michael. She immediately noticed the smell of sickness in the room. Maggie moved across the floor toward Michael's side. A large number of medicine bottles sat on a night stand next to the bed. Maggie slid her hip up onto the bed and reached for his hand. He looked very frail. Though he had large hands, they were pale and lifeless. His breathing was shallow, and she was surprised to find his hand was quite warm. She realized it was entirely too warm. The fever running through his body explained the odor to the room. She moved the blanket down from his chest to his waist and found he was covered in sweat.

Maggie went to the bathroom and soaked a few washcloths. She came back and started to wash off Michael's body with the cool washcloths. The t-shirt he wore was soiled. She washed his hands, and arms, and made her way back up to his neck and face. His eyes opened as she wiped his forehead. He started to cough and she backed away from him a little. Michael looked at her and slowly focused. He coughed again and looked closer at her.

"I'm so sorry, Maggie," he said as he looked her over.

"Oh now, you have nothing to be sorry for," Maggie said, her eyes full of pity.

"Oh, honey, I wasn't talking about me. I was referring to your hair and clothes. What the heck happened to you?" he asked with his brow furled.

They both laughed, and Michael's coughing continued.

"Just rest for now. Let me wash these out and finish what I started." She said leaving his side for the bathroom.

She had finished rinsing out the washcloths when she realized someone was standing behind her. She turned to discover Michael. He leaned against the door jam, haggard and emaciated.

"Do you think you could help me into the bathtub?" he tried to smile and hide his discomfort.

She helped him out of his clothes and into the tub. She started the water quickly as he was already shivering. She laid a towel across his waist giving him some dignity. As the water reached a warm temperature Maggie plugged the drain and added some bubble bath.

"Oh! We're going all out," he whispered in a raspy tone.

Maggie heard a noise in the bedroom.

"I'll be right back. Will you be okay?"

With his eyes closed, he nodded and let the warm waters take him away.

Maggie returned to the bedroom to discover Bill removing the bed clothes. He looked at Maggie and mouthed "Thank you."

Maggie winked at Bill and returned to the bathroom.

She found Michael in bubble bath heaven. Maggie turned off the water, and the only sounds in the room were the tiny bubbles popping and Michael's raspy breath.

"So, how do you like the place?" Michael raised a brow as he ran the washcloth over his face.

"It is amazing! It doesn't look like the same place I remembered. The second floor is brilliant. When did you add that?" She spoke to him like his impending death would never take place.

"Oh, that was Bill's idea. He is a handy one. That's why I kept him around so long. It sure wasn't because of his economic status."

They both laughed.

"We need to talk, Michael. I know you're very ill, but I need you to be very strong right now." Maggie was clearly distressed, searching for where to begin.

"Oh, my! Honey, I'm here for you, well, as much as I can be. Did Bill have you come see me before my last hurrah or something? Because I wasn't planning on checking out just yet."

For a moment, he had a glow about him as if his illness washed away in the bubbles of the oversized tub.

"This has to do with Kylee..." She stopped, waiting for the words to set in.

Michael turned to Maggie, waiting to hear what would come next.

Maggie told the whole story from the very beginning. Halfway through the story, she added more hot water to the tub, as she saw Michael was starting to shiver again. He didn't say much during that time.

The Chain

"So, you thought she came here?" he asked with a dumbfounded look.

"Well, we hoped." She answered as she brought him an oversized bath towel.

Maggie helped Michael to his feet. It was then she saw herself in the mirror. She really was a mess. Her face looked like she had bathed in bacon grease, and her hair was a rat's nest gone wild. She laughed when she looked in the mirror.

"Honey, ain't we a sight?" he said drying his short cropped hair.

Maggie pointed to his pierced nipple. "Nice, is that new?" she asked with a grin.

"I've had that for a while, you jealous crow," he shot back at her.

"I can only imagine what you had to do to get that." She teased.

"And that's why you don't have one!" He teased back with a wink.

"Touché!" she finished with a big laugh.

Just then, Bill poked his head into the bathroom. "Rub a dub dub," he said.

"Bill, could you get my chair please?" Michael asked as he brushed his teeth.

"I... well... Sure I can," Bill responded with a surprised look on his face.

Maggie emptied the tub and returned to help Michael shave around his Goatee. They worked quietly together, enjoying the moment.

Bill finally returned with Michael's wheelchair and some pajamas. He helped Michael get dressed and gently helped him into the wheelchair. Michael held his grip and pulled Bill close. They embraced in a long hug until Michael finally let go. Bill kissed the top of Michael's head and wheeled him out of the bedroom.

Maggie called out, "Mind if I take a shower?"

Michael coughed and yelled back, "Please do. You need it," laughing his cough away.

Chapter Fifty-Two

Jenkins' eyes opened. He could make out Agent Ross's outline above him. Ross was speaking, but for some reason Jenkins couldn't make out what he was saying. It was as if his world was still in slow motion.

"Keeper. Keeper, can you hear me?" Ross asked repeatedly.

Jenkins finally let out a moan and started to move to a sitting position. Ross helped him and offered him a cup of water.

Jenkins took a sip, and looked around the room. They were in the medical facility at Shriever Air Force Base, though he saw no medical staff. He could see Ross's lips moving, but he couldn't hear anything. He drank a little more water, hoping his head would clear.

Jenkins gestured "Stop" to Ross, and spoke very loudly, "I can not hear."

Ross nodded his head and looked around the room for something to write on. He removed a medical form from a clipboard at the base of the bed and started to scribble on it. He handed it to Jenkins.

Jenkins read the scribble that said, "Shell shock," and nodded his head, contemplating what the hell had happened. The last thing he recalled, they were heading for the cars, and he saw his vehicle get violently thrown over a hillside.

He felt dizzy and nauseous and sipped more of the water. The water accidently entered his windpipe, sending him into a coughing spasm. In his head he heard a crackling sound and finally the rush of hospital sounds and white noise filled his ears. He moaned as real life came back into speed. He could hear again. Relief washed over him like a tidal wave.

"Ross, is your team assembled?"

"Yes, but you are in no condition to..." Ross started to reply.

The Chain

Jenkins waved away Ross's concern, "Any injuries?"

"No. We're ready to move on your order," Ross's dark brown eyes gave Keeper a concerning look.

"Give me a minute to get dressed, and then we're heading to Steamboat Springs."

Jenkins found his clothes in a bag under the hospital bed. He hated hospitals. The sterile, cold environment always felt so uninviting. The bathroom offered no reprieve. It also lacked warmth. There might as well have been a sign over the door that said, "Not Welcome Here!"

Keeper washed his face and hands. He looked at the exhausted man in the mirror. He drew closer to the mirror attempting to look deeper into his own tired brown eyes. If the eyes are the doorway to the soul, he imagined opening that doorway and seeing what lay ahead.

The knock at the door, followed by Ross's voice, broke Jenkins gaze.

"Keeper? You okay in there?"

Jenkins opened the door and said, "Of course, Panther. Give me a status report on Team Two."

"They are in place; the secondary nodes have arrived, as you anticipated. There has been no activity, but you did get a phone call from "Papa Bear"?" Ross said in a questioning tone.

Jenkins had his back to Ross during the conversation, and stopped when he heard that statement.

"And what did Papa Bear have to say?" Jenkins asked, as he put on his watch.

He said, "Dinner at seven with the three sisters."

Keeper was fiddling with his watch and cocked his head as if something were wrong. This was an unexpected turn. He stared long at his watch, contemplating the meaning of this new development.

"Keeper? You okay? What does the message mean?" Ross asked.

Jenkins turned to face Ross. "Oh, it's my watch. It seems to have stopped during our previous encounter."

"Keeper, the message?" Ross crossed his arms waiting for an explanation.

"Oh, yes, it appears the Weavers have added a Native American to their party."

Ross was shocked. "How do you know that?"

"Well, it appears I have been invited to dinner, and there is someone of Native American decent invited as well. 'The Three Sisters' is a term used by some American Indians representing corn, beans, and squash. Has Beth reported in?" Jenkins asked.

"Yes, the Weavers have arrived at the destination, and they have an American Indian with them named 'White Eagle'. We ran his tags; he is from the Rosebud reservation in South Dakota."

Jenkins interrupted Ross and said, "White Eagle… Very interesting name. What do we have on him?"

Ross handed Jenkins a printout. Ross watched Jenkins scan the document, noting his focus, and finally the brow movement.

"Wow, this guy was a member of Intertel? That is pretty amazing." Jenkins said as he kept reading.

"Yeah, I saw that. Is that like Mensa or something?" Ross inquired.

"Sort of," Jenkins nodded, "Mensa is the top two percent, but these Intertel folks are the top one percent, and make up many of the greatest minds in the world. It is interesting this guy is also some kind of spiritualist/shaman."

Jenkins put the document in his briefcase and said, "Get us a helicopter. We need to move quickly."

Chapter Fifty-Three

Maggie exited the shower and was greeted by the sounds of roaring laughter from the other side of the house. She dried off with a large bath towel, and wrapped it around her chest and waist. Her hair, though clean, needed attention. She searched the cabinets and found a brush and a blow dryer. She dried her hair and brushed it into a soft sheen. The blonde streaks were fading along with the summer days. Her blue eyes shimmered against her lightly tanned skin. The knock at the door startled her briefly.

"Mrs. Weaver. I thought you might like this, "Stan said, as he opened the door and stepped into the room. He smiled as he handed her a travel bag.

"Why thank you, Mr. Weaver. How's it going out there?" She smiled at him in the mirror as she continued working on her hair.

"Just great. He looks..." Stan searched for the right words, "pretty good, I think?" Stan's shoulders lifted in unison with his eyebrows.

"Yeah, he does. They both do."

After a quiet moment, Maggie finally broke the silence with her best villainess voice, "Now leave me! The beautification process is not complete!" She turned back to the mirror with an exaggerated scowl.

"Yes, my evil queen." Stan bowed and mumbled something about an evil stepmother as he left the room and closed the door behind him.

Maggie rummaged through her bag and found her last pair of clean underwear. She would have to do some laundry tonight. She slid on her panties, and bra, and found a soft pair of Wranglers. She pulled out an equally soft University of Wisconsin Badgers sweatshirt. She liked red. It was a good color for her. Even Michael told her that once, *or was he joking*? She couldn't remember, but would know soon enough. After all, he was the fashion police in these parts.

She chuckled to herself as she carried her things out of the bathroom. She passed by the empty bed that had been stripped and remade. Bill must have opened the windows as there was a slight chill in the air. The mountain breeze blew through, washing away the sick smell that had previously occupied the room.

Maggie walked down the hall, finally arriving in the large open area that made up the great room and kitchen. Michael was seated in a large chair. White Eagle sat to his right. They were having an in-depth conversation that clearly interested both of them. She looked around the room, but neither Stan nor Bill was in sight.

"Michael, pardon me, but do you think it would be okay if I did some wash?" Her brows were lifted, hoping for a favorable response.

"Oh my... I see you are still wearing that thing. I thought we had a talk about that before?" Michael said, baring the fakest Hollywood smile he could muster.

"Oh no, the fashion policeman is on duty! I thought you said I looked good in red?" Maggie sighed.

"Yes, red looks lovely on you, but honey, you have faded that thing so badly that it is now some strange offshoot of orange meets scary. If one of those Wisconsin Badger players saw you wearing that, he might mistake you for a Florida Gator fan." He placed his pointer finger over his mouth and shook his head *no*.

Michael's sarcasm made White Eagle laugh.

Maggie shot back, "Blasphemy!", and then she laughed as well.

The battle was quickly diffused as Bill and Stan came in through the front door. Stan was toting a small travel bag.

Bill announced he was going to be doing some laundry, and Michael took advantage of the opportunity to land the final blow to Maggie. "Please wash the stuff in the bag the Florida Gator is holding. Don't worry about mixing colors and whites. She never bothers with it."

Maggie shot Michael an evil face.

Bill took the bag from Maggie with a confused look on his face and whispered, "I thought you were a Wisconsin fan?"

"I am! I love the Badgers... Michael is a weenie!" she said in a defeated tone.

Bill whispered back, "Yes, he is, dear!"

The Chain

Maggie moved to the big black leather couch to enjoy Michael's company and somehow make her way into the current conversation. The two of them were discussing the lamp on Michael's table. White Eagle was talking about the effect different types of light bulbs had on the glass that made up the shade.

Maggie finally piped in, "That's a stained glass lamp, right?"

Michael turned to look at her and gave a nod.

White Eagle went on to discuss the base, and its construction, and the nouveau period.

Michael was enamored with White Eagle, but Maggie felt completely out of her league. She finally interrupted again and said, "Now that is a Tiffany style lamp right?"

Michael turned to her and said, "Honey that is a Tiffany lamp. It isn't in the style, it is the real deal."

"You mean, like he made it himself?" she asked with a confused expression.

"No, he most likely designed it. He had artisans that made the glass, and cut it and put together the shade. Then the buyer would select a base, and a marriage was made." Michael went on to describe the whole process of how the shade was made, and White Eagle would add a bit here and there.

Maggie was overwhelmed.

"That is amazing. How old is it, and where did you get it?" she asked finally, feeling included in the conversation.

"Yes, do share the story with us," White Eagle said, interested to hear as well.

Michael began to tell his tale.

"I became friends with a fine lady named Mrs. Leona Harper. She was an only child of a prominent family from West Virginia. Her parents had made their fortune in the coal mining industry. Her father moved the family to Wyoming to expand their business. The business grew, but her mother became very ill and lost a long battle to cancer. Not long after that, she lost her father to a heart attack. He left her a fortune.

As a child, her family had vacationed in Steamboat Springs many times. She loved it so much, that she and her husband chose to retire here after settling her father's estate. They built a lovely mansion and made this town their new home.

When Bill and I moved here, we started another landscaping business. We were very busy, and our client list grew quickly. One day, a black Rolls Royce pulls up and this little old lady steps out of the car. She was well dressed and stately. She asked, 'who's the owner of the business?', though she referred to it as an establishment. I told her I was the owner.

She grilled me for sometime about my credentials, and background. She asked why I had moved here, and a bunch of other odd questions. It sort of came to a head when she asked if I was married. When I told her no, she pressed harder and asked me why not. I was getting pretty pissed and said, 'Because they won't let two men get married in this country'.

I thought for sure she would swallow her tongue, climb back in her Rolls, and never be seen again, but instead she paused for a long while and said, 'Well, it takes a while for ignorance to be bred out of people, but it will probably come in your lifetime.' At that, she reached out her hand and introduced herself, 'I am Leona Harper, and I would like to hire your services for my property.'

We became such good friends. She called me Michael, but I always called her Mrs. Harper. She was a true lady. She had lost her husband years before. She had no children. It was something she often lamented. Though we came from two different walks of life, she treated me like a true friend.

We were her personal gardeners. The property was massive. There were several gardens overrun with weeds and overgrown bushes. The trees hadn't been pruned in years. She would often come outside and try to dictate my work, but I knew she did it because she wanted someone to talk to. I remember her reaction after that first year. The following spring our hard work had paid off. Her property looked amazing. It was revitalized. Flowering bushes and lovely tall trees adorned the grounds. Hedges were cut back and shaped, and new boxwoods were planted, providing an introduction to gardens to come. Flowers adorned the walkways, and Holly trees created an enchanted backdrop to the woodland beyond.

Her estate was stunning. We ordered a dozen of these wonderful hanging fern baskets and decorated the front porch and entrance. It made the place appear so warm and inviting. She was so pleased, that she paid to have the exterior repainted. It, once again, became a remarkable showplace.

She would often find excuses to have me come over and look at this plant, or this tree, or ask my opinion about this or that. I quickly real-

The Chain

ized it was more about having company. Eventually, it became a weekly visit to her home. She would have tea and would make scones. She was quite a lady.

In the late fall that year, we were having tea, and Mrs. Harper decided we were going to have a small dinner party. She wanted to pull out all of the stops. I remember coming over the day before to help her prepare. We polished silver, and laughed. She told me about the old days. She was very entertaining. We shared everything, and kept no secrets. Mrs. Harper had a great knowledge of many things; we shared stories into the late night over a glass of Bourbon. She loved her Bourbon, and we were known to have a little 'Honky Tonk', as she called it, from time to time. That was the day she introduced me to Pappy. She would say, 'Sharing the evening with me and Pappy is what made her happy.'"

Michael paused for a moment. He looked out the front windows. His face showed a great love and respect for this woman. It was clear that he missed her dearly.

"Who was Pappy?" Maggie asked with a curious look.

White Eagle spoke, "Pappy Van Winkle?"

"Well, yes it is!" Michael was shocked and pleased with White Eagle.

He leaned over to Maggie and said, "Maggie, I love your friend. Can we keep him?"

They all laughed.

Bill and Stan returned to the room. Bill raised his hands to get everyone's attention, "How about I open a bottle of wine?"

"Excellent!" Michael yelled back.

Michael leaned over to White Eagle, pointing towards Bill and whispered, "I love that man."

Stan sat next to Maggie on the large couch and placed his arm around her. She kissed him on his cheek and whispered in his ear, "Michael is telling a great story."

They both turned to Michael to hear more.

"Okay where was I? Oh yes, Pappy Van Winkle. Excellent Bourbon, and not cheap. But then, everything she had, and did, was top shelf."

Michael pointed, directing everyone's attention to the lamp.

"This lamp was in her living room. Last winter, I got worried about her. She was living up there on the hill all alone. Her driver wasn't much younger than she was, and I would check on them often. It was a Saturday. I woke up early and made a couple of apple pies. She always watched her sugar, and so I made her one with this great recipe that used Splenda. When we pulled up her long driveway, I knew something was wrong. I kept telling Bill something was not right. The house looked too dark. She always had the lights on in the receiving hall. We rang the doorbell and knocked several times. The front door was locked. I knew where she hid the key to the backdoor, so we made our way to the back of the house. She had one of those fake rocks in her yard, and the key was placed neatly inside. When I finally opened the back door, I saw her on the floor. She had on her pajamas and robe. There was a broken tea cup on the floor. She had apparently been like that for a day or two. It broke my heart to see this fine lady of great dignity like that. The coroner report said she suffered a massive stroke.

We later found that driver had taken a two week vacation to visit with a sister in San Diego. It was such a sad loss. She was an exquisite lady and my good friend."

Maggie looked at Michael, clearly waiting for him to finish.

Michael looked at Maggie, confused.

"What? Oh that lamp... I forgot what I was telling. A few weeks later, I get a phone call about the reading of Mrs. Harper's will. I know she planned to leave a small fortune for cancer research and a few other charities. When the attorney read the will, he only named the driver and me. She left her driver five hundred thousand dollars. He retired and moved to Florida. I honestly didn't expect her to leave me anything. She knew we were doing okay financially. When the attorney said she left me the lamp, I was floored, but not nearly as floored when he said that her estate would pay all of our current outstanding debt and provide an additional sum of money."

"Wow!' Maggie said, "That is amazing! So?"

"So, what?" Michael asked.

"So, how much did your friend leave you?" Maggie pressed him, loving the idea of actually seeing him squirm.

"Maggie Weaver. Have you no scruples?" Michael gave her the evil eye.

At that, Bill returned with a bottle of wine and wine glasses. Bill poured the wine and said, "I can answer that. More than we could ever spend in this lifetime."

The Chain

Michael looked away, then back to Maggie and said, "It's sad, isn't it? All this money, and I can't really enjoy it. I'll tell you, I would rather have my health than the money, but enough about me," he said, fanning his hand. "I want to hear more about your fascinating friend, Mr. White Eagle."

White Eagle shared a little about his life growing up on a reservation, and his travels. The conversation finally turned to sports, and White Eagle, Stan, and Bill found a common ground to digest. Michael motioned for Maggie to follow him to the kitchen.

"Where are you going, Michael," Bill inquired with a concerned look.

Michael smiled at him, shaking the empty bottle of wine, "To get a fresh bottle of wine from the kitchen, and get some girl talk in with my cousin."

Bill winked at him, and the men went back to the upcoming football season.

Michael directed Maggie around the kitchen. He had her collect a large white serving dish from the cabinet while he pulled out two large tomatoes from the massive stainless steel refrigerator.

"So what are we making?" she asked.

"Oh, a little something to nosh on before dinner. Can you hand me one of those knives there?" he asked, pointing to a butcher block like none she had ever seen before.

She pulled one out and brought it to the granite topped island. Michael washed the tomatoes and began to slice them. He then topped each one with a slice of white cheese.

"Oh, that looks yum! What kind of cheese is that?" she grinned.

"Goat cheese. Have you ever had it before?"

"Naaa," she bleated.

He topped a tomato and handed Maggie a fork.

"Try it," he insisted.

She cut off a piece of tomato, put it in her mouth, and closed her eyes. It was clear she was in heaven as she hummed, "Mmmmmm."

"Ha ha, I told you," he grinned as he tasted some as well.

Michael finished decorating the tomatoes and delivered them to the cocktail table where the men were sitting. They all liked what they saw. Maggie brought little plates and forks for everyone, with a bottle of wine under her arm.

She and Michael made their way back to the kitchen. Michael handed her napkins and the wine bottle opener, "Uh oh... They can't drink wine without this. Would you mind taking this to them? I'm going to run out to the garden real quick. I will be right back."

"Ahh... okay? Will you be alright? Want me to come and help?" she asked.

"No, I will be fine. Go enjoy the munchies before the boys eat it all."

With that, she returned to the great room to find her way into the football conversation.

* * * *

Michael went outside in his slippers and pajamas. He had on a long bathrobe that repelled the cool mountain summer air. The sun was descending the valley and soon would be hidden by the mountain across the lake. He had pruning shears in his hand, and a vase. He smiled when he reached the sunflowers. They were wide open with stunning yellow petals, and a brilliant glowing brown center. He knew, in a few weeks, the centers would be nothing but bird food for the local seed eaters. He cut some red and yellow roses and added them to the vase. He knew there would be plenty of white daisies in the back and made his way to the far end of the garden. There were so many to choose from, and it saddened him to know that in a month, this would all be a pile of mush. Butterflies were making their rounds, and hummingbirds were topping off before the long journey south. The birds seemed rather active in the garden, more than he remembered in the past. Their songs seemed to increase in volume. He turned to see what the commotion was all about and was taken back by the sight of Kylee.

He gasped. Sparrows were on her arms, and shoulder. All around her feet were doves, and other birds. It was like something out of Wild Kingdom, except this was *his* garden in *his* backyard.

"Kylee. Kylee, can you hear me? Is that you, honey?" Michael asked as he approached.

She smiled at him and said, "Auntie Michael, what kind of outfit is that?"

"Oh this?" he asked, looking down at his robe and slippers. He couldn't think of a quick comeback.

The Chain

He looked at her with tears in his eyes and they both laughed. At that, the birds lifted and flew to other parts of the garden. Kylee approached him and hugged him. He hugged her back and breathed her in like the finest flowers.

"I have missed you so much, and thought about you every day." He sobbed in her arms.

"Oh, Michael, there is no reason to cry. Everything is alright." She pulled away and wiped away his tears.

Kylee led him to a concrete bench in the garden, and they sat and talked. She asked him all about Colorado, and he told her all about the lake, and the mountains, and the animals there. He also told her about the fabulous shopping, and how she and her mom needed to go shopping with him in town sometime. Kylee was excited about the idea. He couldn't recall feeling better.

Kylee helped him gather more flowers, and they made their way back to the house. Michael walked in first and announced to everyone, "I have a surprise!"

Stan, happy with his wine, responded first, "And what might that be?"

Michael stepped aside and all you could see was a massive vase filled with flowers with two legs behind it. Maggie gasped and ran to Kylee. Michael took the flower vase and handed it to Bill, who gave a questioning look.

Stan came to their side and they all hugged. Maggie kept asking Kylee if she wanted water, but she politely declined. They introduced Kylee to Bill. Kylee seemed to be mesmerized by the Native American man.

"Wow, you look cool!" she said.

"Well, so do you." He smiled back at her.

She came close to him and he bent over to get a closer look. She looked at him like he was the most amazing creature she had ever seen.

"Your hair is beautiful, may I touch it?" Kylee asked.

"Sure you can," and he sat down on the chair and let her come close. She ran her hands down it. Then, with her pointer finger, touched his hand. She blushed when she did so.

"White Eagle, you are a special man. I can tell." She smiled at him as he hoisted her into his lap. He was surprised she knew his name. He wondered if Michael had told her.

Kylee said, "Oh, Mommy! Tomatoes! Can I have one?"

"Of course, you can," everyone responded in unison. She ate the tomato and said, "Mommy, I want to be an Indian." With that, the room burst into laughter.

Chapter Fifty-Four

The one hour forty-five minute flight seemed to last forever. Jenkins had no idea what awaited him, but he knew his destiny was about to unfold. It would be a close call making dinner. Hopefully, there would be leftovers.

The black Chevy Suburban made its way around the large lake, and up the mountain side. Halfway up a gravel road Ross stopped the SUV to let Clepto and Gopher out. They exited the vehicle, traveling in opposite directions, one to the east and the other to the west.

Ross continued up the road, until he saw the peaks of the two-story cabin. He slowed the SUV and looked to Keeper for a response.

Keeper nodded and Ross positioned the Suburban directly behind White Eagle's car ensuring no one was leaving soon.

"So, this should be fun, "Ross said sarcastically, reaching for his gun.

Jenkins waved it away, "You won't need that."

Ross raised a brow at Keeper, and put his gun back in his holster. They departed the vehicle and made their way to the front door.

Jenkins knocked, but no one responded. He could hear people laughing from behind the house and the smell of the grill. He knocked again and Michael answered the door.

"May I help you," Michael asked.

"Yes, I think you can. May we come in?" Jenkins smiled

Michael gave a confused, concerned look as he eyed these two men dressed in black suits, and was joined by Bill.

"Oh, hello, Agent Jenkins. Please come in," Bill said as he nodded to Michael that everything was okay.

"Bill, I would like you to meet Agent Ross." Bill shook Ross's hand, and escorted the men in through the front door.

Michael was concerned and confused, "Bill, what is going on?"

Stan and Maggie walked into the kitchen from outside, carrying their wine glasses, laughing over one of White Eagle's stories. They heard people talking and looked up to see Jenkins. Maggie gasped, and Stan hissed, "Jenkins!"

"What the hell do you want? Why can't you people leave us alone?" Maggie was ready to draw blood.

White Eagle held the door open as Kylee came into the kitchen. Everyone turned to see her. Maggie wanted to run to her daughter's defense, but Kylee ran across the room to Jenkins and yelled, "Keeper! I am so glad you came!" She wrapped her arms around his waist, and he reached down and picked her up.

He always felt like he knew this child, but this was an awkward meeting for sure. He had many questions, but there would be a time for that later.

"Well. Hello. Kylee," he said with a surprising smile.

"Oh look! Panther is here too… Ohhhh. Very cool." She gave Panther the thumbs up.

Maggie and Stan's jaws hung wide open. They were both unable to grasp what was going on. Finally, White Eagle stepped forward and said, "Hello, I am White Eagle."

Jenkins placed Kylee on the ground, and shook White Eagle's hand. Jenkins introduced Agent Ross.

"Look folks, I just came to talk. Nothing more, nothing less." He assured them, waving his hands, palms out.

During the whole commotion, no one had noticed that Michael had slipped away. Even Jenkins hadn't expected it when Michael came in so quickly from the front door behind him. The coolness of the double barreled gunmetal against his neck confirmed that maybe he was getting too old for this. He wondered if you really felt pain when your head was blown off. He hoped he wouldn't have to find out.

"I don't know who the hell you people are, but I'm a dying man and won't think twice about putting a hole in your heads." Michael's eyes stared wildly at the back of Jenkins' head.

Bill yelled at Michael, "No, Michael. Wait. Stop. Don't kill him. Trust me he is a friend."

"Someone better start talking and telling me what the hell is going on!" Michael's finger moved over the trigger and the gun was shaking in his hand. In the movies, it was always a sign that the gunman was chang-

The Chain

ing his mind, but the truth of the matter was he is getting closer to doing the deed.

Jenkins finally spoke, "Michael, I know more about you than you know. I know that you are HIV positive, and I know that you didn't abduct Kylee, and I know that your partner loves you very much. I know more about you than you can imagine. Who do you think provided your healthcare, and paid for all of those medications? Didn't you wonder how you were able to get health insurance so cheap, much less at all? How many insurance companies do you know that will pick up someone with HIV?"

Michael had tears in his eyes and started to lower the gun. He cried to Bill, "Who *are* these people?"

Ross saw his chance to seize the weapon and made his move, but before he could secure the gun, he felt his holster's snap release and in an instance cold metal pressed against the side of his head. White Eagle's hand didn't shake. He spoke clearly and calmly, "Agent Ross, hand the gun back to Michael."

Ross handed the shotgun back to Michael, and raised his hands.

Kylee approached Michael, "It is going to be okay, Michael. I promise." She turned to White Eagle and had tears in her eyes, "You have to trust me, Mr. White Eagle. It's going to be okay. They aren't going to hurt us."

White Eagle lowered the gun. Michael walked around them and handed the shotgun to Bill. He hissed at Bill, shaking his finger in his face, "William, you have some explaining to do!" He then continued past Bill and went to the bedroom.

Bill followed Michael to the bedroom, only to find him sitting on the bed with tears streaming down his face.

"Don't cry, Babybear. You know I love you and would never hurt you. Please don't cry." Bill sat next to him and placed his hand on Michael's.

"Who are these people? Are they agents? Are you an agent? Have you lied to me all this time?" Michael looked down at their hands, shaking his head, unable to comprehend what was going on.

Bill started to talk, "Back in Wisconsin, it was just you and me. The police were after you, and they were about to pin you for Kylee's abduction. You were so afraid that the world would find out we were lovers. I was stupid back then. I was so worried about being 'outed'. Here I was, this middle aged man dating this young man. We both know how the world has this twisted view of gay people, and assume we are all child molesters. It was a witch hunt, Michael. Those detectives were about to arrest you and put you in jail."

Michael just nodded his head and looked at his hands, allowing the tears to roll down his cheeks.

Bill rubbed Michael's hand and continued, "One day, Conrad Jenkins knocked at my door. He told me that he was with the government, and that they were investigating the incident. He knew all about both of us. He claimed he knew who took Kylee, and that it wasn't us or a family member. Mr. Jenkins was very kind, and it was him that had the detectives stop their pursuit to prosecute you. That check I get every month has nothing to do with my retirement from the postal service. It is from the government for keeping an eye on things. They are the ones that arranged for your healthcare. We could never have afforded your medications and doctor visits before Mrs. Harper's inheritance gift. I did this for you. I did this for *us*."

"What do you mean by 'keeping an eye on things'?" Michael looked at Bill, very concerned.

"I called in once a month and gave an update on us. For some reason, they always thought Kylee would show up. They knew how close you two were. I was asked to let them know if she should return, with the promise that they wouldn't take her or hurt her," Bill looked down at his hand on Michael's.

"And you believed them, William? This is the government we're talking about," he pointed out, rolling his eyes. "You trusted them?"

Bill had tears in his eyes and finally said, "Did I have any choice? We had already lost Kylee; I wasn't going to lose you too. Hadn't you been through enough? Hadn't we all been through enough?" Bill sobbed on Michael's shoulder.

"I just want to know one thing, William Brandt. Are there any other secrets you are keeping from me?"

"No, you know everything. You are my everything. I love you, Babybear."

"I love you too, Papabear," Michael said, holding tightly on to Bill.

"Can I be Goldilocks?" Kylee said, surprising them both as she drew near.

Michael and Bill both laughed out loud. Michael reached his arms out to her and pulled her to him, "You can be anything you like!"

The Chain

"Oh, crap!" Bill sat up.

"What's wrong?" Michael asked.

"I got meat on the grill. Let me get back out there. Will you be okay?" Bill asked.

"Yes. Yes, go ahead." He waved him away. Then focusing all his attention on Kylee, he said, "Goldilocks and I will get cleaned up and be out shortly."

Bill walked down the hall and stopped midstride as he ran into Maggie. She had tears in her eyes and hugged him. "I had no idea. Thank you so much for taking care of Michael. I know I shouldn't have eavesdropped, but Kylee wanted to see Michael, and..."

He shook his head, "Don't worry about it, Maggie. But I have to run; I left meat cooking on the grill."

"Oh, don't stress. Chef Boyardee, AKA Stan Weaver, is out there saving the day." Maggie giggled.

Bill let out a sigh of relief, "Okay, let's turn this event around and get smiles on everyone's face. Deal?"

She nodded, "Deal!"

Maggie returned to the living room and found White Eagle and the agents standing around talking.

Bill called from the kitchen, "Who'd like a beer?"

There was a brief moment of silence, then in unison they responded, "Me!"

Maggie helped divvy out the beers and escorted everyone outside to the patio area. Expensive outdoor furniture adorned a large covered patio area. The gas grill was part of a beautiful outdoor kitchen.

Bill took over the cooking tasks, while Stan made his way around that patio area, lighting the various candles and citronella laced Tiki torches.

The mood was settling down, and Michael and Kylee finally made their way outside. He had changed into a pair of jeans and a sweatshirt. Kylee carried a basket of rolls, and he followed her, toting a large bowl of pasta with tossed vegetables that had been marinating in Italian dressing.

It was a beautiful evening, and the cool air was a reminder that the summer was coming to a close. The lighthearted conversation was centered on the beauty of Colorado, and the current events in the news. Maggie sat with Michael and Kylee, discussing the idea of going shopping in town the following day. White Eagle seemed to be enjoying the company of Conrad Jenkins. They discussed many things and got up to stretch their legs a bit. They made their way around the perimeter of the large vegetable and flower gardens. Once they were far away from the crowd, White Eagle finally asked, "How many do you have in the woods around us, besides the woman?"

Jenkins was caught off guard, and wondered if Ross had discussed the two teams that surrounded the house. "I have two teams of four here. Excluding me and Agent Ross, we have seven agents within earshot of the house."

"What are you hoping to achieve here, Agent Jenkins?" White Eagle pressed him.

Jenkins thought about that a long time. The unseen man he reported to had become very quiet, but wanted him to bring Kylee in. Yet, these entities had their own agenda. One faction wanted the girl, and the other wanted her protected. Assuming she is the gift they referred to.

He finally answered, "The truth."

White Eagle responded, and "What truth do you seek?"

"I want to know what this gift is, and what its purpose is, and how the hell am I supposed to protect it." Jenkins chewed on a piece of grass for a moment then spit it out on the ground.

"It sounds as if we have the same agenda," White Eagle said, patting Jenkins on the back.

Back at the patio area, Stan helped Bill clean up the grill area, and gather empty plates. They made their way into the kitchen with hands full.

Maggie excused herself to help cleanup while Michael and Kylee continued their important shopping conversation.

Maggie was followed into the kitchen by Agent Ross. Their hands were full of utensils and empty beer bottles. Bill rinsed out the sink while Stan loaded the dishwasher.

"Bill, I thought you said Michael wasn't doing very well?" Maggie asked in a perplexed tone.

"Maggie, he hasn't been out of that bed in two weeks. I'm amazed. It is like a miracle." He shook his head in disbelief as he wiped down the kitchen counters.

Maggie shot Stan a glance. He acknowledged her look and raised his eyebrows.

White Eagle and Jenkins helped Michael extinguish the candles and Tiki torches, and they made their way inside.

The Chain

"Miss Kylee, you need a bath, and we need to get you in some pajamas, "Maggie insisted.

"Oh, Mom." Kylee sighed.

"Come with your auntie, I will introduce you to my lovely tub full of bubbles and surprises, "Michael winked at Maggie as he escorted Kylee down the hall.

Everyone else gathered around the fireplace. Bill pressed a button on a controller, and the gas logs ignited. There was a minute of awkwardness, and Jenkins finally broke the silence.

Looking at White Eagle, he said, "May I ask how you and the Weavers became acquainted?"

White Eagle and the Weavers shared their stories. Jenkins, though careful, shared what he knew as well. Many of the gaps were filled in. The conversation became very quiet, when Jenkins revealed that he was to protect the gift. Everyone, with the exception of Ross, was surprised to hear this.

Maggie finally put things in perspective, asking, "Do you think these things are angels or something?"

Jenkins shook his head, "No, they are far from angels."

White Eagle had a look of surprise and asked, "Why do you think that?"

"Because we have been watching and documenting them for years. Kylee isn't the first abduction case. There have been several abductions. Often these beings use their biological entitics to do their dirty work. I'm sure you have seen the UFO stories on television and in books about 'The Greys'. They have very large eyes, and grey skin, and are short. They are like genetic robots, but the real minds behind it are these entities we saw. They are aliens; you can trust me on this."

Jenkins realized he had shared too much already, but he was exhausted with it, and needed answers.

White Eagle spoke again, "And these 'Greys' were associated with this case somehow too?"

"Well, not specifically, but we're fairly confident they are associated."

Jenkins dark brown eyes searched White Eagle, concerned that he knew more than he told. Maybe he wasn't the only player at the table holding his cards closely.

"I forgot to close the windows", Bill said as he excused himself. Agent Ross got up to help him. They made their way around the room, and into the kitchen.

Ross said, "It smells like it is going to rain."

Bill looked out the window into the darkness and nodded.

Maggie made her way back to Michael's room. He and Kylee were sitting on his bed watching Beauty and the Beast. They were mesmerized as Belle and the Beast danced around the large ballroom.

"Don't mind me. I'm just going to close the windows. It looks like we have rain coming," Maggie whispered as she closed the first window.

"Rain? There wasn't a cloud in the sky out there? I don't think it was in the forecast. Oh well..." Michael hunched his shoulders and returned to the lovely dance before him.

* * * *

Gopher sat quietly in the brush. The coolness of the evening had set in. He ate a snack bar, wishing instead he had one of those steaks from the grill below. He never saw the silhouette of Rudy and Deloris behind him. Nor was he meant to.

One by one, each agent was relieved of their post. Rudy and Deloris knew it was just a matter of time until the gift would be theirs.

* * * *

Maggie returned to the great room where the men were rehashing the events that lead them all to this place. She sat among them, quietly noticing Agent Ross had gone into the kitchen area. She whispered to Stan, "What's wrong with him?"

He whispered back, "No idea. Maybe this storm rolling in."

"Oh, my God!" Maggie gasped as she jumped out of her seat and ran down the hallway. As she turned into Michael's room, she yelled, "Move now! Come with me." She grabbed Kylee, and ran down the hall toward the great room. Michael was right behind them.

"What's wrong?" Stan asked started by her sudden movement.

"Smell the air, Stan!" Maggie yelled.

"They are coming, Mommy," Kylee said holding her mother's hand as the foundation of the house started to lightly shake.

The Chain

Jenkins and Ross pulled out their guns, and Jenkins called into headset,"Team one report!"

There was no response. He tried again, "Teams one and two, Report!"

His headpiece filled with loud static, forcing him and Ross to both remove their earpieces.

The glasses in the cabinets were clattering along with the pots and pans and dishes. It felt as if a freight train was running through the house. The lights in the house were flickering, as everyone tried to steady their feet.

All at once, it stopped. You could hear the hiss of static from the earphones hanging down the front of Jenkins and Ross.

Jenkins instructed, "Everyone move to the center of the room."

Both agents shut off their earpieces and listened to the silence. There was nothing to be heard. It was eerie. There was no wind, no sound of the woodland. It was as if they stood in a void. There was nothing natural about it.

The empty silence was finally greeted by a loud knock on the door. Ross darted across the room, and peered through the draped window. He gave a hand signal and Jenkins opened the door.

"Clepto, why didn't you report in?" Jenkins asked, staring into the man's pale face.

Clepto fell through the door and slumped in Jenkins' arms. Jenkins quickly closed the door behind him. Stan helped Jenkins place Clepto on the couch. He was hardly breathing.

The front door flew open with such force that the hinges bent away from the doorway. The crack of the wood and whine of the metal hinges bending startled everyone. Standing outside the door stood Rudy and Deloris. Rudy gave a hand sweeping gesture, ushering Deloris into the room.

"Surprise!" Deloris said with a warm grandmotherly smile.

"Party!" Rudy yelled like a college kid at some frat party. Deloris adjusted her outfit as she looked around the room, "Look at who's here. All my favorites, and there's my kitty!"

Agent Ross never had a chance to shoot. With a swift hand movement he was at her feet. He screamed as her hand rested on his shoulder. You could see her start to squeeze as his bones began to break under her strength.

Jenkins yelled, "Run!" as he threw himself at Rudy. Rudy was caught off guard and fell to the ground laughing. His laughter shook the windows in the house. Conrad Jenkins knew this was a mistake as Rudy gave him a bear hug. He whispered into Jenkins' ear, "You always were a frail puppet. Your strings have been pulled entirely too long. It is time for you to break free."

Jenkins felt the extreme pressure as his back popped and finally broke. He knew it was just a matter of time now, but he bit Rudy's face anyway just to leave his mark.

Everyone ran for the front door, but stopped at the sight of Clepto holding a gun. It was pointed right at Kylee.

His voice was like the voice of many, speaking at once, "How appropriate, Beauty and the Beast! I guess you're Belle? So that must make me..."

As he spoke, his features changed and he morphed into a horrible, in-human creature. His skin had a tortured burned look. His mangled long fingers were bent in odd directions and almost appeared too large for his hand. His large skull housed two blood shot eyes that seemed to know death without pity or remorse.

He continued, "The Beast!" He wailed in roaring laughter that made the foundations of the house shake.

Kylee spoke in a very confident calm tone, "You don't scare me. It is you that should be afraid."

"Afraid? *Me*?" he asked, hitting his chest, "Of what! A little girl? Come with me, and I will show you a mansion that Belle only wished she could live in." He laughed as his body once again morphed back into Clepto.

"He is coming, and you are in big trouble," she said, pointing her finger at him.

"This is my realm, he has no say here." He pointed to Kylee, "If you want the rest of these people to live, then come with me now!"

"Never," she said.

"Then no one shall have you, child," he said as he raised the gun and pointed it at her.

White Eagle knew this was his destiny as he threw himself in front of the racing bullet. He heard Maggie's scream as the bullet penetrated his heart. It felt like a pipe had hit him in the chest, but there was no pain; instead there was a peace that surpassed all understanding. He had done his part, he had fulfilled his obligation. He remembered seeing a

The Chain

great white explosion of light, and watched the three dark entities writhe in pain as they were shackled and carried away by several of the other beings. He recognized the two entities that had appeared in his car. It was odd looking around the room seeing the commotion. Michael and Maggie held each other as they watched Stan tending to Jenkins. He finally saw Kylee. She was lying on top of someone. White Eagle then realized it was his body she laid on. His long, flowing, white hair was sprawled on the floor with broken stained glassed all around. For a moment, he was saddened, knowing that his efforts to save the girl had destroyed the lamp. It had endured a lifetime, only to succumb this event. He watched as a little old lady walked into the room. She was surrounded by light. She looked at the broken lamp strewn across the floor then back at White Eagle. She smiled at him and nodded. Then he heard a voice and it said, "Restore to them that which was destroyed" and he awoke to Kylee saying, "Wake up, White Eagle. It's not time for you to go to sleep."

He opened his eyes and took a deep breath. He reached his hand to his heart, but there was no pain. Though there was some blood on his shirt, there was no wound. It was completely healed.

Conrad Jenkins was amazed he could stand. He ran his hands down his back, but felt no pain. It was as if the event never happened. Ross gave him a nod and said, "Much better without the water thing."

Jenkins smiled and said, "I bet."

The house began to vibrate with a tone. It was a pleasing tone. The entity named Raziel said, "Come, please." He wore robes that glimmered in iridescence. He had a golden sash.

They went outside. The mountain side was covered with thousands of brilliant lights. Maggie gasped at the spectacular view. The lights filled the yard and surrounded the house as well. As they made their way out further, they realized the lights were these beings. They lit the mountainside. Their faces glowed as they looked upward. Everyone looked up. Two objects were in the sky, hovering over them. They made no sound, and didn't move, but appeared to be spinning. They were a soft, glowing, golden color, and pleasant to view. One object was much larger than the other. A great peace fell over everyone.

Jenkins pointed to the larger object and said, "That must be the mother ship."

White Eagle responded, "And the little wheel run by faith, and the big wheel run by the grace of God"

They heard a noise coming from the house. A bright blue light emitted from the interior as the vibration increased. As they approached, they witnessed the stained glass lamp reassemble and restore to perfection. Every plate, broken glass and fallen object was completely restored to order. The vibration increased and a loud tone, like the loudest trumpet was heard from above. They turned and watched as the beings ascended into the two objects above.

As the final being ascended, another horn was heard and the objects vanished in a blink of an eye.

Chapter Fifty-Five

Two weeks later, Agent Jenkins delivered Stan, Maggie, and Kylee Weaver to the airport. Their final destination was St. Helena, California, nestled in the Napa Valley. Bill and Michael decided to move as well. They wanted to stay close to Kylee and the Weavers. They would make the journey after they prepped their house for the upcoming winter. White Eagle planned to join them as well. He was going home to pack his things and ask his daughter if she wanted to accompany him.

Their flight had stops in Denver, and Phoenix, then the drive from Los Angeles to their new home. Jenkins made all the arrangements, and found a nice place for them. Michael and Bill purchased the adjacent home, which included a large grape vineyard, and winery. There was a guest house on the property, and they offered it to White Eagle.

Panther and the Chameleon sat in the last two seats of the plane. They watched the Weavers board, and finally find their seats. Stan took the window seat, and Maggie took the aisle. Kylee sat between them, excited about her first plane ride.

The plane took off without incident. The flight attendants prepared the beverage carts, and snack boxes.

"Mommy, I have to go to the bathroom, "Kylee embarrassingly whispered.

"It's okay, honey, I will take you, "Maggie said, unbuckling both of them and directing Kylee towards the back of the plane. Kylee moved slowly, placing her hands on the various seats as she passed each row. Maggie had the bathroom in sight, but Kylee stopped. She turned to a very large black woman sitting in the aisle seat. She had on a black skirt, and a flowered print top. She didn't look very comfortable in the small plane seat, but appeared to be making the best of it.

Kylee said, "I know you. Your name is Esther."

The woman had a surprised look on her face and said, "You do? Well, I don't know you, but that is my name. What is your name, precious?"

"My name is Kylee. You have good things a comin," Kylee said and gave the woman a hug. Esther Johnson looked up at Maggie with a questioning smile on her face as she hugged Kylee back. The woman next to her said, "Aww, isn't that just the sweetest thing. Gawd gives us the greatest blessing through our children."

"Yes. Yes, he does, "Maggie said as she rubbed Kylee's back, "Come on, honey, the bathroom is back this way."

Kylee backed away and waved goodbye. Ester and her friend waved goodbye too. Maggie leaned over and said, "It's her first flight. Sorry, ladies."

"Oh, no need to apologize. It's our first flight too. She sure is a fine one." Esther said as Maggie chased after Kylee.

Maggie waited outside the restroom for Kylee. She knew that the two agents would be on the plane, but the fact that they were holding hands told her more.

Kylee came out and they made their way back to their seats.

No one really seemed to notice the two tall men in the back. Their skin was pale, and gaunt, and their faces were expressionless. They watched the family the entire flight, yet the Chameleon and Panther weren't aware.

"Kylee, how did you know that lady?" Maggie asked.

"The Big man showed her to me. She has a chicken farm in Alabama. She has 'good things a comin. That's right... good things a comin'."

Maggie looked at Stan and mimicked Kylee with her brows raised, "Good things a comin."

Stan was watching both of them. He smiled at Maggie and kissed Kylee on the head.

Kylee said, "Make a chain with me!"

With that Stan made a circle with his thumb and pointer and connected it with Kylee's thumb and pointer. Maggie, in turn, did the same with Kylee's right hand. The chain had grown stronger and larger, and though it had been stretched, it held true.

* * * *

The Chain

Keeper answered the phone, "Jenkins."

"Is this line secure, Agent Jenkins?" the voice asked.

"Yes, Sir." Jenkins answered.

"And is the gift secure?" the faceless voice questioned.

"Yes, Sir. It is being hand delivered as we speak, "Jenkins spoke assuredly.

"Excellent, Give me an update when you arrive in California." The voice said in a confident tone.

"Will do, Sir."

The phone in the tiny office of the Vatican was placed back on the receiver by an older man's hand, yielding a stunning gold ring.